Rebecca's Hope

Book One of
Endless Sea Series

᪻

Elizabeth Elliott King

Published and Distributed by:

GRANITE
PUBLISHING & DISTRIBUTION L.L.C.

Granite Publishing and Distribution, LLC
868 North 1430 West
Orem, Utah 84057
(801) 229-9023 • Toll Free (800) 574-5779
Fax (801) 229-1924

Cover Design by: Tammie Ingram

Cover Photo by: Stacey Fife

Page Layout and Design by: Myrna Varga, The Office Connection Inc.

ISBN: 1-932280-53-7

Library of Congress Control Number: 2004113232

First Printing November 2004

10 9 8 7 6 5 4 3 2 1
Printed in the United States of America

Dedication

❧

To my husband Jim and my children Jane Wagoner, Allen King, Victoria Jones, Elliott King and Tom King, and to their families who have always been so very supportive of my writings over the past twenty years. And to so many of my friends who have encouraged me not to give up.

Acknowledgment

☙

In appreciation of Michelle Scott-Chiodo, my "attorney-in-fact," who has made the publishing of my work a reality. Not only did she see the potential in me as a writer and the story as worthwhile reading, but further vowed to do everything in her power to help me have it published and through her effort it has happened. Thank you, Michelle.

Elizabeth Elliott King

Rebecca's Hope

A story of Love and Adventure

by

Elizabeth Elliott King

LIST OF CHARACTERS

IN AMERICA

William Stewart of Stewart Hall
Stewart Hall is a wealthy plantation in Virginia.
He is brother to Rebecca Ann Stewart-Lathrope.

Rebecca Ann Stewart-Lathrope
The beautiful young widow of Jeremiah Collins Lathrope

Jeremiah Collins Lathrope
Husband of Rebecca Stewart-Lathrope and Captain of a whaling ship and resident of Nantucket Island, Massachusetts.

Nathaniel Jeremiah Lathrope (infant)
Child of Rebecca and Jeremiah Lathrope and future Captain of the whaling ship, MORNING STAR.

Toby
A freeborn man, a servant and friend to the Lathrope family

Betsy
The Lathrope's loyal housekeeper

Steven Cummins
Virginia Vicar

Jonah Pierce
Virginia doctor

Captain Henry Black
Friend of Jeremiah Lathrope who married Jeremiah and Rebecca on the high seas.

Aggie Starbuck Black
Wife of Captain Black and Mid-wife/friend/mentor to Meghan

In Ireland—the Village of Kilcrohane, County Cork

John McGonigal
Husband of Kathleen and father of Meghan

Kathleen Benfield McGonigal
Wife of John and mother of Meghan

Meghan McGonigal, AKA Marty Ryan
Runaway daughter of John and Kathleen McGonigal

David McGonigal
Jilted brother of John. Betrothed to Kathleen before she married John

Cavin McGonigal
Son of John and Kathleen and loving brother to Meghan

Squire Brian O'Shea
Arrogant, detestable widowed Irish oaf who intends to marry young Meghan.

Nora Murphy O'Shea
Deceased wife of the Squire O'Shea

James David Murphy
Father of Nora

Julianne Allen
Childhood friend of Meghan/Wife of Cavin McGonigal

Hugh Francis Miller
Shopkeeper and Director of County Cork Registry for Nannies

Father James Ryan
Catholic Parish Priest

The Most Reverend Mr. Jennings
Missionary to Maui in the Hawaiian Islands and Meghan's employer

Mistress Jennings, Robert and Elizabeth Jennings
The Missionary Jenning's family

Kilcrohane Villagers
Willy Jawn
Tavey Connolly

ON THE SEA AND ON THE ISLAND OF MAUI

Caleb Pratt
Cook on the ship going to Maui.

Leah Kamiya
Meghan's island native friend on Maui

Nelson Leigh
British Trader

The Most Reverend Mr. Bainbridge
A suitor for Meghan

Mildred Bainbridge
The Reverend's mother

CHARACTERS ON THE WHALING SHIP MORNING STAR

Nathaniel Jeremiah Lathrope (grown up)
Ship's Captain

Marty Ryan
Crewman
a/k/a Meghan McGonigal and 'Marty Girl'

Jeremy Haws
First Mate of the MORNING STAR

The Whaling Men
Samuel Tracy
Henry Johnson
Donald Matthews
Daniel Riley Timmons
William Blake

Levi Simmons nicknamed "Cookie"
The MORNING STAR cook

Jacob Milton Higgins
Young Whaler and
Adversary to young Marty Ryan.

Prelude

❧

Nantucket Island – 1788

An enclosed carriage rambled over the cobblestone lane; its horses in full gallop as the driver snapped a whip over their heads. As the rig neared a group of out buildings a man emerged from one of the sheds and stared after the conveyance, his eyes showing the terror he felt.

"Oh, Lardy," he moaned. "Couldn't ye keep 'im away a bit longer?" He ran up the slope toward the house and hid in the shadows of the porch just before the driver opened the door to allow a tall, well-dressed man to disembark.

He watched as that man retrieved a silver snuffbox from a pocket in his blue satin jacket and with a delicate swirl of his fingers, placed a pinch of the white powder at the opening of each nostril and breathed deeply.

"You have my instructions," he said, dabbing away the residue with a silk-laced handkerchief before he continued, "at my signal make sure they are carried out. Is that understood?"

The driver nodded and returned to his perch.

PULLING HIS CLOAK about him, the man turned his attention to the massive three-storied log home standing alone on the cliff. Reaching the top of a stone staircase, he quickly made his way to the immense oak door. It never occurred to him to knock. He lifted the brass handle and arrogantly pushed it open. The highly polished oak floors and walls gleamed in the sudden sunlight, yet it meant nothing to him.

"Who might ye be?" a woman asked as he came into the foyer. "And what right do ye have to enter without the bother of a knock?"

"And who are you to question me?" the man inquired in high temper.

"I'm the housekeeper. Betsy is my name. And the Captain left me in charge of his household."

"Very well, Betsy," he sneered, "take me to my sister."

"Yer sister? Ye mean Missy Rebecca?"

"Of course. Now, where is she? I have a carriage waiting!"

"In her room at the top of the stairs. But ye can't be goin' up. She's in bed," replied the woman, trying to block him from going to her mistress' room.

"Up the stairs, you say." He brushed past her, mounting the steps two at a time; the woman right behind him. Once on the second floor he stopped to ponder which of the four doors might be his sister's.

The housekeeper rushed past him and braced herself in front of her mistress' room. "Ye can't be goin' in," she cried. "Ye can't be botherin' her, now!"

He pushed her aside and entered the room. A pale young woman lay in a huge four-poster bed, her petite body diminutive amidst the quilted blankets; her eyes were pools of fear.

"William, what are you doing here?" she managed to gasp.

"I have come to take you home," he said, walking closer to the bed.

"Didn't you get my letter? I wrote you not to come. I promised to have Jeremiah's child here, on the Island."

"You're having his bastard! Isn't that enough?"

"My child is not … a .. a … what you say. We are married! The document is there," she cried, pointing to a rolled parchment lying on the oak dresser just beyond her reach.

William read the elaborate hand-written document. After he had finished, he held the paper by one edge, his nose pinched slightly as if smelling something repugnant.

"And who exactly is this Captain Black who married you?" He did not wait for her reply. "Someone, no doubt, Lathrope hired to perform the 'so-called' marriage." He tossed the paper to the floor. "It hardly matters, Rebecca, whether you were married or not. I ask you—what is a promise to a dead man?"

"I gave my word, William. Isn't that enough, even for you?"

"No, dear sister, it is not. Besides you are not yet of age, therefore, I am still responsible for you, and you will do as I say. You are coming back to Virginia with me; back to your own kind.

The man from the shed appeared in the doorway. "Missy Rebecca, I'm 'ere."

Rebecca, her eyes pleading, cried out, "Toby! Tell my brother that I must stay on the island."

Before Toby could speak, the man turned to face the servant, "I am William Stewart of Stewart Hall, and I am here to take my sister away from this god-forsaken place."

Toby stepped inside the room. "I know who ye be," he said, "but ye best let Missy Rebecca be, Mistah Stewart. The Cap'n wanted 'is youngun born on Nantucket."

"You dare to argue with me?" the man asked, his face flushed with anger. "You say another word and I'll have your hide."

"William, you must not hurt him," she pleaded. "He is a friend and a free-born man."

"And, I suppose, you have a paper to show that?" his voice dripping with venom.

"He doesn't need one," she insisted. "He has always been free."

Toby took another step closer to the couple, followed by the housekeeper who stood quietly by the side of the bed. "Ye best be goin' Mistah Stewart," Toby said. "Missy Rebecca won't be leavin' this place."

William's voice was calm and without a trace of emotion as he responded, "Rebecca, do you want this person taken into custody? My driver has been instructed to go for the law if I so order. When the authorities arrive, I'll swear to the fact that you are harboring a runaway slave from Virginia. And you know what will happen to your Toby if that occurs."

"You can't mean that. Oh, William, even you cannot be so cruel as to swear to a lie."

"Dear sister. You know me better than to doubt my word. I told you not to see your captain again and you disobeyed my order."

The young woman lay back on the pillows exhausted. "I don't have the strength to fight you, William. But I beg you to allow me to stay until after my babe is born."

William turned to the housekeeper. "Get your mistress ready for the journey. We will be leaving as soon as her things are packed."

"If ye be goin' Missy, I be goin', too," insisted Toby.

Alarm clouded her features. "No, Toby! You must stay here."

"Beg yer pardon, Missy, but Cap'n Jeremiah told me not to leave ye," Toby insisted.

Rebecca searched her brother's face for some sign of pity and found none. William looked down at her, his eyes void of expression. She attempted to touch his arm, he pulled away and his expression remained hard and cruel. As she reached out again to touch her brother, begging, "Will you allow him to go with me?" she pleaded.

"He can go, but I'll brook no interference. If he tries, I'll have him hung."

After Rebecca's things had been packed, William carried his frail sister out of the room. Toby, unobserved, retrieved the marriage document and hid it under his shirt. He picked up the trunk and two valises and followed William and Rebecca out of the house. He stayed a moment on the front porch, his eyes lovingly taking in the home he had helped his captain build.

"Wall, Cap'n," he whispered. "I'll be lookin' after yer lady as promised, but I think she'll be joinin' ye soon."

A week after arriving at Stewart Hall, a baby boy came into the world. Rebecca's lips trembled as she kissed his pink cheek.

"Where is Toby?" she asked. "I must see him."

"Rest now," soothed the elderly doctor.

She smiled. "That will come all too soon. Now, I must see Toby."

The doctor opened the door. "Come in, boy," he said, motioning toward Toby. "Your mistress wishes to speak with you, but don't stay long. She is very weak."

Toby had seen the face of death, both on sea and land. Tears filled his eyes as he recognized its presence in the room of his beloved captain's lady.

Rebecca touched his arm. "Promise me that when my son is old enough, you will take him to Captain Black."

"I'll be gettin' 'im thar," assured the man.

Rebecca looked at the vicar, who had followed Toby into the room. "My son's name is Nathaniel Jeremiah Lathrope. His father was Captain Jeremiah Collins Lathrope. It's my hope and prayer that he will bring honor to the name we give to him."

A smiled touched her lips. She held out her arms. "Jeremiah," she whispered, then slipped into the eternities.

The doctor checked her pulse. "She has departed this life."

"For a much better one," voiced the vicar.

Once more the door opened and William entered.

"I could not save her, Stewart," the doctor told him. "However, the boy is alive."

Showing no emotion, William looked at the two men, ignoring Toby. "My sister died of fever; there was no child. If I ever hear any different, the pair of you will suffer. You have my guarantee of that!"

Neither man replied.

William glared at Toby. "Take this pup to the slave quarters. Give him to the wench whose babe died this morning. She is to wet nurse him, and raise him as her own." His countenance was full of vengeance. "Listen to these words, for I intend to carry them out. I'll destroy anyone who dares reveal what has just transpired. Now, all of you get out! Leave me with my sister."

In the foyer, the vicar sighed. "If only they had come to me, I would have gladly joined them in marriage. Now all I have to record is her death."

"Am I to understand," the doctor asked him, incredulously, "you'll not record the birth of her son?"

At that moment a look of determination came over the vicar's features. Straightening his shoulders, he answered, "By all that is holy, I'll record the birth."

"And what about Stewart's threat?" inquired the doctor.

The vicar looked up. "I must do the duty God has given me. I can do no less."

Toby smiled. He retrieved the paper from his shirt where he had been keeping it and handed it to the vicar. "My Cap'n married 'is lady. Here be the paper to prove it."

While reading the document, a smile came over the vicar's face. He entered the following in the book of records:

"Born this day, fifteenth of May, 1788 to Rebecca Ann Stewart Lathrope and Captain Jeremiah Collins Lathrope, husband and wife, a son, Nathaniel Jeremiah Lathrope, I hereby do declare.

Signed Steven Cummins, Vicar

He handed the paper to the doctor, who wrote below his signature.

Dr. Jonah Pierce, witness

"Can I be keepin' the papers?" asked Toby.

The two men looked at each other, and then the doctor gave the papers back to the black man. Toby placed the two documents under his shirt, knowing they would be needed when the lad was old enough to understand their importance.

Chapter One

❦

Ireland – 1811

Night was coming to the village of Kilcrohane. Candles flickered in brown-thatched cottages throughout the glen to greet the men coming in from the fields. The sun flamed orange; leaving behind a trail of color to fade into the darkening sky as it disappeared from view. For an instant the valley was bathed in shadows; then clouds slipped apart, allowing the moon to cast its silvery beams through misty rain.

The deep purple of the far mountains reflected on the mirrored surface of a small lake where a mother duck gathered her young safely beneath her wings and glided to the water's edge. A cat, followed by her brood, dashed across the meadow and darted into a barn. A flock of sheep neared a break in the stone wall, at their sound a cottage door opened and a woman stepped out onto the cobbled porch. Her auburn hair, fixed in a bun at the nape of her neck with soft wisps curling in about her face, its brilliance warming the ivory of her skin. Her dress was modest, simple, and dark in color. The white starched apron was stark against the background of the garment.

"Meghan," the woman called out, "Hurry along, child. Soon yer da will be home, and 'tis help with the sup I be needin'." Her voice reached the ears of the girl at the head of the flock.

"Just as soon as Old Woolly decides to go in, I'll be comin'," she called back.

"Drive him through the gate, child. There's no need to keep yer da waitin'."

Kathleen McGonigal turned and re-entered the cottage, closing the door behind her. Her own heart was heavy, for she feared this night would be the beginning of a lifetime of heartache for her daughter. And she knew there was nothing she could do to stay it.

Outside in the misty rain Meghan knelt beside the ram, her hands tugging the wool at each side of its neck. "Did ye not hear me mum?" she asked.

Old Woolly tossed his powerful head and freed himself. Laughing, the girl gave him a hug, rose to her feet, and grabbing his bell strap, began pulling him toward the gate.

"Meghan, stop yer playin'. Run them through to the pen, now!" cried her mother, leaning out of the open window. "'Tis a fit yer da will be havin' if all is not prepared by his return."

Meghan's strong, slender hands clenched into fists; her brow furrowed as she faced her pet. "Do ye want me to give you what for?" she asked the ram, her voice tinged with anger.

Again Old Woolly tossed his head but stood his ground. Meghan leaned forward, her lips close to his ear and whispered. "Soon the Wee Folks will be about, and if it's a stray they think you be, 'tis into little pieces they'll be carvin' ye."

Still he balked.

"'Tis enough of your stubborn way," Meghan hissed, losing all patience. "Stay here and see what's yer reward. 'Tis a roast on a spit ye'll be. Me da will see to that."

With a sudden bleat the ram bolted in, the rest of the flock close behind. As Meghan closed and latched the gate, she turned sharply and slipped on a moss-covered rock and sprawled full-length in a puddle of murky water.

I don't think me mum will be amused, she thought as she hurried toward home.

Kathleen met her daughter at the door. "Oh, Meghan, what have ye done?" She joined her daughter on the porch. "Why, tonight of all nights, must ye be so careless?"

"What be so important about this night? 'Tis only himself comin'; and no matter what, he'll be findin' fault."

"Enough of yer sass," her mother replied. "Now, take off yer shoes. I won't be havin' ye track mud through me clean rooms. A guest be comin' for the sup." A note of sadness came into her voice causing Meghan to look sharply at her mother. The woman avoided her daughter's eyes. "Yer bath water be warmin' on the hearth," she told her daughter.

"Mum?"

"Not another word till ye clean yerself."

Meghan took the bucket of water and walked the few steps to her room behind the hearth. Once there, she poured the water her mother had placed beside the bed into the tub. She had removed her outer garments when a terrible feeling of doom struck her. *It couldn't be!* she thought. No! *It wasn't time yet.*

Meghan came slowly around the hearth and back into the common room, containing both the living area and the kitchen. She found her mother staring into the fire. "Who be comin' for sup?" she asked, her voice trembling.

Her mother turned to face her. Then, at the look on her mother's face, the girl cried passionately! "I won't be doin' it. Nothin' me da can do will make me marry that horrible man."

Meghan slumped into a chair, her face buried in her hands. Tears poured through heavy lashes and streamed down her pale face. Was it only a moment or two ago that she had been playing with her pet without a care in the world? Now that world lay still and broken about her. Kathleen went to Meghan's side. The year since her man promised their daughter to wed Brian O'Shea had rushed by like leaves in the autumn breeze. Now that time was nigh and her beloved child would be the wife of the most feared and hated man in the countryside. Little did she care that he was also the most powerful and rich. So immersed in her own anguish, the mother could find no words to ease her daughter's pain. Gradually she cleared away her own grievous thoughts. This was not helping her precious child and at all cost she must do that.

"Meghan, me darlin'," she finally said, caressing the girl's long auburn hair, "I wish I could be sayin' the words ye yearn to hear, but I cannot. 'Tis the Squire O'Shea who be comin' this night." Kathleen kissed her daughter's eyelids, then the tip of her nose before continuing. "His year of mourning be over and he's comin' to ask for what's been promised him."

"'Twasn't me that promised such a dreadful thing, and I'll not be givin' meself to the likes of him. I'd take me own life first."

Tears leaped to Kathleen's eyes, but her voice did not quiver. "Nay, nay, Meghan. Never be sayin' such a frightful thing. To be takin' yer life be a mortal sin, and ye be knowin' that as well as I."

"Oh, Mum, be there not a widow in the glen who'd take him for her man?"

"He wants ye and the sons ye'll be bearin' him."

Meghan's back straightened her head up. She stood facing her mother. "I'll leave this cottage, and none will see me again. I mean it, Mum. I won't be his wife, now or ever."

"I've been meditatin' on Mary's Crown," continued Kathleen, looking into her daughter's eyes. "She'll not be lettin' any harm come to ye. Now, back to yer room and get dressed. There's no use fightin' before the time is due."

Meghan expression changed. An impish gleam came into her tear-stained eyes as she muttered, "Maybe the King of the Wee Folk will be gatherin' me into his arms and fly me off to live in his grand castle." She laughed and it was a grand thing to hear. "Not even the Squire, himself, will be able to find me there."

"Aye, maybe he will at that," agreed a smiling Kathleen. "Now, you best be addin' more hot water to yer tub. 'Twon't be long till they are here. And we can't be havin' them see ye in yer pelt. If the Squire were seein' ye like this, nothin' could hold him back from takin' what he thinks is his."

Meghan's face flamed. "He'll never be seein' even the turn of an ankle let alone what ye see before ye." So saying, Meghan hurried back around the hearth.

Quickly she climbed into the tub and bathed. After finishing, she wrapped a large towel about her wet body and looked about the room, so cozy and warm from the coals in the kitchen fire. The Irish lace on top of her dresser had been given to her mother on her own wedding day. Meghan knew she should have put it away for the time she went to a cottage of her own, but it was so beautiful with its raised rose border that she could not part with looking at it.

Even the rag rug she was standing upon was full of memories. Parts of it were cut from remnants of dresses given to her over the years. Her favorite was from a dress her Granny Berry had sent on her third birthday. The material, once of emerald green, was faded now, yet she could still pick it out from the others.

Meghan had a choice of two dresses that she could wear this night. One was a beautiful shade of green, which brought out the gold flecks in her green eyes and the highlights of her long red hair. The other was of a dull shade of gray. It wiped out the color in her cheeks and made her look older and dreary. She grinned as she put the green dress away.

"Someday there'll be a lad for this one," she whispered to herself.

Meghan dressed, pulled on long black stockings and slipped her feet into worn slippers.

She peered into the cracked mirror on the wall, pulled back her hair and studied her reflected image. Freckles still bridged across her nose and cheeks, and she wondered again if they would ever fade away. Her skin was free of any other blemish, her neck long and slender. Because of the crack, one eye appeared higher than the other did. She could not help giggling. "If the Squire could see me as the mirror does, he wouldn't be wantin' to marry me."

Meghan brushed her tangled hair until it shone. Her hair was her one prideful possession, and, not even to make the Squire think her ugly, would she neglect giving it one hundred and ten strokes with the brush.

When Meghan returned to the kitchen, she set the table with their finest china, then gave a quick dusting to the wooden furniture and a swift turn of the broom over the highly polished floor. She had just finished as John McGonigal opened the door and stepped over the threshold, his eyes took in the sparkling condition of the room and the woman and girl standing in front of him. He did not say whether he was pleased with what he saw or not. He removed his cap. His dark brown hair, touched only at the temples with gray, curled over his ears and at the nape of his neck. He crossed the room, sat down beside the table, and stuck out one leg. Meghan hurried to help him take off his boots; Kathleen handed her his slippers.

"The sup ready?" he asked crossly as Meghan finished her task.

"Where be the Squire?" questioned Kathleen.

"He insisted on comin' by wagon." Turning his thoughts to Meghan, he demanded she stand before him. "And be bringing along the lamp." His cold, green eyes raked over her attire. Before he could comment there was a heavy knock at the door. "'Tis the Squire," he said. "Go let him in, Meghan. And be givin' him yer sweetest smile or 'tis the back of me hand ye'll be feeling."

O'Shea's massive form filled the doorway. Where McGonigal was tall and lean, O'Shea was built like a bull. His legs were far too short for his thick-barreled chest; his wide, short neck supported a large, round head full of unruly red hair. His small eyes accentuated the huge nose, red now from the nip in the crisp air.

When Meghan did not give O'Shea the hearty welcome her father had ordered, he called out, "Come, pull up a chair, the sup be on the table."

"Good evenin', one and all!" boomed O'Shea. "'Tis that glad I am to be here." He pulled out a chair and sat down. Leaning toward McGonigal, he continued speaking. Only this time his voice was a bit lower. "Have ye told them the good news?" He jerked his head toward Kathleen and Meghan.

"The matter can wait till after the sup," McGonigal said, dishing up the meat, boiled potatoes, and cabbage onto the plates in front of him.

Kathleen sat opposite her husband while Meghan, with downcast eyes, sat across the table from O'Shea.

"How do ye fare, Meghan?" Not waiting for her answer, O'Shea proceeded to fill his mouth with food, some of it oozing down from the corners of his mouth, then he repeated the question.

This time Meghan did reply her voice barely above a whisper. "I be fine."

"I not be hearin' ye," complained the man, taking another bit from his plate.

McGonigal looked at his daughter, his eyes narrow with impatience. "Meghan, answer the man and be doin' it so he can be hearin' the words."

"Perhaps the food in his mouth be pluggin' up his ears," was her impish reply.

"McGonigal," O'Shea's eyes narrowed to slits, "Is this how ye allow yer child to speak to a guest in yer house?" McGonigal did not answer.

O'Shea jumped to his feet, his voice demanding, "Did ye not hear me?"

"If it not be for the howling of the wind, the whole glen is hearin' ye!" shouted back McGonigal.

Kathleen hurried to close the shutters to muffle the voices from the ears of the villagers. As she returned to her place at the table, her husband laid aside his fork.

"There's somethin' that needs be said, and I'll be sayin' it. Meghan, look at me!"

The girl raised her head to meet her father's gaze.

"'Tis nearly fifteen ye be, and 'tis time for ye to be married and carin' for a cottage of yer own. And since 'tis me duty to find ye a husband, I have chosen Brian O'Shea. I see no reason to have a period of courtin'. Ye know the man, and he knows ye, so the marriage takes place within the month."

Meghan rose to her feet. "I'll not be havin' him for m'man," she said, her voice clear and without a trace of fear.

O'Shea's chair fell with a crash as he jerked to his feet. "What's that ye say?" He glared first at Meghan then back to her father. "Since when does a colleen tell her da what she will and will not be doin'?" he demanded. "Tell her here and now that she has to marry me."

McGonigal's face contorted with rage, his hands clenched into tight fists as they slammed upon the table, his feet firmly planted on the wooden floor. Leaning across the table, inches from O' Shea's startled face, he snarled, "Brian O'Shea, this is me home, and 'tis only me that does the demandin'." Neither his face nor eyes softened as he looked into the pale features of his wife and daughter. "Now, sit down all of ye."

O'Shea righted his chair and sat down, his eyes fixed on the head of the household. He smiled. He knew he had nothing to fear from John McGonigal. The man wanted the *promised land* far too much to let his daughter stand in the way. It was not the usual way for a dowry to be paid—from the groom to the parents of the bride—but he wanted to have her far too much to let convention stand in his way. And besides, what could McGonigal give him he did not already have, aye, and have more abundantly? No, O'Shea knew the marriage would take place. To Meghan's father, the land was the most important thing in the world. He was enjoying himself. There was nothing he liked better than to see another man crumble before him.

McGonigal cleared his throat, his eyes drilling into his daughter's. "Meghan, me mind is made up and I'll be havin' no more words upon the matter. Is that clear?"

Meghan looked at O'Shea before facing her father. She made no effort to control the fire flaming in her own eyes.

"The truth be standin' in front of ye. Dead, I'd sooner be, than be any wife of his."

O'Shea looked at the beauty of the girl in front of him, her skin glowed with anger, her eyes molten pools of hatred. Words sprang to O'Shea's lips and burst forth. "Aye, I like spirit in me women, 'tis all the more to tame them."

Meghan swirled to face him. "'Tis not the truth ye be speakin' and all the room knows the lie for what it be. 'Tis known to all here that ye beat the spirit out of yer poor dead wife. I imagine she was that pleased to have death claim her wretched soul rather than live any more with the likes of ye." Her words shot out like deadly daggers. "And me own da would be puttin' me into yer foul hands."

"Ye'll be doin' as yer told," her father barked.

"And if I don't?" Meghan demanded.

"Then 'tis out of the cottage with no more than what's on yer back! Can the meanin' be clearer than that?"

Kathleen had remained silent during the entire exchange. Now, she rose, her hands in fists upon her slim hips. She looked directly at her husband.

"Nay, John. Ye'll not be drivin' the child out as ye did her brother. He was well equipped to care for himself, so I did not stand in the way, but Meghan, be different. If she goes, she will not be goin' alone. 'Tis me who'll be goin' with her, and 'tis more than the clothes on our back we'll be takin'. All the fine things I brought with me on our weddin' day will be goin' with us. Now, be thinkin' it over. Does she stay, or will I be leavin' too?"

For a moment McGonigal appeared stunned. The room stilled, not a sound could be heard as the occupants looked at him. Finally he spoke. "She can stay but only until the weddin'."

"John, knowin' how she feels, ye'll still force this weddin' upon her?"

"No earthly threats will keep it from happenin'," he replied, picking up his fork and stabbing another piece of meat from the main platter.

Wordlessly, Meghan fled from the cottage and out into the night.

Chapter Two

❧

T he cold night air chilled Meghan to the bone, yet she continued in her flight until she reached the edge of the lake. The night was quiet, and the wind had ceased its race across the meadows.

"I'll not be marryin' that dreadful man," she sobbed, hating Brian O'Shea far more intently than she would have believed possible; far more than she feared her father. If only she knew where to find her brother. He would help her, she was certain of that.

It was Gavin who taught her to climb her first tree. Other girls might have been afraid but not Meghan. She loved to sit on the highest branch and see the valleys and dells below. She remembered the time she had almost fallen but was caught by her brother's strong arms. It was not until then had she realized he had always stayed on a branch just below in case such a thing might happen.

Her first memory of going to the fish traps was with her brother. Afterwards, they would walk along the shore, and sometimes Meghan would talk about her desire to go out in the fishing boats with the men and boys in the village.

Gavin would laughingly say, "Dear little Meghan. 'Tis not a boy ye be lookin' like."

"Well, I wish it all the same," was her standard answer.

Her mind continued to roam in the past. She thought again of that winter's night when she witnessed the awful fight between her father and brother. They were in the yard, she in the cottage. She could not hear their words, but from her bedroom window she saw her father strike Gavin and Gavin draw back his hand as if to retaliate. But the blow never came. Dropping his arm Gavin ran past his father and into the loft. In a few minutes he came out with his canvas bag slung over his shoulder. That had been three years ago. Since then she had seen him only three times. He had told her to send him word if she ever needed him. If only she knew where to find him, now!

The sound of galloping hooves interrupted her troubled reverie. O'Shea must have finally given up waiting for her return. She could go back now. Meghan prayed with all her might that her father had retired for the night.

Upon arriving at the cottage, Meghan silently opened the door and stepped inside. Just as quietly, she closed the door behind her. Embers glowed in the hearth casting shadows into the room. Her parents were no where in sight.

Angry voices came from beyond the curtain partitioning of her parents' room. Upon hearing her father's heavy footsteps, she hid behind the settle and watched in silence as her parents stepped through the curtains.

"Please, John," her mother pleaded. "Won't ye be tellin' me what has angered ye so? There was a time ye'd ordered Brian O'Shea out of the cottage. Don't ye remember how ye loved our little Meghan? Tell me what has happened to change ye so?"

"Just be puttin' yer mind to it," her father replied sullenly, "and I'm sure 'twill be comin' to ye."

McGonigal rummaged in the cupboard for the whisky bottle, found it, and poured himself a drink. He quickly downed the fiery fluid and poured another before turning back to his wife.

For a long moment he stared at her anguished face, suffused by the rosy glow of the dying fire. With a strangled sob he reached out, and pulling her into his arms, crushed his lips to hers. She struggled to free herself.

"Stop it, John, and answer me question." she repeated, her lips trembling. "Why do ye hate me so?"

"Hate ye? Oh, Katie. Can't ye be seein' the truth of it. If only ye would tell me . . ." he paused.

Meghan held her breath waiting for him to finish his sentence.

"But who be knowin' it better than ye?" he growled.

Walking to the door, McGonigal took his cap from the hook and slammed from the cottage.

Kathleen slumped in a chair; her face in her slim hands. Meghan rushed from her hiding place to kneel at her mother's side.

"Mum, please don't be crying," she begged.

Startled, her mother looked up. "Meghan! Where did ye come from?"

"I was hidin' behind the settle. I couldn't help hearin' the spoken words. Oh, Mum, can't ye be seein' he isn't worth one little tear in yer blessed heart?"

"Yer da is a man full of sadness," answered her mother, drying her tears. "Oh, child, be ye rememberin' the times he was kind and gentle? Then do ye remember when he changed so?"

Meghan shook her head.

"'Twas the day he smashed yer lovely little cart. Now, 'tis it comin' back to ye?" urged her mother.

An uninvited smile crossed Meghan's lips as the memory of that cart flashed into her mind. She had been wondering that Saturday morning what her father had been doing so long in the locked shed.

In response to his call, she came running from the cottage, and there before her was the most beautiful pony she had ever seen. It was light brown with a golden mane and tail. She had gasped with pure delight as he brought out the cart, its wood polished until she could see her features in the glory of it. He had painted colorful flowers around the borders of the cart, and to Meghan it looked as though the pony pulled a little garden.

Her father lifted her into the cart and handed her the reins. He got in beside her and placed his large hands over her little ones and off they rode. Meghan turned back to see her mother wave as they drove down the lane toward the village.

Everyone they met had smiled and said how wonderful the cart was. Meghan remembered how some of the village women's eyes lit up as they smiled at her father. "And why not?" she had reasoned, "for wasn't he the most handsome man in all the glen."

On the way back home, he had stopped to chat with a neighbor and his wife while Meghan stroked and crooned to the pony. Suddenly, without warning, she was snatched up and sat roughly into the cart. Her father, his eyes blazing, his face drained of color, his hands shaking with fury, whipped the pony mercilessly and the cart careened perilously toward home. Meghan could not even imagine what might have angered her father. But whatever it was had changed him.

Once home, he lifted Meghan from the cart and ordered her to the cottage. He unhitched and rolled the cart into the shed and bolted the door from the inside. Meghan heard the sound of smashing wood and ran to find her mother.

"Please, be quick! Da's gone daft!" she cried.

Kathleen ran past her frightened daughter. She banged on the door until, at last, her husband opened it. His face twisted with such pain and anger that Meghan hardly recognized the beloved features. For a moment Meghan thought her father would strike her, but then, with a cry, he dropped his hand and stumbled from the shed. Her mother stood stunned and silent.

Tears streamed down Meghan's face; she stooped and picked up one tiny wooden flower, miraculously left intact, and carried it back to her room where she hid it in her marriage chest.

That night her father returned to the cottage, neither speaking nor looking at Meghan. And in truth, he was never to speak a kind or loving word to her again.

Her mother's voice, sad and low, brought Meghan back to the present. "There was a time," her mother was saying, "that yer da was so full of life. And a more handsome man ye'd not be seein' anywhere in the glen. At the time of our meetin', I thought meself in love with his younger brother David. In fact, the banns had been posted.

"I had been milkin' the cows when yer da, who had been livin' in Limerick, came with his father to visit our farm. While the older men were talkin', yer da came up behind me, all quiet like while I was doin' the milkin'. He spoke to me, and I was that startled. I fell backwards off the stool into a pool of murky water. He laughed. I got up, took a swing at him and missed. And then, do ye know what he did?"

Meghan shook her head.

"Well, I'll be tellin' ye. He pulled me into his arms and right then and there he kissed me. It fair took me breath away. When I could speak, I told him the truth of it. The banns had been posted for me weddin' with his brother. Yer da turned deadly white, yet never a word said he. He turned and left me standin' there with me skirts drippin' wet and the feel of his lips still on me own."

Kathleen stood by the window, looking out into the night. The moon moved behind a cloud as the mist grew heavy over the moors.

Her daughter joined her; neither of them spoke. Minutes ticked by before Kathleen spoke again.

"The next time I saw him 'twas at the village dance. He came in and stood for awhile by the door. The other colleens at the dance were all about my age, yer da bein' some seven years older, and I watched them try to capture his eye. He danced with one or two of them, but all the while I could tell he was watchin' me. David said that he was that surprised to see John there, and he insisted I dance with him. Yer da took me into his arms and we flew across the room. 'Twas as if I could have danced upon cobwebs and never bruised a one. He danced me out of the room. Once outside, he pulled me away from the light. Me heart was beatin' so hard, I could barely breathe."

He said, "Ye feel it too, don't ye?"

"Feel what?" I asked, me voice trembling with excitement.

"'Tis not a time for playin' games," he replied, his lips close to me ear. "I must be knowin' the truth of it."

"Oh, how could I admit that me heart had fairly soared from its restin' place to nestle in his chest, there I knew it would remain forever in his keepin'. All I could do was nod me head, but 'twas enough for him."

"'Oh, Kathleen,' he continued, holdin' me close, "'ye can't be marryin' me brother now—not when we know we love each other. For ye do love me, don't ye? Please be sayin' the words I've been longin' to hear since I first laid eyes on ye and took ye into me arms.'

"He kissed me again, only this time his lips barely pressed against mine. I told him I did love him and would never stop the longin' I felt for him. He would forever be in me heart, and I could never forget him. I also told him I must never see him again, and I begged him that after David and I wed, he would stay away.

"I broke free of him and did not look back until I was standin' in the entrance to the hall, but I shall never forget the look of him. It was as if death had struck him, with eyes like black holes burned into a white blanket.

"I could not bear it. I returned to the dance. A little while later he came back in. Me heart ached as he twirled the others around the floor. Each colleen would smile up at him, and every now and then one would laugh as if he was tellin' some precious secret. I could bear it no more, and I asked David to take me home. He said we couldn't leave now and wanted to know what be the matter with me. I couldn't be tellin' him I loved his brother, so I said 'twas all the excitement of our comin' weddin', and he laughed and pulled me into his arms.

"He called out to the others, 'Kathleen is tired and wants to go home'." He winked. "'Twill not be long until the colleen will only be doin' what I want, and 'twon't be makin' any difference, be she tired or no.'

"Everyone laughed, that is, everyone except yer da; his face looked like chiseled stone. He came over and told David there be no use in both of them leavin', and since he was on his way back to Limerick, he would take me home. I told them both, if there were to be a fuss, I would stay until David wanted to go. David said he really couldn't be leavin' his friends so early in the evenin', and it would be fine if John took me home. There was nothin' I could do but go."

"Would ye be wantin' a cup of tay?" interrupted Meghan.

"Aye, 'twill warm me a bit, at that," Kathleen replied.

The women were silent as Meghan took the cups from cupboard. The tea was soon prepared and she filled the cups and gave one to her mother. Then she took her own and came back to sit beside her mother.

As Kathleen sipped her tea, Meghan urged her to continue with the story. In the past she had heard how her parents first met, but never once had her father's brother been a part of the telling. In fact, until this very moment, she had never known that she even had an Uncle David. She wanted to ask her mother why his name had never been mentioned, but she didn't want to break the spell of her mother's words and so remained quiet.

In a few moments Kathleen put aside her cup. She did not look at her daughter as she continued her story. "We did not speak in the buggy nor did he say a word as he helped me down. He walked with me to the cottage door, waited until I opened it and stepped inside, then he was gone."

"And the next time ye saw him?"

"'Twas the very next day and I had gone for a walk amongst the rocks by the sea.

I was fairly bowled over seein' him sittin' on the sand, his gaze toward some far shore. At first he'd not seen me, and 'twas a shock for him when he did. The look of him fairly tore out me heart; it was so full of sadness. I turned to leave, but my foot slipped on a rock and I fell, landin' on the sand below. He was that quick upon his feet, and the next thing I knew he was kneelin' by me side. I was that embarrassed, I was. I turned my head away, so he couldn't be seein' the longin' in me eyes. He cupped me chin in his hand and forced me to look at him."

"I tried to fight the risin' desire within me but I couldn't. He knew that, too. He sat down beside me and pulled me into his arms. The next thing I am knowin', we were both lying on the sand, his arms wrapped about me. It was as if we were the only two in the world, not thinkin' about anythin' except our love.

"'Twas only later that I worried about our bein' seen. We did not fulfill our love, but 'twas unseemly lyin' there and kissing, just the same.

"We both knew I could never marry David now. It would be seen as a sin in the eyes of Heaven to marry one man while lovin' another.

John said he would speak with me da and then to his brother. Oh, how I dreaded that meetin'."

"'Twas a shock to them, us wantin' to wed, and not only to our families but also to the whole glen. Me da was a kind and lovin' man. He spoke to John's family, and in the end they gave their consent. All, that is, but David. He was a bitter man and vowed that we would never find a minute's peace if we did this terrible thing and bring shame to him. Then came our weddin' day. I was that surprised to see David at the church, but there he was. Me heart perked up when I saw he had a smile upon his lips, but plunged to the depths of despair as I looked into his eyes, they were so full of hate. Oh, I hope never to see such a look again.

"He walked over to where we were and asked John to go with him. They were gone so long everyone began to whisper, and I started to fear the worse. When yer da did return, he was alone. He held me close. I could feel the poundin' of his heart and asked what be the matter. He asked if I were sure it was he that I loved and not his brother. I told him, as I had before, that until I met him, I thought meself in love with David. I then laughed and told him I'd never lain on the sand with anyone but him. Suddenly, he laughed, too, and all the worry left his face."

Meghan laid her head on her mother's lap. "Oh, Mum, if he loved ye so much that he defied the whole glen for ye, what could have happened when I was little to make him change so?"

"I don't know, and can hardly be guessin'," was the reply.

Gently Kathleen lifted her daughter's head, and then rose to stand by the window, where Meghan joined her.

"Please leave me now," Kathleen said. "I can't be speakin' anymore. 'Tis been a long day, and I'm weary."

Meghan kissed her mother and went to her own room and bed.

She lay for a long time listening to the faint patter of rain against the window-pane. Finally, she fell asleep.

When she awakened the fiery flame that had enveloped her earlier that evening, had burned out. She felt cold, empty, and alone. Her throat grew tight, her chest hurt. She had to do something or die. She left her bed and went in search of her mother. Her mother could make things right. Always her mother had been there, her shelter from the storm.

Meghan's eyes quickly searched the darkness of the common room. Her mother was not there. She quietly crossed to her parent's room. Before any words left her lips, she watched her mother open the chest at the foot of the bed and remove a picture from a small wooden box.

"Oh, John," her mother moaned, clasping the picture to her bosom. "Whatever happened to that smilin' couple?"

Meghan turned from the tragic scene. With tears rolling down her own cheeks, she knew that it was time to find her own safe harbor.

Chapter Three

❧

Bryan O'Shea sat on the edge of the bed, a bitter taste in his mouth and an ear splitting roar in his head. *It must have been all that ale I drank last night*, he thought, pulling on his trousers. After all Meghan had put him through, it was no wonder he had taken a nip or two. Even now he could still see her standing so straight and tall, her eyes blazing with anger, her body pulsating with hatred; but marry her, he would. He could see it now. Following the departure of their guests, he would leave the room for her to make ready for bed. When he returned, she would still be dressed. He would tell her to remove her clothing; she would refuse and demand that she be taken home. And that was something he would never do. He wanted her to be mistress of his home and to bear his sons and daughters, and most of all he wanted her in his bed.

Meghan was right in saying he had beaten his wife, but what he did was no one's business. No one would be allowed to question him. What he did away from the farm was his affair, nobody else, least of all a wife's.

He looked about for his slippers. When Nora was alive, at least everything was in its place. He ran his fingers down the nearest bedpost, then looked at the thin layer of dust upon them. The heavy drapes about his bed needed a good wash and the braided rug needed a scrubbing. Well, as soon as he married Meghan that would all change. She would take charge of the household and make sure his wishes were carried out. Her pride would see to that.

He felt a gentle breeze; it enticed him to the veranda. As far as he could see the land was his, and he was rightfully proud of what he had accomplished. His home was another thing that fed his enormous ego. A whitewashed, thatched roof cottage was not good enough for him. He had seen the original house on a trip to England and decided, then and there, that he must have it duplicated for his own. He also knew that it would impress Nora's family. He led them to believe they would benefit from the union of their daughter to a man they felt was socially inferior to them. It had cost him a small fortune to obtain the plans, and to bring the craftsmen here. Well, he had showed them. As soon as the marriage took place, he financially ruined James David Murphy, Nora's father. Her family left the glen in disgrace. Nora hated him for it, but he did not care. He had the land from her dowry and that was the important thing.

Once down the curved staircase to the lower floor, O'Shea saw his cook and ordered breakfast. He was not sure he would be able to eat, but he ordered it just the same. No use in paying the lazy lot for doing nothing. Assured that the meal would not take long, O'Shea stepped outside into the misty rain. He lifted his face; the air felt cool against his hot skin, although it did nothing to help his throbbing head.

He looked across the emerald fields where a flock of his sheep grazed. Soon it would be time for the shearing, and afterwards more coffers would be added to his fortune. He turned at the approach of a servant. "The geeusafry, ye ordered be ready," the old woman told him.

O'Shea stepped into the dining hall. At the sight of fried eggs, bacon, and bread, his stomach revolted. He waved the food away. With a servant's help, he went back to his room and lay across his bed, aching.

Chapter Four

❧

Meghan awakened late, the sun was up yet there was a chill in the air. She dressed quickly then found her mother at the kitchen table.

"Mum, 'tis that sorry I am for causin' ye grief last night but after tellin' me all ye did, ye can see, can't ye, that I could never be marryin' a man I didn't love?"

"Aye, I've done a heap of thinkin', too. And maybe ye won't be marryin' one Bryan O'Shea."

"Oh, Mum, ye found a way?"

"Aye, that I do." Seeing Meghan about to speak, she hastened to add, "No!" Don't be askin' questions. Now, be eatin' a mite before yer chores. I must be off to the village."

After eating Meghan hurried out of the cottage and ran to open the pen. It was not long until she and the flock headed down the lane where the hired boy was waiting to take the sheep to pasture. With a wave and a promise to return by dusk, Meghan headed for the sea-shore to tend the fish traps with her closest and dearest friend Julianne Allen. She found the girl lying on the sand, looking up at the sky.

"'Tis a fine time of the day to be comin' to the fish traps," Julianne said. "I've been here for hours."

"I'm thinkin' ye've been here only minutes, and there's no use in ye denin' that fact," replied Meghan.

"Well, it seemed like hours to me," the girl exclaimed, sitting up.

Julianne took one look at her friend and gasped, "What has happened? Ye look like death itself."

"'Tis a visitor we had last night, one Brian O'Shea." Meghan went on to explain the reason for his visit.

For a time neither girl spoke. Then Julianne asked, "What can ye be doin' to stop such a dreadful thing?"

"I don't know and that be the truth of that."

"Ye could be marryin' someone else," ventured Meghan's friend.

"And who would that be?" Meghan wanted to know. "For there's not a man betwixt young Willy Jawn and old man Tavey Connolly that I'd be havin'."

The ever practical Julianne replied, "Well, maybe marryin' the Squire won't be so bad. I hear tell he's rarely at home, and besides, there's not a man in all the glen who has more riches." Her eyes widened. "Why, ye could be havin' all yer heart's desire." Then added, "I hope me da will be doin' as well by me."

"Ye can't be meanin' that!" cried a horrified Meghan. "Ye must be knowin' that I'd rather be dead than feel his clammy hands upon me bare skin."

With an impish grin and sparkling eyes, Julianne replied, "Ye could close yer eyes and pretend he be fair."

"'Tis nothin' but foolishment ye're speakin'." Meghan's words were so bitterly spoken that the girl was quick to answer.

"Dear Meghan, 'tis that sorry I am for hurtin' ye so." The girl put her hand on her friend's shoulder. "I only spoke in jest. I had hoped to make ye laugh."

"There's no laughter in me anymore," Meghan sighed.

From beyond the bluff the breeze carried the faint sound of voices, and both girls rushed to the very edge of the cliff to satisfy their curiosity. To their amazement the largest boat that either of them had ever seen lay anchored in the bay.

"What could it be doin' here?" wondered Julianne. "I've only seen fishin' boats comin' up the channel."

"Silly goose, it won't be comin' up the channel. See, a smaller boat is bein' lifted over the side onto the water."

They watched as six men climbed down the rope ladder into the waiting small skiff. Then a man and woman being lowered over the side in wooden chairs soon followed them. Once all were settled into the boat, the men rowed toward the narrow channel.

"They must be goin' to the village," said Julianne. "And I can't help wonderin' why."

"I only wonder where they'll be goin' after they leave our shores."

"Some wondrous place, no doubt,'" quipped Julianne. "Wouldn't it be grand to be goin' with them?"

"Aye, it would at that," agreed Meghan.

The boat was now near enough for the girls to plainly see the occupants.

"The woman has a look of anger about her," declared Julianne. "'Tis that glad I am that it's not me she's on her way to see."

"Let's go find out."

Julianne quickly looked at Meghan. "Why?" she asked.

Ignoring the question, Meghan declared, "If we run all the way, we'll be to the village before them."

"But if we leave the fish traps, 'tis trouble we'll be in."

Things were spinning in Meghan's head. She had to be there, but why she did not know.

"I must go," Meghan said. "Please come with me, Julianne."

The look on Meghan's face drew Julianne along as if she was hypnotized. A gentle rain began to fall and broke the spell. Julianne stopped. "'Tis a devil ye be," she gasped. "Ye'll not be weavin' yer spell over me!"

"What foolishment be ye sayin'?" Meghan asked, a look of bewilderment on her face.

"Foolish or not, I'll not be goin' with ye," was the other girl's reply.

"Please, Julianne. Come with me."

"I said I'm goin' back, and goin' back is what ye best be doin', too."

With stubborn determination, Meghan declared, "Ye can go back, but there be somethin' I must be knowin'."

"Meghan, what must ye be knowin' that's important enough to risk the wrath of yer da?"

Meghan did not reply.

"Answer me," her friend pleaded. "Has the devil put in yer mind a plan for yer goin' away in that boat?" Julianne said, pointing toward the ship.

"Who's talkin' crazy now?" Meghan asked. "How could I be doin' such a thing?"

"I don't know," cried her friend. "But ye have a look about ye that frightens me."

Meghan smiled. "Then ye best be comin' with me, to keep me out of trouble."

"I durst not. If me da finds me gone from the traps, 'tis a whippin'

I'll be gettin'. And after he tells yer da, ye'll be gettin' one, too," declared Julianne.

"Me da won't be hittin' me."

Amazed, Julianne replied, "Aye, but he will and 'twon't be the first time!'

"Aye, but 'tis a blemish free body he'll be wantin' to hand over to the Squire," the bitterness clear in her voice.

"I fear for ye, Meghan. Please, don't be doin' anythin' fierce. 'Tis only trouble ye'll be headin' for."

"Aye, better trouble than belongin' to a man I detest."

"I fear for you," Julianne repeated. "Oh, Meghan. Please be careful."

Meghan smiled at her friend. "Don't be worryin' yerself. 'Tis fine I'll be."

By the time Meghan arrived at the village the couple was no where to be found. She popped her head into several shops, but they were not there. She had just about given up hope of finding them when a door opened a few feet away and the man and woman came onto the porch, they were followed by Mr. Hugh Francis Miller, a man that Meghan had known all of her life. Her heart pounded as she listened to their conversation.

The woman's eyes flashed with indignation.

"I hold you personally responsible for this . . . this inconvenience," she said to Mr. Miller, "You'll have to find someone else and immediately. It goes without saying, of course, she must be suitable and capable of helping the children with their studies. We shall be waiting on board the ship. And remember this! My husband has persuaded the captain to wait two hours, but that is all. If you have not sent someone by then, I shall let it be known that your Registry for Nannies is a farce and should not be taken seriously." The couple turned and left.

Mr. Miller was about to re-enter his shop, when Meghan called out to him. "Mr. Miller! Wait! Please! Wait!"

Mr. Miller turned around with a look of surprise on his face. "Meghan, is that you?" He removed his glasses, wiped the lenses across his sleeve and put them back on. He peered at her again. "Ah, I see that it is."

"Mr. Miller, I must speak with ye."

He did not slow his pace. Back in his office he hung his coat on a clothes peg and returned to the chair behind his desk.

"I saw your father earlier, and he told me the grand news. 'Tis a lucky colleen you'll be, with a grand house and servants to be lookin' out for your needs and desires." He reached in a drawer, pulling out a ledger. "You must be goin' to see the Widow Gaines about your weddin' dress, so I'll not be keeping you." He began scanning the pages before muttering "No, there's not another one that I can be sendin'. Oh, what will I do? That blasted woman will ruin me with her tales."

Meghan leaned across his desk. "Mr. Miller, please listen to me. I did not come about a dress. I came to see you about that man and woman. The ones I saw comin' from that big boat in the channel."

"Meghan, they call such as that, a ship, not a boat."

"Aye, a ship, then. What did they want?" Meghan continued to plead with the man until he finally put the ledger away.

He packed the bowl of his pipe and lit it. "'Tis a nanny they want, Meghan, but the colleen I hired didn't come. I'm thinkin' she didn't want to leave Ireland, when it came time."

A glow spread over Meghan's face and there came a wild beating to her heart. "Leave Ireland? Where are they goin'?"

"To a far piece from here," was his answer. "But 'tis no matter if I can't be findin' another to take her place."

Meghan moved around the desk and stood by his side. "Are they kindly people?"

"What interest do you have in the answer to that?"

"No interest for meself. Just wonderin' where they be goin' and about the colleen ye were sendin'."

"Bridgett Connolly."

He leaned forward, put his pipe down and once again opened the ledger on his desk.

"Please, Mr. Miller, just answer me this, and I'll be on me way," she assured him. "What be her duties?"

"Learnin' the wee ones readin', writin', and doin' their ciphers. Now, if you'll excuse me, I've but two hours to find another to take Bridgett's place."

"Mr. Miller, ye can be sendin' me."

That got his attention. "You? And what would your father and the Squire be sayin' to that bit of foolishment? Now, go about yer business or the widow will have closed her door."

Meghan started to speak, but he stopped her.

"There's no more time to waste," and waved her away. With downcast eyes Meghan left the office.

"Well, well, if it's not me intended."

Startled, Meghan looked up to find Brian O'Shea grinning down at her.

"Have ye come to tell me that ye'll be marryin' me, willin'ly'?"

"Nay, I have not!" cried an outraged Meghan. "Nor will ye ever be hearin' such words from me."

O'Shea laughed. "There's nothin' ye can be doin' about the fact that within the month ye'll be me wife. Yer da will see to that. Willin' or not, soon all yer beauty will be mine for the takin'." Still laughing, he turned and went into the pub.

Meghan shook with fury. How dare he speak to her as if she had no thought or will of her own? She would show him! She would show them all. She would leave the glen and never return.

Chapter Five

❧

A tall young man, broad of shoulders, and with a look of strength about him, opened the side door of the chapel and stepped inside. He walked quickly to a woman sitting alone near the back and gently placed his hand on her shoulder. She looked up and smiled.

She placed a finger on her lips and led the way to a door on the opposite side of the chapel from where the young man had entered. She took a key from her pocket and unlocked the door leading out into a garden, protected from view by three sides of the church. The fourth side was opened to the sea.

Meghan's brother, Gavin McGonigal sat on one of the wooden benches facing the sea watching his mother. The mist grew heavier. Kathleen drew her shawl over her head and about her neck and shoulders. The sound of the crashing waves brought back a flood of memories. She thought of all the times she and John had stood on such a bluff and watched the ships far out to sea. He would have his arms about her waist, his heart beating against her back; and they would talk about their future and all the things he wanted to do for her. Sometimes he would spin her around and kiss her, other times he would just brush the hair off her neck with his lips and kiss the side of her throat.

"Mum," Gavin said, breaking the spell, "I know ye didn't send for me to sit here with ye gazin' out to sea and not a word spoken betwixt us."

She did not turn around. "I sent word, my son, to ask help to spirit yer sister away before yer da could make her marry the squire."

"Then what I've been hearin' is true?" He joined his mother. "I didn't want to believe da could do such a foul thing. What is wrong with da? First he drives me, his only son, from his home and now my sister, too. Mum, we can't be lettin' this happen. Not to our little Meghan."

"Meghan is not so little anymore, Gavin. There be a beauty about her that comes from a pure heart. If he can, I know that terrible man will smother that beauty. No, I'll not be lettin' that happen."

"Then ye have a plan?"

"She must be taken away from the glen."

"But where in all of Ireland will she be safe?

With tears brimming in Kathleen's eyes, she said, "She must be taken from Ireland."

"Will ye be goin' with her?"

"Nay, Gavin. I cannot be leavin' yer da. Somethin' it is that's wrong. He's carryin' a heap of hurt upon his shoulders, and the day will come that he can no longer hold it within. I can't be leavin' him to face that day alone."

❧

BY THE TIME Meghan ran to the cottage, she was gasping for air. She opened the door and stumbled inside, calling out "Mum! Mum! Where are ye?"

Receiving no answer Meghan dropped into a chair until she could catch her breath. As soon as she was able, she looked around for her mother; she was not in the cottage. She ran out to the barn, followed by a dash to the kitchen garden, her mother was no where to be found.

A terrible thought pierced her heart. If her mother did not come home before she had to leave . . . if she couldn't say goodbye! No! The thought was too dreadful! Her mother would return in time, and with that thought in mind, Meghan hurried to her own room.

Taking the carpet bag from under the bed, Meghan quickly packed the few belongings that she could take with her. She had to leave behind the precious items in her wedding chest; and if her plan to leave on that ship were accomplished, she would never see them again. Tears spilt at the thought of never seeing the Irish linen sheets and pillow covers, the soft quilts, the crystal glasses and chinaware again. But her deepest regret was leaving behind her beloved rag rug of memories.

She took one last look about and wondered afresh why her father had forced this upon her, and prayed he would not take her disobedience out on her mother.

Then a dreadful thought came to her. Now that she was leaving who was there to help her mother with the chores, to read with her by the hearth at night, to help in the garden, to take her turn at churning the butter, and to go with her to visit the sick and needy?

Meghan found paper and pen and wrote a note to her mother. In her hour of heartache Meghan thought of her friend. Julianne could take her place beside her mother. Her own mother had passed beyond the veil. Meghan quickly added a postscript to her mother that Julianne needed her. Now, where to leave it? If her father came back and found the note before the ship sailed, all would be lost. She smiled. She would leave the letter with the good Father, James Ryan.

Meghan gathered her things together and ran to the church. She found the priest standing by the chapel door.

"Meghan, my child, what brings ye here?" he asked.

"Be givin' me time to catch me breath," she gasped, taking the letter from her pocket and handing it to him.

"What is this?"

"A letter to me mum."

"A letter? Why would ye be writin' her a letter when ye can be seein' her in a matter of minutes?"

"I can't be waitin' and that's the truth of it."

With those words said, Meghan ran down to the sea and jumped into the waiting boat.

Father Ryan waited by the garden door until Kathleen and Gavin came out. "'Tis a letter I have for ye," he said, giving it to her. "And I've a feelin' 'twill be better if ye read it now, with the two of us by yer side."

"A letter for me," asked Kathleen. "Now who would be writin' to me?"

"It came from Meghan," replied the man.

"Meghan? Why would she be writin' to me? I'll be seein' her soon."

"Best ye be readin' it, Mum," Gavin said after looking closely at the Father's saddened face.

When she didn't answer, the priest asked, "Tis it help ye need with the readin'?

'Tis with the writin' I need help, Father, not the readin'."

Kathleen's eyes clouded over with tears as she finished reading the letter. "The matter we were discussin' no longer exists," she said, handing the letter to her son.

Gavin quickly read the letter. "Can't we stop her?" he asked.

"And bring her back to what? A life of anguish and bitterness awaits her here."

"Mum, if we don't, ye may never see her sweet face again."

"Life can be hard at times, but it could not be that cruel. No, lad. I shall surely see her again."

"A brave colleen, she be," Gavin said. "And what a grand adventure she'll be havin' for herself."

Chapter Six

✧

Meghan looked back toward the village, and when she saw her mother standing on the bluff, prayed the words would reach her. "Mum, I love ye!" She shouted, then added, "I'll be writin' ye." Then turned her back on all she held dear, to face what lay ahead.

Once on board ship she faced the Jennings. The woman's voice was harsh and cold. "You are quite late," she stated, "and I do not like to be kept waiting."

The man stepped forward. He gently laid his hand on the woman's shoulder. "I am the Reverend Mr. Jennings and, of course, you have just met my wife, Mistress Jennings."

He beckoned to a boy and girl standing nearby. When they stood by his side, he introduced them to Meghan. "This is our son Robert and daughter Elizabeth." He looked down at them. "Dear children. This is your new nanny."

Meghan thought Robert must be about twelve and his sister around nine. She was to later learn, she was right about their ages. Meghan smiled and curtsied. "Robert, is it? Why, ye be nearly as tall as me." Looking at the girl, Meghan continued with, "and what a little beauty

I behold in ye, Elizabeth." Then to both, "I know we'll be the best of friends."

"It is not required that you become friends," advised the woman.

At that precise moment the sails caught the wind; the ship slipped further out to sea. Meghan turned back to watch the land disappear. When she once again faced the woman, her eyes were red but tearless.

"Your name is Bridgett, is it not?" asked Mrs. Jennings.

"Bridgett did not come. Me name is Meghan McGonigal. And 'tis the same who'll be teachin' yer young'uns."

"Meghan McGonigal?" The woman turned to her husband. " Mr. Jennings, did you hear what she said?"

"Yes, my dear, I did, indeed."

He looked not unkindly at Meghan. "Can you explain why Mr. Miller sent you, instead of Miss Connolly?"

"She did not want to come." Meghan looked at the woman. "And 'twas ye, yerself who said, if Bridgett did not come, Mr. Miller was to find someone else."

"But we know nothing about you! Did you bring references?" insisted the woman.

"'Twas no time to be collectin' such things. Ye gave Mr. Miller but two hours for the findin'."

"What the child says is true," interlaced the Reverend Mr. Jennings. "Now, my dear," turning his attention back to his wife, "I believe the children should be taken below; the wind has become quite brisk."

"But Mr. Jennings, we have not finished our discussion!"

Mr. Jennings smiled. "I believe we have, my dear." He turned to Meghan. "Mistress Jennings will show you the way to your room."

Without looking directly at Meghan the woman said, "Come with me, Miss McGonigal. I want the children to rest before the evening meal. Also, there are your duties to discuss."

The seething anger was evident in Mrs. Jennings' manner, and Meghan was not looking forward to the discussion, which was to follow.

Mrs. Jennings hurried the little group down the flight of stairs to the deck below. At the end of the corridor, she opened a door and ushered Meghan and the children inside.

Meghan looked about the room. It contained three single beds, two chests of drawers, a nightstand with a bowl and pitcher of water on it, and four chairs around a small round table.

"Miss McGonigal, this has been a great shock to me. I hardly know what to make of it."

"Miz Jennin's," started Meghan, but she was not allowed to finish her sentence.

"My name is Mrs. Jennings, not Miz Jennin's. Now, try it again."

After several failed attempts, Mrs. Jennings realized it would take Meghan time to speak as she felt the girl should, and on their first day together there was no use in having them both upset.

"That is quite enough for now," Mrs. Jennings told her. "You must practice each day, and I am sure it will soon become quite natural for you to speak correctly. Now, shall we get back to Mr. Miller and why he sent you?"

"Mr. Miller didn't want ye to be put out."

"But he checked your references? Or, did he?"

"He be knowin' me all me life as he has me mum and da."

"Did he tell you about our destination?"

"No, Ma'am, he didn't," admitted Meghan.

Mrs. Jennings appeared stunned. "And you came not knowing where you would be going?" She was now inches away from Meghan's face. "Are you wanted by the authorities for some crime or another?"

Meghan gasped. "Of course not," she answered.

"Then why did you come on a trip with perfect strangers, not even knowing your destination?"

"I came on account of ye needed someone, and I had no other place to go. And that's the honest truth for all the world to know," Meghan answered.

"I simply don't know what to do." Mrs. Jennings replied." I cannot have just anyone caring for my precious ones. No, I cannot have that at all."

"I be tellin' ye the truth," Meghan replied. "I don't know what else I can be sayin' to put yer fears to rest."

The woman looked into the girl's eyes and saw the truth mirrored there. What else could she do but accept the situation? "Very well, Miss . . . what was your first name?"

"'Tis Meghan, Ma'am," came the response.

"Now, as I was saying, Meghan, since there is nothing else to do, the matter shall be dropped."

Mrs. Jennings turned her attention to her children. She stood facing them. "Robert, Elizabeth, remove your coats and shoes. Lie on your bed, and rest your eyes while I discuss Miss McGonigal's duties with her."

"Yes, Momma," they said in unison.

She turned to Meghan. "Let us sit over there, away from the children. They must have their rest." Mrs. Jennings sat down, and motioned Meghan to sit in the adjoining chair.

"As you will soon learn, my husband, the Reverend Mr. Jennings, is a saint. He has devoted his life to the searching out and destroying evil wherever he can."

"Our destination is an island in the middle of the ocean. We learned from a former missionary that the natives won't give up their sinful ways. Therefore, he was not successful in routing out their wickedness. But that will change when the Reverend Mr. Jennings takes them in charge. And I am determined that nothing will stand in his way."

She looked at Meghan's attire. "It seems I also have a challenge in you. Stand up, Meghan, and remove your shawl and bonnet. Just place them on the chair. Now turn around, I want to have a good look at you."

Mrs. Jennings glanced up and down the length of Meghan's body. A look of exasperation came into her eyes. "Your hair is worn much too long. It must be kept in a bun on top of your head or at the nape of your neck. Now, let me look at your dress. Your skirt is too short. I can actually see your ankles and that will never do. Your arms must be covered at all times as well as the area below your throat." A frown deepened the lines about the woman's face. "Are all your clothes fashioned is such a brazen manner?"

Meghan's lifted her face. "I have but two others, and 'tis that proud I am of them; me mum's own hands made the stitches."

Mrs. Jennings brought the hem of the skirt closer to her eyes. "I must agree that she did an excellent task. If we were going to a civilized place, I am sure they would be very suitable for one in your station of life."

Meghan's face whitened. "What be yer meanin', not civilized?"

"As I told you, it is an island, a place called Maui. And I understand that the natives have not seen many white women. Their own women wear little or nothing above their waist or below their knees. We must set the proper example for them. They must learn to dress to our standards and not continue in their heathen ways. Even on this ship, we must dress properly. You shall wear a shawl whenever you go on deck, and your bonnet is a must to keep the sun and wind from burning your face."

"Me skin has never burnt," insisted Meghan, barely over the shock of hearing where they were going.

"As we both know, Meghan, the sun rarely shines in Ireland. I have been there enough times over the past years to know it is cloudy, misty, or rainy. So when you leave this cabin, you will dress as I have stated. Is that clear?"

Memories of standing before her father and hearing his commands flooded to mind. Her first reaction was to scream, *"I won't be spoken to in such a manner!"*

Instead, she bit her lip, nodded her head, and said nothing.

"Very well," responded Mrs. Jennings. "Now that we understand each other, you may take this opportunity to put your things away. I believe this chest will give you ample room."

She looked across the room. "I see the children are fast asleep. You will not have any trouble with them. They are perfect in every way. I have seen to that. They have had problems in the past with nannies that were not used to highly, intelligent children.

"Now, it has been a strenuous day for the Reverend Mr. Jennings and myself; therefore, we shall have our evening meal in our rooms. I will see to it that your food is sent here. Make sure the children eat their portion, fully." With that announcement, she left.

Meghan leaned against the closed door, and thought, *"What have I gotten meself into?"* pounding in her mind.

Robert, who had been lying with closed eyes, suddenly sat up. "Why can't we eat with Father?' he asked.

"Yer parents are tired," Meghan replied. "I'm that sure they'll be seein' ye before ye go to bed. Now, I'm thinkin' we should be joinin' Elizabeth in takin' a small rest."

Some time later heavy knocking on the cabin door brought Meghan out of a deep slumber. She straightened her skirt and hurried to the door but did not open it.

"Who might ye be?" she asked through the door.

"I'm the cabin boy, Miss," was the answer. "I have your meal here."

Meghan opened the door. A lad of perhaps thirteen smiled broadly as he walked across the room. He took the food off the tray and placed it on the table.

"Might that be all, Miss?' he asked, bowing before her.

"Aye that be fine," she replied and curtsied.

They both laughed and he walked backwards out the door, closing it behind him.

The smell of hot beef, combined with potatoes, brown gravy, thick slices of freshly baked bread, jelly and fruit brought a surge of hunger to her.

"Robert, Elizabeth, 'tis time to be wakin' up and eatin' this fine meal."

"I'm still sleepy," the boy replied.

"Me, too," chimed in the girl.

"Then 'tis the more for me," Meghan told them, "for I'm that hungry, and can't be waitin' for ye."

Meghan poured cool water from the pitcher into the bowl and washed her hands and face. After drying on one of the towels she opened a porthole and threw the water out. Robert climbed out of bed.

"How come you can eat your first night out when we were so sick on ours?" inquired the lad.

"'Tis not me first night out," declared Meghan. "Many the times I be out in a fishin' boat and be tossed about somethin' fierce. Why compared to that, this ship 'tis hardly more than a feather movin' gentle-like though the air."

"You were on a fishing boat?" Robert asked.

"Aye, 'tis what I said. Now, ye best be washin' up, or I'll be eatin' all the food by meself, for 'tis sinful, indeed, to be wastin' it."

Robert looked at his sister. "We had better do what she says, or we won't be eatin' until breakfast."

Two hours later they were summoned to join the Reverend and his wife in their stateroom, for the evening devotional.

◌ℬ◌

BACK IN IRELAND, John McGonigal had returned home. He put his cap on the peg by the door, looked at his wife and said "Is the sup ready?"

Instead of answering, Kathleen spoke boldly. "John there be somethin' to be said, and I'll be sayin' it now."

"Can't it be waitin'? 'It's been a long day and I be hungry."

"It cannot!"

"Then be sayin' it."

"John, Meghan has left, and she'll not be comin' back."

John grasped her shoulders, his eyes piercing, his jawbone taut, and his voice demanding, "What's that ye say?"

"Meghan is gone," Kathleen repeated, returning his glare.

'Woman, tell me where she be, and I'll have her back tonight." His fingers dug into her soft flesh.

"She's gone to a place where neither of us will ever see her again."

"And who dared to whisk her away? Was it Gavin?" He did not wait for her to answer. He released her to take his rifle from the closet. "I'll not have him defy me. He'll be bringin' her back, or 'tis death that will claim him."

"She's safe from the likes of Brian O'Shea. Can't ye see, John? That's all that matters.

"Nay, that's not all." He thought for a moment, "Has she gone to me brother?"

"Why would ye be askin' me such a question? Where he be, I know no more than ye."

"Be that the truth?"

"John, I have never lied to ye."

"So say ye, but there be some who knows better."

A dazed Kathleen looked into her husband's stormy eyes. "Tell me when I have lied to ye, for I know not."

"It started before we were wed and hasn't ended to this day."

He put the rifle back and retrieved his cap from its resting-place and left the house without another word. Kathleen stared after him, a look of bewilderment on her face.

Chapter Seven

❧

The following days were pleasant enough; the routine varied little. The sea rolled gently toward the empty horizon. After breakfast both children had three hours of study; then Robert was allowed to walk freely about the ship while Meghan and Elizabeth, if they wanted to go on deck, were forced to stay in a secluded part of the ship next to where the vegetables were kept.

Meghan's resentment grew under what she considered unfair conditions, although Elizabeth didn't seem to mind at all.

"'Tisn't fair," Meghan fumed. "Since we be colleens we're prisoners on this ship. We should be allowed to walk on the deck. But never mind, Elizabeth, I'll be thinkin' of somethin'."

"I don't like the sun," Elizabeth pouted. "I like shade. It's nice and cool here."

But Meghan was not listening to the child. She would not be a prisoner on board ship. She was determined to find a way to be free no matter how long it took.

In less than a week, she found the answer. Each afternoon the children spent an hour with their parents and she was left on her own.

Why not put on Robert's clothes and pass off as a boy? In that way, she could also have the run of the ship and taste a bit of freedom. Even if she was discovered, they could not take away the memory of that hour. She decided it was well worth the risk of discovery.

The very next day Meghan put her idea into action. Robert's clothes were somewhat short but she did not care. She tied her hair in a knot on top of her head and put on one of Robert's caps.

When dressed to her satisfaction, Meghan eased open the cabin door and slipped into the passageway. Finding it empty, she sighed with relief. She tiptoed past the Jennings' quarters and climbed up the ladder to the upper deck.

The feel of the sun was wonderful. A gentle breeze blew a spray of seawater into her face, and she licked the salt off her lips. She wanted to shout with joy at her newfound freedom. If only she dared remove the cap allowing the wonderful air to swish her hair about her head but she had not the courage. Meghan made one round of the deck without anyone even looking in her direction. She spent some time watching the men climb up the rope ladders, and even had the opportunity of handing one of them an empty bucket that he had asked her to fetch. Long after the children went to bed that night, she relived her new secret life of the day.

The next afternoon was uneventful, but on the third day a man came out of the cook shack and called out to her, "Lad, would ye give old Caleb a 'elpin' 'and?" and held out one of the buckets he was carrying out to her. Startled, Meghan took the bucket and followed him to the railing. After he had emptied his bucket into the sea, she did the same with her bucket.

"Bring et along,'" he commanded, walking toward the cook's shack located in the midsection of the ship. "Ye be a 'eap stronger than ye look," he said. Staring hard at her features, he took a step closer. His mouth dropped opened in amazement. "I thought 'twere the Jennin's lad, but I can see now thar be no truth to that. 'E would not 'ave 'elp, no, not the likes of 'im. Now, who be ye?"

Trying to draw his attention away from herself, Meghan lowered her voice and, trying to imitate his accent, asked, "Whar be they goin'?" pointing to some men climbing up the ropes.

"Thar be a rip in one of them sails. But 'tis no use askin' me questions. 'Tis answers, I be wantin' from ye. Now, who be ye?"

Meghan tried to think of an answer, which would satisfy him, yet not tell him the truth.

The look in his eyes told her he was no fool, but she thought she saw a twinkle in them, too.

Meghan took a deep breath. "I was a lad watchin' the sheep in the glen near me cottage in Ireland. I was wishin' on a sea voyage. I spied the King of the Little People and hit him over the head with me staff. I tied him up proper, I did, and when he came back to life, he found himself bound hand and foot."

"What did ye do that for?" he asked me, trying to sit up.

"''Tis but a wish I be wantin','" I told him.

"'And what might that be?'" he asked, still trying to get loose.

"I told him of me dream of sailin' over the seven seas, and that I would let him go if he be grantin' me a wish."

"'e said he would grant my wish, so I let him go. But he had the last laugh, he did. As ye can see, he turned me into a colleen and in the employ of an English family, instead of the employ of a kind and carin' man, like yerself."

"Lass, ye think me a fool to believe in such a tale?"

"Would be kind, indeed, if ye would," replied Meghan.

"Wall, I don't. So let's hear it again, and 'tis the truth I be wantin' to hear."

As she told her tale of woe, her shoulders slumped with despair. He laughed. "Wall, the first story 'twas a bit more entertainin'."

"Aye," Meghan giggled, "I thought so meself." Sobering, she continued, "Ye won't be givin' me away, will ye?"

"Nay, I won't be doin' that. But 'tis the last time ye'll be foolin' me. Now, off with ye. I won't 'ave ye gettin' me into trouble."

"But who's to be the wiser?" she asked, trying desperately to be allowed to remain on deck.

"I'll be knowin' and so will ye. So that makes two."

Although tears came into Meghan's eyes, her lips did not quiver as she continued speaking. "I be dyin' if I'm denied the sky and the pure air. Please, won't ye be lettin' me stay? If I be caught, 'tis the blame I'll be taken." Her hand reached out to him. "Please, let me stay."

"Now, don't be tryin' yer Irish ways with me." His voice was stern, yet Meghan saw the twinkle come back into his eyes,

"Ye'll not be turnin' me away, will ye?"

"Nay, but I can't be callin' ye by a lass's name." He stroked his short gray beard.

"I had a lad once. 'E be named Martin. I called 'im Marty. Might be I'll call ye Marty. Be it all right by ye?"

"Marty . . . Marty . . . ," repeated Meghan. "Aye, I like the sound of it."

"Then Marty 'tis," he said, "and ye can call me Caleb."

The next few days were the happiest Meghan had known since leaving Ireland, but to her dismay the charade ended three days later. Mrs. Jennings left her cabin early that afternoon to retrieve a sweater from the children's room and found Meghan gone. Not wanting to bother her husband, Mrs. Jennings went in search of her missing nanny, and to her dismay, found her not only on deck but also in Robert's clothes.

She snatched the cap off Meghan's head.

"What is the meaning of . .this . . this deception?

Why are you here talking to this . . . heathen, and out in the open for all this riffraff to see?"

"I can't be stayin' below all but one hour a day. Me spirit needs freedom."

Mrs. Jennings bristled. "I refuse to discuss anything more in front of this . . . this man.

Miss McGonigal, come with me!"

Mrs. Jennings led the way to a secluded place behind the bulkhead. Once they were away from Caleb, the woman continued her tirade. "Child, deceit is a wicked thing to behold. I am deeply hurt you have resorted to such a deception. I just can't understand what you were thinking of to expose your body in such a wanton way.

"Yet, I am not entirely without sympathy for your plight. I can understand confinement must be hard on one who has been allowed to run free of proper restraint. However, you must now realize you cannot conduct yourself in such an unladylike manner. You are now a member of the Reverend Mr. Jennings' family and not some peasant girl who can do anything she likes, is that understood?"

Meghan swallowed hard to keep the fury she felt under control. "I not be runnin' wild," she finally managed to say.

As if Meghan had not spoken, the woman continued, "I will not punish you this time for trying to live a lie; the Lord will do that in His good time. As for now, the deed has been done. I will not suffer you to remain secluded in your cabin. You may go on deck alone for one hour each afternoon. However, you will wear your own clothing. And,

Meghan, if I hear of you making bold with any of the men, you will be punished and punished severely."

Relief flooded through the girl. "Can I be talkin' to Caleb, the cook?"

"I will allow that, but only with the old man. I will not have you carrying on with any of the others. And I'll not have him tell any of his tall stories and scare the children, is that understood?"

Meghan trembled with relief. "Thank ye, Ma'am."

"I was not going to speak to you on the subject as yet, but now I feel I must do so. Meghan, I will not allow you to teach my children your Irish way of speaking. Once and for all, it is you, and not ye. And your, not yer. Is that understood?"

"I'll be doin' me best," came the reply.

"And it is my best, not me best," insisted Mrs. Jennings.

"How can ye . . you be expectin' me . . . my to change at the drop of a hat?

"Meghan! You are really trying my patience. Of course, there are times when one does use the word 'me'. You must learn to speak properly, as the English do."

"But I'm not English. I'm Irish and mighty proud of it. So who's to say which be the better of it?"

"In this case, young woman, I do," replied Mrs. Jennings. "And while we are on the subject, your 'g's' are no longer to be dropped."

Meghan took a deep breath; the anger within was closing off her throat. "I'll be sayin'. . . . saying no more."

"That, Meghan," replied the irate woman, "is a very good idea. Now, come along with me. I think it will do you good to stay with the children while they are being counseled by their father, on the proper behavior for young men and women."

Chapter Eight

❧

"Caleb, have ye..you ever been to Maui?" Meghan asked one afternoon.

"Aye, Lass, that I 'ave. And thar's many a tale I could be tellin' ye, if ye had the mind to listen."

"I be havin' an hour to listen," Meghan replied. "I deem it an honor to be listenin'. . . listening to you."

"Then seat yerself over thar," Caleb pointed to a shady spot near the bulkhead, "and I'll be tellin" ye a tale ye'll not soon be forgettin'."

He took several puffs on his pipe before continuing. "Somewhar on the island thar be a pool whar witches live. Some be good witches and some be bad. Some can tell a man's future just by lookin' into the water as if 'twere a crystal ball. Others can be drivin' a man mad."

Meghan leaned forward, her eyes dancing with excitement. "Caleb, have ye seen them?"

Caleb laughed. "Ye be slipping back, lass. Ye must remember to say you."

She shrugged her shoulders "I don't have to be anythin' but meself with ye," Meghan replied.

"Ye can't be two people, Lass, or ye be torn apart. Ye must be the same to all."

"I know ye. .you're right, Caleb. I'll be trying harder."

"Aye, that's me Marty. Now, back to yer question. I wasn't fool enough to go. But I be knowin' others who did."

"What happened to them?"

"One was never the same as 'e were before. Sort of out of 'is 'ead, 'e was."

"And the other ones?"

"Some left the sea. Some say they all be crazed in one way or another. One man be a friend before 'e went, but 'e nary said a word upon 'is return. Ye listen to me, Marty. You stay clear of that evil place, because that's not all they be doin'. Why they can turn themselves into devils. Maybe they'll be changin' ye, too."

Meghan shook her head. "They be doin' naught to the likes of me. Why, I'll just be callin' on the King of the Wee Ones, and he'll come to my rescue."

"Ye ain't no match for them. Ye better listen to Old Caleb. 'E knows what 'e's talkin' 'bout."

"I promise to be real careful," replied Meghan, giggling.

"'Tis not a laughin' matter," Caleb said. "It be best if ye take me words for the truth. 'Tis not some fairy tale, I be tellin'." Caleb stood up and emptied his pipe into the sea. "Now, be off with ye. Thar's work to be done, and no time to be wastin' me words on one who won't be listenin'."

"Please, don't be angry, Caleb. I promise that if I find the pool, I'll be careful and remember yer . . .your words of reason."

Caleb smiled. "Ye be doin' that, Lass. It'll be savin' ye a heap of trouble, if ye listen to me tales."

The next afternoon found Meghan, once again, listening to the cook weave his stories of adventure.

"Sit yerself down, Marty," he said, "and let me tell ye a story that was told to me years and years ago. The island that ye be goin' to was named after one of them Polynesian gods, not a great one, mind ye, but one that got himself into a peck of trouble. Now, young Maui was no spirit like some of them gods. No, by dang, 'e be mortal like ye and me. And 'e be likin' a good joke, now and again.

"'E be tired one day, but 'e wanted to do a mite of fishin', so 'e takes 'is brothers with 'im. Ye see, 'e wanted them to do the rowin' while 'e leaned back in the canoe and did the fishin'. Now, Maui had a magical fishin' line, and 'e could catch anythin' 'e had a mind to. But on this day, the hook latched onto somethin' mighty fierce, and 'e couldn't pull in the line. 'E told his brothers to stop rowin', but they got scared and rowed faster and faster.

The line grew taut and then, low and behold, it broke loose, pullin' a part of the ocean bottom with it. Aye, the greater part stayed on 'is line, but the other part broke off into seven pieces. Those pieces are called islands. The biggest one is named Hawaii. I forget the other names. The place ye'll soon be callin' home 'twere called Maui since he be the one that brought it up out of its slumber."

He stopped talking, staring over Meghan's head. "Appears ye be wanted, Marty."

Meghan turned to see Elizabeth coming toward them.

"Mama said it's lesson time," Elizabeth said.

"But my hour is not up," insisted Meghan.

A look of spite came into the child's eyes. "Mama said to come, now! Then added, "You're just a servant." She made a face, "Mama told Papa that you must do what we say."

Leaning over, Caleb whispered, "Ye best be not rilin' the woman. She can be making yer life unhappy."

"But my hour isn't up. She has no right to be ending it."

"Right or no," exclaimed Caleb, "she be cap'n over yer soul."

A light came into Meghan's eyes. "I'll go, but I'll be adding the time on tomorrow's hour."

Those times Meghan spent with the old seaman were the happiest times in the long voyage to her future home. One afternoon they passed several larger ships, and Meghan asked Caleb what kind of ships they were.

"Thar be whalin' ships, Marty," he replied with a grin, for he had not reverted to using her own name. "Most come from the land of America, and they be sailin' round the world lookin' for beasties."

"Beasties?"

"Aye, lass. Thar be whales they're huntin'. The bigger the better."

"And when they find them, what then?" "Wall, lass," he said, "they'll be killin' them. Whar else be ye thinkin' comes the oil for the lamps, and the perfume for the ladies?" He leaned closer to her ear. "Whar do ye suppose Miz Jennin's get the bones in her corset if it be not from whales?"

Meghan shook her head, her eyes expressions of wonderment as he continued his tales of adventure.

Once or twice he started to spin some yarn or another when the children were about, and Meghan would have to remind him he was not to say anything to scare them. However, to the running of a ship or position of the stars, etc., she allowed the children to listen to every word but only when they were good.

Robert had not been obeying Meghan of late, but since Caleb began telling his tale of the sea he was on good behavior. Even Elizabeth stopped fussing so much about wearing petticoats or the dreadful heat.

Through Caleb they all learned how to tie seaman knots, and to spot the different types of whales. They learned the difference between the bottle whales, blue whales, killer whales, and that it was the elusive sperm whale that was the most sought out by the whalers. It's enormous head made up a third of its body and contained a large reservoir of pure spermaceti. This oil was needed for making fine candles, ointments, and perfumes.

One morning as Meghan and the children came on deck; they saw the crew pointing toward a huge whale that was surrounded by a group of boats bobbing on the churning sea. Robert and Elizabeth ran with her to the ship's railing. Suddenly, harpoons flew from the boats to lodge into the whale's enormous body.

She leaned down to the boy. "Robert, run for Caleb. I saw him enter the cook shack.

No! There he is standing by the railing. Ask him to come and tell us what is happening!"

Robert ran to Caleb and the man waved for Meghan and Elizabeth to join them.

"Ye'll be seein' a killin' for sure this day," he told them, his eyes dancing with excitement. "Look over thar! See all them whales? When they travel together, they be called a 'pod'. 'Tis a sight ye'll not likely see again. Now, can ye see them thar lines acomin' from the whales back to the boats?"

All three shouted, "We see them!"

"Look over thar!" He said pointing to a boat racing behind a large, blue whale. "Do ye see that big blue devil a cuttin' through the waves? 'E be pullin' a boat behind 'im."

"I see it! I see it!" cried Robert, jumping up and down.

Caleb chuckled at the uninhibited behavior of the lad. He wondered what his mama would say if she saw him now. "They be callin' that a 'Nantucket Sleigh Ride," he continued. "See how the boat cuts through the waves? Now, be lookin' at the men! They be hangin' on for dear life!"

His voice pitched higher and higher as the adventure unraveled before their eyes "The water cuts into a man's face, and the wind fairly takes his breath away. Look ye now! Heed the man at the bow of that green boat?" They nodded. "'Tis an officer 'e be. Look at what 'e's holding; 'tis called a lance. That's what 'e kills the beastie with. 'E'll jab it just below the monster's eye. If 'e misses and the brute takes off, the boat be pulled under the waves and sometimes disappears forever. Aye, many a lad who goes out, never comes back."

Robert looked up at Caleb. "How do you know so much about whales?"

"I ain't always been a cook," exclaimed Caleb, leaning back against the railing. "When I be young, I left Scotland goin' to a place named New Bedford, in America. Thar I set sail on a whalin' ship, its crew bein' from Nantucket. Aye, and what a life! Still thar came a time when I longed for me 'ome in Scotland. After my third hunt I went back and married a sweet lass. 'Twas a grand life we had. When she died, my world died and I returned to the sea. Not to me whalin' life, but 'ere aboard 'THE MORNIN' GLORY,' and 'ere I stay till I be joinin' me lass."

"What is the meaning of this?" shrieked the voice of Mrs. Jennings. The three turned around to face her. They had been so engrossed in the telling of Caleb's story, none of them knew of her approach until she had cried out. Now, she continued in her tirade, "Meghan, I thought you could be trusted! And here you are allowing my little angels to see such a terrifying sight? I'll not have their dreams disturbed by such violence. Take them below, immediately! And as for you," she hissed at Caleb, "I have a good mind to report you to the captain."

"Oh, please, Mrs. Jennings," begged Meghan. "Don't be doing such a thing. 'Tis my fault he be here. I asked him to explain what was happening. I thought it would be doing the wee ones good to learn about boats and the men of the sea. Men who risk their lives bringing back the oil for lamps and to make yer . . . your perfume and the bones for your corsets."

Nearby men hearing the conversation, roared with laughter; Mrs. Jennings flamed with embarrassment. "Meghan, I can't believe you would mention such personal things in front of this riffraff. Now, do as I say and take the children below." Again she turned to Caleb. "And as for you, I shall forget this incident, however, if in the future you never let me catch you telling your stories to my children."

"Aye, Missy Jennin's, 'tis a true thing ye be sayin' and I'll not be lettin' ye catch me, again." Caleb winked at Robert and Elizabeth, and they winked back.

Every day was like a new adventure for Meghan. Her times with Caleb were treasured ones. Caleb taught Meghan about the different parts of the ship, and she memorized the names. There was the aft, the bow, the starboard, the midsection, the bulkhead, the bridge, and the stern. She learned the ropes were called lines or sheets; the ladders made of ropes were called riggings. The place where the men stood to look out to sea was called the crow's nest; it was located just below the main mast. The place where the captain might stand his watch was called the masthead.

Sometimes at night she would slip on deck to see the fires blazing from the deck of the whaling ships. She asked Caleb all about why so many fires burned and learned the meat of the whale was called blubber and it was stripped from the whales and cooked in the frypots until they gave up their oil. The blubber was then skimmed from the pots, and the pure oil poured down a passageway that led directly to the vats in the hold of the ship. When she asked why the fire didn't burn up the ships, Caleb told her about the tunnels under the frypots that were filled with water so the flames could not reach the wooden decks.

"What makes ye so curious about those ships?" Caleb asked her.

"I don't know and can't be guessing," she told him, for hadn't she asked herself that very same question?

Chapter Nine

❦

The weeks rolled into months of sea, wind, rain, and blazing sun. Meghan's fair skin burned, blistered, and burned again until, at long last, it became golden in color. Looking into the mirror she could hardly recognize the image before her. It looked nothing like the girl who had smiled at her in the cracked mirror at home. Moreover, her face wasn't the only thing about her that had been recreated from that girl in Ireland. Her arms and legs had grown out of her dresses and it was near impossible to tie the short ribbon lacing her bodice. Her body had changed from a pretty young girl into that of a young woman. She wondered if anyone else had discovered the transformation and the prospect frightened her.

Barely a week had passed before Mrs. Jennings came to Meghan. "Child, if you'll come with me, there is a matter that we must discuss." Meghan followed the woman below deck. Once in her room, Mrs. Jennings told her, "I have something for you. Open the package on the table, and you'll find some material I secured from a seamstress on board the ship. She has pictures of gowns appropriate for someone of your station and said she would be happy to assist you in making one or two gowns of your choice. It is more than apparent you can no longer wear what you have. I have also ordered the children new clothes."

As Meghan opened the package, tears sprang to her eyes. Mrs. Jennings patted her on the shoulder. "Now, Meghan," she said, "there is no reason to become emotional. I simply saw my duty and acted upon it. There is no need to thank me." Mrs. Jennings walked out of the room, closing the door behind her.

"Thank her, indeed," Meghan said, looking at the two pieces of heavy broadcloth in dull, lifeless colors.

The door opened and Elizabeth came in. She also had a package in her arms. "I saw what Mama brought you," she said. "Here, Meghan. My Granny gave this cloth to me. Said I was to have a fine dancing gown when I became of age." She made a face. "Mama said it wasn't proper for a minister's daughter to be wearing such a dress."

Meghan opened the package to find a beautiful glossy fabric inside. She held the lovely cloth to her face. The emerald color brightened her eyes and bronze skin. "It's the most wonderful gift anyone has ever given me," she told the girl, as she handed the package back to Elizabeth. "No, 'tis that sorry I am, but I can't be keeping your present, it wouldn't be seemly. I'm just a hired girl."

"Don't say that," wailed Elizabeth. "You're my friend, and I want you to have it. Please, take it."

"Elizabeth, your mama would be very angry if she saw me wear such a dress."

"Mama doesn't know I still have it. She gave it away, but I got it back." The girl began to dance around the room. "Please, please, Meghan, take it and make it into a dancing gown."

"It is a perfect color," Meghan told her. "I don't know how I can ever thank you, Elizabeth."

"You don't need to thank me. I want you to have it so you won't be hating me for all the times I was mean to you."

"I've never hated you, Elizabeth. 'Tis a sin to hate. But I must be admitting that at times you could be riling a saint, and I'm far from that."

"Then you forgive me?"

Meghan put the cloth into her drawer. She turned around and held open her arms. Elizabeth rushed into them. "I'm so glad you're our nanny," she whooped. "Robert is glad, too."

After the girl had left, Meghan did a bit of dancing herself. She imagined dancing with a tall, dark man with his arms strong about her. Then she caught sight of her reflection in the floor length mirror and wondered if her mother would recognize the golden creature living in the mirror. And with the vision of her mother came the vision of Ireland. How she longed to see her village with its green rolling hills; but most of all, she longed to see her mother, and sit once again in the cozy kitchen watching the embers in the hearth slowly lose their color.

There were times when she was not sure leaving home was the best idea she ever had. But at those times, she remembered the look of Brian O'Shea and knew she made the only decision she could have.

The next day Meghan went to the seamstress and had the dreaded black and gray material made into dresses. She had some of the black made into a bodice for the gray and the gray into a bodice for the black. During the time of fittings, Meghan became a friend with the seamstress and the woman made the emerald material into a dancing gown, keeping the knowledge to herself.

At long last land was sighted. Never in Meghan's wildest dreams had she ever imagined a place more emerald in color than her beloved Ireland, yet before her eyes was an island of such grandeur that it fairly took her breath away. Instead of the green, rolling hills of home, she saw gigantic mountains covered with ferns and foliage of every shade of green she could imagine. And the sandy beach was far more shimmering than the stretch of land beneath the cliffs at home. Here the green towering mountains loomed high above her head until, it seemed to her, they reached heaven, itself. Water fell from the top of the mountains, dropping hundreds of feet to hide in the mist and greenery below.

Meghan rushed to find Caleb. Just as soon as she did, she threw her arms about the old man's neck. "I never thought I would ever be happy away from my own dear valley, but I'm thinking I'm going to be living in a place befitting a princess." She paused. "Still, I'll be missing you something fierce. Oh, my dear, dear friend, I'll never forget all the things you have told me, and the day may yet come, for what reason I do not know, that I'll be needing to know those very things."

He laughed. "Nay, lass, nothing' old Caleb told ye will ever 'mount to much. Howsoever, I did dearly love to share with ye the things that I be knowin'." He kissed her on her forehead. Caleb saw the Jennings family approach and whispered, "Marty, ye best be off."

Meghan smiled. "I'll love you, always," then turning hurried after the family.

With a pounding heart, Meghan climbed down the rigging to the bobbing boat where the family was already seated. She looked up at the ship's railing, saw Caleb and waved. One adventure had ended and she was looking forward to the one about to begin.

It had been a long time since Meghan had experienced seasickness, however, on this long boat ride her stomach rebelled, and she found herself leaning over the side. Several of the seamen laughed, but it was not a laughing matter to Meghan. She looked over at them, her face pale and eyes glazed. "'Tis ashamed I am to be sick," Meghan said.

"Sorry, lass," one of the men said and glared at the others. They nodded their heads in agreement and stopped their laughter.

Just as soon as the party neared the shore, the men jumped into the knee-deep water and pushed the boats onto dry land where Mr.

and Mrs. Jennings were helped from the boat. Not waiting for assistance, Meghan and the children took off their shoes and stockings, Robert rolled up his pant legs, Elizabeth and Meghan pulled up their skirts and all three stepped down into the cool water, much to the chagrin of Mrs. Jennings.

"Meghan, how dare you allow Elizabeth to pull up her skirt in front of the men. Oh, I have never been so mortified in all my life."

"Tis that sorry I am if I offended you," Meghan said, letting down her own skirt. "But it has been so long since my feet has touched land that I couldn't wait another second. Please, don't be upset with the children, 'tis my fault for setting such a bad example."

"We are all tired," interjected the Reverend. "Let's say no more on the matter."

Mrs. Jennings took a deep breath before saying, "Meghan, you and the children may walk a bit to get the stiffness from your legs. Nevertheless, do not wander off. As soon as the carts are loaded with our belongings; we shall be leaving the shore. One more thing, Meghan, be careful with whom you speak. I have no idea which ones are saved."

As Meghan and her charges neared the dense foliage fringing the beach, she could see the leaves were not all the same color or size and shape. Some of them had little ruffled edges while others looked sharp enough to cut you. And the flowers! How magnificent they were, in every color imaginable and in all their various shades. The birds darting about were but a continuation of the flowers. The only difference she could see was that the birds could fly and the flowers could not.

"Meghan," Mrs. Jennings called, "bring Robert and Elizabeth along. The carts are waiting to take us to our new home."

There were three carts waiting. The luggage and supplies were in the first cart; Mr. and Mrs. Jennings in the second, and third cart waited for them. As they rode along, the sight of the swaying trees and the feel of the gentle breeze soon lulled Meghan asleep. She did not wake up until they arrived at their destination.

"Meghan," Robert said, giving her a poke in the side. "We're here. See Mama and Papa are ready to go inside." He and Elizabeth hurried after their parents.

The cart had stopped in front of a high stone wall. Meghan left the cart to follow the others through an open doorway and with an open mouth and wide eyes took in the splendor that lay before her. Green moss covered the ground and flowers and ferns lined the pathway to a large house that she would soon be occupying for how long, she could not even guess.

Seagulls soared overhead while dark-skinned men, dressed only in a cloth wrapped about their waists, helped carry their things into the building, not so unlike the cottages in Ireland, only much, much larger.

"Meghan! Stop your gawking and come here."

"Aye, Mrs. Jennings, I'm coming," Meghan assured her.

"Take the children for a walk. They'll only be in the way here. However, stay within the walls of the parsonage. I don't want you getting them lost."

Meghan and the children walked around the building to the back yard.

"Let's go down that path," she said and they quickly agreed.

"It looks like a jungle I once saw," piped Elizabeth.

"And how would you know that?" asked Robert. "You've never seen a jungle."

"I have too," insisted the girl. "Our last nanny had a storybook telling all about the jungle."

"That's different," commented her brother. "You said you saw a jungle."

Meghan looked at them both. "This is our first day on land. Let's not have a fight and spoil it . . . please!"

Robert glared at his sister and in response; she stuck out her tongue. Ignoring their childish conduct, Meghan took Robert's left hand and Elizabeth's right hand and made them skip down the path leading deeper into the dense foliage. The overhead tangling soon cut off their view of the sun, and a bend in the path made it impossible to see the parsonage. Elizabeth became frightened.

"I want to go back," the little girl cried. "I don't like it here."

Robert replied, "She is right. Let's go back, now!"

At that precise moment, they heard their mother's voice. The trio ran back around the bend. Mrs. Jennings was standing at the head of the pathway.

"Come along. It is time for refreshments and a rest for us all. Meghan, you should have realized how tiring it would be for the children to take such a long walk in this heat. Just look at their damp foreheads."

"It wasn't really that hot," exclaimed Robert. "It was like being in a cool tunnel."

"A cool tunnel, indeed," responded his mother.

"I was frightened," declared Elizabeth.

"Of course you were, my dear," agreed her mother. "Now, you both run along with Meghan." As an after thought, she continued, "We have been assigned servants from the village. They have prepared fruit and cool drinks on the side verandah. Your rooms are just beyond. Oh, by the way. Be considerate of the servants, nevertheless, remember who your father is and act accordingly."

"What did your mama mean by 'act accordingly'," Meghan asked as they walked to the verandah.

"Oh, that," quipped Robert. "She means we must never say or do anything that would embarrass our father."

"That must be ours," declared Robert, looking at a table laden with fruit. "Let's eat. I'm starved."

❧

MEGHAN POURED COOL water into three glasses and selected various fruits for the children. One was not quite round and a lush green color. She peeled the skin and found a soft creamy substance that they spread on the warm bread. They later learned its name was avocado. A bunch of yellow bananas (they had eaten those on board ship) hung down from the porch. Berries, both white and black had been placed in the center of the table. Another strange fruit they had never seen before was round and yellow. Once it was opened, they saw large black seeds in the center. They removed the seeds and sucked in the creamy substance; it was very good. Meghan never did learn what it was called. After they ate their fill, Robert and Elizabeth went to their rooms and soon they were fast asleep.

Meghan had removed her bonnet before they had eaten, now she pulled out the pins holding her hair in restraint; it fell across her shoulders to her waist.

She rubbed her scalp vigorously until it tingled from the assault. She unlaced her bodice revealing her throat and upper shoulder. She leaned back against the post and closed her eyes. A warm breeze caressed her face and neck. Meghan felt rather than heard the approaching footsteps. She opened her eyes. A girl about her own age was gathering the dishes from the table.

Meghan smiled. "Hello," she said to the girl.

The girl returned the smile, but said nothing.

Meghan quickly laced her bodice. "My name is Meghan," she said, winding her hair back in place. "And your name?"

"My name is Leah," replied the girl hesitantly. "I serve here."

Meghan brightened. At long last she would have someone to talk with besides the Jennings. "How wonderful! You speak English."

Leah smiled and repeated, "My name is Leah. I serve here."

Meghan's smile faltered. "Is that all the English you know?"

The girl shrugged her shoulders. "My name . . ."

"I know," said a downhearted Meghan. "it's Leah."

Leah waited for a moment and when Meghan did not speak again, the girl cleared the table and left. Meghan stared after her for a minute before she too left the porch and went to her own room.

Meghan was quite envious of Leah's skimpy attire and her golden skin.

Her dress was bright red with large yellow flowers. The material came just above her breasts, leaving her neck, shoulders, and arms bare. The skirt ended mid-thigh revealing long, golden legs. She wore nothing on her feet. Although Meghan's face and hands were as golden as the girl's, the rest of her body was as white as the day she left Ireland. A smile tugged at the corner of her lips. If only she dared to follow the plan that was even now taking root in her mind.

The next morning found Meghan and the children resuming their walk of the previous day. "Listen to the music," Meghan instructed them.

"What music?" they asked.

"Can't you hear the birds?" Meghan asked.

"I can hear them," they cried.

"What else can you hear?" Meghan inquired.

"I can hear water," declared the boy.

"So can I," chimed Elizabeth.

"Pretend the birds are violins backed by the roll of drums."

"It does sound like music," Robert voiced. "But where is the water?"

They hurried around the next bend to find water flowing into a large pond set above a small waterfall. "Where does the water come from?" inquired the boy.

"I imagine from the mountain down to here through those ferns," said Meghan pointing to the back of the compound.

"Can we go closer?' the children asked.

Meghan smiled. "Let's go." She led the way through giant ferns until a wooden fence stopped them.

"Lift me up," pleaded Robert. "I want to see the other side."

"We'll drag that wooden chair to the wall, and you can stand on it," Meghan told him.

Robert climbed ups on the chair; then balanced on the arms and peered over the fence.

"I want up there, too," wailed Elizabeth.

"No, you are much too young. You'll fall and hurt yourself," Robert said, trying very hard to act unafraid.

Elizabeth howled even louder.

Ignoring the girl's cries, Meghan asked, "What do you see?"

"It looks just the same," he told them. "And I can't see where the water comes from on account of all the flowers."

Robert jumped down. "Can we take our shoes off and wade in the pool?" he asked Meghan.

"We'll be doing better than that," Meghan said. "I'll ask permission for you to swim."

Their smiles disappeared. "We don't know how to swim," they protested.

"Well, I do and I'll teach you both," Meghan promised.

That evening Meghan asked if she could teach the children to swim. After much discussion between the parents, she received their approval. By the end of the week, both children could paddle across the pond. In another week, they were actually swimming in front of their parents.

"Well done, indeed!" Mr. Jennings called out. "I'm proud of you both."

"It is time for you to prepare your Sunday message," Mrs. Jennings whispered into her husband's ear. "We had better go back to the parsonage."

"Of course, my dear," he replied.

Mrs. Jennings took her husband's arm and they left the youngsters without saying goodbye; the children did not notice them leave.

"Meghan, watch me." Robert stood on the rock edge of the pool. He jumped into the water and did not come up. If Meghan had not investigated the depth of the pool, his actions might have alarmed her, as it was, she merely waited until he surfaced.

"That was very good, Robert," she said. "However, you only have another half hour to swim, I don't think you ought to waste it playing."

Meghan removed a writing tablet from her bag and began to write a letter to her mother. When she had finished it was time to go back to the mission. She gave the letter to Mr. Jennings who said he would be glad to mail it for her. She thanked him and hurried off to meet with Leah. The two young women had become fast friends, each attempting to teach the other her language.

One evening after the children were asleep, Mrs. Jennings went in search of her husband. She found him in his office. "Mr. Jennings," she said quietly. "May I have a moment of your time?"

"Of course, my dear, what is it?"

"I am quite worried about Meghan. I really don't think it quite proper for her to associate so much with the servants."

"And which servant concerns you, my dear?"

"Leah."

"I have spoken with Leah on several occasion," he told his wife, "and I cannot imagine any harm coming to Meghan by the association."

"If that is your decision, Mr. Jennings. I will say no more on that matter," replied his wife as she picked up her needlepoint and sat in her chair by the window.

Chapter Ten

❧

Meghan spent as much time as she could with Leah. As the girl taught Meghan the Polynesian language Leah learned to speak English—with an Irish brogue.

One afternoon when Meghan was free of her duties, she asked Leah if she could borrow one of her sarongs, the red one with the yellow flowers. "I want to sun by the pool,"

Meghan said, confidently. "I'll be putting it on in my room and I'll cover up with a shawl to walk to the pool. And, as you know, Mrs. Jennings has forbid anyone other than the family to go there, so it's not likely I'll be seen."

"Tis fear I'm feelin'," Leah said.

"I promised no one will find out," assured Meghan.

Reluctantly Leah went to her room and returned with the cloth. Together they went to Meghan's room where Leah showed Meghan how to wrap it about her slim body. "Please," Leah begged. "Don't let anyone see you."

By the end of the month Meghan's entire body had turned the same shade of gold as had her face and hands. Not many days later Meghan had another idea, one that alarmed Leah even more. "We are almost the same shade of color. If I were to stain my hair in the juice of the black berries, we might pass as sisters. What do you think?"

"I'm thinking you better stop before trouble comes upon you," Leah replied.

"What trouble could there be pretending we are sisters? I think it would be fun."

"Meghan, I want no part of your play acting."

"Leah, what harm could it be?"

"What harm? If we're found out, we'd both be punished and you know it."

"We won't be found out, that is, not if we are careful. You know the family goes into seclusion for an hour or two in the afternoon. We could leave for a walk and return before they know we have been gone."

"And if the berry stain won't wash away, what then?"

"I've all ready tried it on the ends of a curl and it did wash away."

"I won't be taking you," cried Leah. "I'm afraid of what might happen."

"Nothing will happen," promised Meghan, taking Leah's hand into hers. "And as soon as the Jennings' retire," she continued, "I'll meet you at the pond, and 'tis a bit of a swim we'll be having before we leave."

Meghan had been swimming for some time before Leah finally came. "What kept you?" Meghan asked. "I was beginning to fear you would not come."

"I told you I'd come," Leah said. "Cook had me doing some extra things." She slipped into the water beside Meghan.

"Leah, could you be telling me about the magical pool?

"What magical pool?"

"By the look of your face, you know about it. Now, tell me where it is," insisted Meghan, climbing out of the pool.

"It is only tales to be repeated on a dark night, and to be believed by the foolish and the very young."

"We have such tales in Ireland," said Meghan. "And who's to say they not be true?" Meghan looked earnestly at her friend. "I bet you could find out where it is."

With downcast eyes, Leah promised to try.

A week later Meghan appeared at the pond with her hair stained with berry juice and wearing her native costume. "Is it truly me?" Meghan gasped, looking in the mirror of still water. Then turning to Leah, added "I told you I could pass for your sister or maybe your cousin."

"Except for your slender nose and green eyes, one could hardly tell the difference," Leah agreed in amazement. "But if they do see your face, then all is lost."

"If anyone comes that close, I'll turn my face away. Satisfied?"

"I'll take you to the path leading up to the pool, but I'll not be going any closer.

It's taboo for any of us to go there."

"But why?" asked Meghan.

Leah looked into Meghan's eyes. "Witches live in the pool."

"Are thcy bad witches?"

Leah did not answer. They continued walking through the dense foliage until they came to a fork in the path. "'Tis as far as I be goin'," Leah told her.

"You will wait, won't you?" Meghan asked.

"Aye," declared the frightened girl. "I'll be waitin', but you best be back before it grows dark, or I won't be here when you return."

"I'll be back, I promise," Meghan assured her.

Meghan enjoyed the walk. The birds were radiant in color and in voice. The flowers along the pathway shimmered in the sun's rays. As she neared an opening in the trees, the air grew still, and the birds no longer sang their song. It was as if she had entered a hallowed place. A sense of peace invaded her being. "There's nothing to fear here."

She looked up through the leaves and could see the bright blue sky with only a scattering of fluffy white clouds floating quietly by; the crisp cool air so unlike the heat that baked the compound of the mission. The only sound she heard was the rustling of leaves.

Meghan sat on the edge of the shady pool, her feet dangling in the cool water, her eyes closed. A bird lit on her bare shoulder. The soft pecking of its bill on Meghan's lips forced her eyes open. The startled bird flew to a nearby branch, its head cocked toward her.

"There could be no witches in all this beauty," she said aloud. "But just the same, I best be getting back. There's no need in frightening Leah. The next time I come," she vowed. "I come alone." Meghan pulled her legs out of the water and dried her feet on the soft covering of moss.

Leah breathed a sigh of relief when she saw Meghan walking down the path toward her. "What took you so long?" she asked. "I was that scared, I was. If you want to come here again, you'll be coming alone."

"Those are my thoughts, exactly. Now, do you want to hear of its beauty?"

"Nay. I want to forget I was ever here," Leah replied.

"Leah, there was nothing to be afraid of. It was truly a wondrous place, and I'll be going back as often as I can."

Leah was just as adamant. "Like I said. If you do go, you'll be going alone."

The girl did not go with her to the compound pool while Meghan washed the color out of her hair, metamorphosing it a radiant red, once more.

Meghan went to the small lagoon as often as she could and dreamed of home and her dear, sweet mother. She wondered over and over again what her father might have done to her mother. Had he struck her, or had he ordered her out of the house? If only a letter would arrive and let her know that everything was all right with her mother.

Chapter Eleven

༄

Pacific Ocean – 1815

Trade winds moved the massive square sails of the whaling ship MORNING STAR, moving her steadily over the waves in search of the elusive sperm whale. During the past forty-eight months she had crisscrossed her way over the Atlantic Ocean, around Cape Horn, and up the coast to Galapagos; now she headed for the islands. Her round-bowed 410 tons was the home of twenty-eight men and, except for her captain, Nantucket men, every one.

Soon it would be dawn, and her sleeping whaling men would be awake, but for now only three men kept vigil: Samuel Tracy, her youngest crewman, searched the far horizon from the crow's-nest, his body within three circles of iron. Her helmsman, Daniel Riley Timmons, gripped the large wooden wheel, as the responsibility of keeping the ship on course rested in his hands. The third man, Captain Nathaniel Jeremiah Lathrope, made his way toward the ship's bow.

The STAR's deck rolled beneath him, yet he moved with ease, his leather boots soundless on the wooden deck. Every now and then, a pensive look stole over his finely chiseled features as a growing apprehension gnawed within his lean frame. At the bow, he looked down into the black, churning sea and then at the sky. The sails billowed in the light breeze; the full moon shone brightly; the stars danced in the cloudless sky; yet this feeling of something amiss grew stronger.

He realized how very tired he and his men were. It had been many long months since they had touched land. Nevertheless, he knew his tiredness was more than that. He was tired of the endless sea, of the smell of rancid blubber in every breath he drew, and he had seen more death on this trip than ever before.

Why do I stay? the words sprung unbidden to his mind. *Why don't I leave this blasted ship when we return to port and never sail her again? I want a wife and sons; I want some place to call home; why does this dream always elude me?*

Even as the question came to mind, Nathaniel knew the answer. The lure of the sea was more powerful and seductive than any woman he had ever known. He had been first mate on the STAR at sixteen, her captain at twenty, and today was his twenty-sixth birthday. After this hunt he would have saved enough money to buy the ship, thus becoming not only her captain, but her master as well. The STAR was his life—his reason for living.

A chill wind blew across the deck. The weather was changing, yet the moon was still bright and the sky without clouds. He stared toward the far horizon. Was there something there? Or was his imagination playing tricks on him? He paused in the shelter of the bulkhead to bring out his pipe and tobacco pouch. The tobacco was a blend specially made for him in Jamaica. He filled the bowl, packed it down and lit it. For a time the aroma blocked out the pungent stench of the ship. After all these years at sea, the smell of blubber had managed to seep into the seasoned wood of the ship; it reeked from his clothes and followed him into his cabin. He could not even escape it at night, for it invaded his dreams.

Nathaniel returned to the bow. He saw nothing ahead, yet continued to feel the presence of pending doom. It meant only one thing; somewhere on the far horizon a storm was building. He did not know when it would be encountered, but there was not a single doubt in his mind that the storm would hit and it would strike before daybreak. His watch was almost over and soon Jeremy Haws, his first mate, would be on deck. Another ten minutes and the man did appear.

"Keep a sharp look out," Nathaniel warned him, "There's trouble ahead, and it will come before daylight. Alert the watch for the first sign of the approaching storm."

Haws looked at the moonlight reflected on the calm surface of the water and the stars dancing in the cloudless sky. He stretched. "Thar's nothing to fear this night, Cap'n."

"Fear, you say?" The hair on the back of Nathaniel's neck bristled, his jawbone tightened. With narrowed eyes, he faced the other man. "Fear!" he repeated the word, his voice lashing about Haws like a whip. "Since when has good judgment been mistaken for fear? If Stevens and Billings had known the difference, they might be alive today. And, Mistah Haws, since when have you taken to questioning my orders?" Not waiting for an answer, he continued. "Well, Mistah Haws, do you issue the order to the men, or must I?"

Haws' face drained of color. Never had he seen his captain so angry. "Aye, Cap'n, I'll be giving the command."

The order given, Nathaniel spoke again, his words clipped and crisp. "When the storm hits, Mistah Haws, send for me immediately. Is that clear?"

"Aye, Cap'n," replied Haws. "'Tis clear enough."

Nathaniel turned on his heel, leaving his stunned first mate on the deck. Once inside his cabin, he undressed in the dark, tossed his clothing toward a nearby chair, then laid on the bed. He closed his eyes but couldn't sleep. He sat up, running his fingers through his thick, blond hair. Finally, he pulled on his trousers and went to the cupboard. He lit the lamp and taking down his charts spread them out on the desk. If his calculations were correct, and he had no reason to doubt them, they would be sighting land by the end of the week. However, if the storm blew them off course, there was no telling what their destination would be. His concern was for the men. He'd had to break up several fights in the past five days, and there was no telling what their reaction would be to the added delay. He sat deep in thought. He smiled. Perhaps a storm would be well received. It would certainly give the men something other than each other on which to vent their frustrations.

Whenever Nathaniel was extremely exhausted, the scar on his left hand throbbed.

Tonight was no exception, and his thoughts flew back to the place of his youth. The scene in the barn had been branded forever in his memory. It was not the first time that he had run away, only to be caught and brought back to face the Master of Stewart Hall.

"So you have come back?" the man had snarled. Without taking his eyes from the six-year-old, he commanded someone to bring Toby into the barn. When the black man arrived, Stewart ordered, "Strip the boy to the waist, and tie him to that post."

Fear registered in Toby's eyes, yet he had the courage to reply, "No, Mastah, I won't do it."

William Stewart's nostrils flared. "You dare defy me? His whip snapped up, stricking Toby across the face with such force the man fell to the ground, unconscious.

Stewart turned back to the small boy. "Do you remember what I told you would happen if you ever tried to run away again?" Six-year old Nathaniel stood at attention, his arms at his side, his eyes straight ahead and said nothing.

Nathaniel forced his mind away from the scene. There was too much depending on his clear thinking to waste his energy on the past. He blew out the light and returned to his bed. This time sleep did claim him.

An hour later the storm hit. Haws had been taken completely by surprise. True, he had issued the order to the crow's nest, but never for one minute had he believed the storm would come. Haws wondered why he had not. Had the captain ever given an order that had proven unnecessary? He had been the captain's first mate these past five years and was his second mate before that. Well, there was no use worrying about it now, not with the storm heading in, and it looked like a bad one, at that.

Without warning a tumultuous wall of water rose some two hundred feet ahead of the ship, and black as pitch. Haws managed to shout, "Johnson alert the Cap'n" just before the ship was engulfed with tons of crashing water-sending men sprawling across the deck. Haws grabbed hold of a line and pulled himself to his feet.

"Mistah Haws," a seaman shouted after him, "are we goin' sink?"

"Nay, lad! We'll win the battle." Haws pulled himself along the deck to the ladder leading to the hold to make sure their precious cargo of oil was secured. If they lost it, the last four years would be for naught.

Nathaniel was pulling on his boots when a knock came on the cabin door. "Enter!" he commanded. The door opened and at the sight of the young seaman asked, "Where is Mistah Haws?"

"'E said to tell ye, e's gone below to see about the cargo."

"How bad is the storm?" Nathaniel asked, grabbing his hat and slicker off the hook by the door.

"'Tis as if the gates of 'ell opened its mouth and the demons be making sport of us, Cap'n," replied the youth, his eyes pools of terror.

"Any of the men lost?"

"Don't think so, Cap'n."

Nathaniel laid his large hand on the lad's shoulder. "The STAR has never lost a battle," he said. "Besides, I promised your mother I would return you safe to her keeping."

Johnson gave a feeble smile. "Aye, Cap'n. Thank ye, Cap'n." Some color came back into his face as he followed Nathaniel out of the cabin.

Just as the captain stepped on deck a wave came over the bow, and hurled toward him. "Hang on," Nathaniel shouted down to Johnson. "We're about to be hit." Nathaniel grabbed hold of a line and swung clear. Poor Johnson was not as fortunate. The force of the water hit him, and he toppled back down to the passageway below.

Nathaniel peered down. "Are you hurt, lad?" he shouted.

Johnson looked up at his captain. "I'm fine, sir," he said.

Nathaniel threw a secured line down to the lad. "Take the line and hang on. I'll pull you up." Soon Johnson stood by his side.

Low swirling black clouds, laced with lightning, shrouded the ship and joined the sea in making havoc with the STAR. Together they tossed the wooden ship back and forth between them, like children playing catch. One minute the ship would be upright then in the next minute, it would be struggling to stay afloat.

Nathaniel pulled his hat lower, trying to stop the thousands of tiny javelins of salt from cutting into his face. The raging wind tore at his rain gear, pelting his body not unlike the assault of an enemy in battle. And that was exactly what they were facing, a battle to the death. The combatants on one side were the wind, the rain, and the sea. On the other side of the battle was the STAR and her whaling men.

Adrenaline pumped through Nathaniel's veins, strengthening his muscles, forcing his legs to move against the violent attack of the elements. With each steps his determination to win grew stronger. The storm was not going to destroy what he had worked a lifetime to achieve, nor was it going to kill or maim any of his men, that is, not if he could help it. The thunder was deafening; the lightning crackled across the deck and struck the main mast.

For a time the sail held the wooden pole in place; then, with a ripping sound, the sail tore, the mast toppled, missing several whalers by mere inches. The massive sail, now freed, whipped dangerously overhead.

Nathaniel started toward the bridge. However, before he could reach the ladder, the force of the tempestuous wind sent him back three steps for every two that he had taken. "You're not going to defeat me," Nathaniel shouted, "nor are you going to destroy my ship or my men."

The wind roared across the ship knocking him first one way then another. He managed to get to the ladder and had climbed two rungs before he slipped, striking the side of his head against the next rung. Blood gushed from the wound, spreading across his forehead and down into his eyes. Anger flashed through him. "That's something a cabin boy would have guarded against," he grumbled. Back on his feet, he conquered the next four rungs before the force of the storm half-keeled the ship.

The sudden movement sent him tumbling back down the ladder and across the deck like a runaway keg. Matthew, the first mate, saw Nathaniel's plight and cried, "God Almighty, save the Cap'n," Matthew prayed as he made his way toward Nathaniel.

A water keg broke loose from its lashings and careened toward the two men. It missed Matthew, but the captain was not so fortunate. The keg struck him on the back of his head. Blood spurted freely from the new wound, and Nathaniel sank into unconsciousness.

Matthew's screams for help fell helpless in the gale. If they were to be saved, Matthew knew it would be up to him. He anchored one arm around a secured line, made a vise of his own legs around his unconscious captain, and pulled him from the hungry sea. Doors, ripped from their leather strapping, flew toward them. A whaling boat, freed from its restraint, toppled from the bulkhead and splintered on contact with the deck.

"We're goin' to be killed," Matthew cried out.

But fate stepped in. The bow plunged deeper into the sea, hurtling both Nathaniel and Matthews toward a coiled mound of lines, and in the process knocked two whalers off their feet. One of those men was Jeremy Haws who quickly took in the urgency of the situation. He grabbed a secured line and tied the free end around his waist. He fought against the elements as he made his way to the stricken men, their bodies wedged between two barrels. A lucky break came when the wind ceased its race across the deck. And in that lull, another group of men came to their rescue having heard Haws' shouts, "Save the Cap'n, first." ordered Haws, as he hung on to Matthew.

Unfortunately for the group, the turbulent sea had not eased it's strength. A huge wave cut across the deck, knocking the men to their knees. The added jolt brought Nathaniel back to his senses. He saw the men struggling to keep him afloat. "Release me," he commanded, "and save yourselves." The men did not. "Let me go," Nathaniel demanded. Another wave crashed over them; salt water rushed into Nathaniel's mouth and down his throat. He struggled for air. Matthew remained unconscious. Nathaniel relaxed his muscles. The men loosened their grip thus enabling Nathaniel to break free. He spun, then tumbled toward the bulkhead, grabbed a line and pulled himself upright.

"Take Matthew below!" Nathaniel commanded. "My ship needs me."

Nathaniel's head ached. Momentarily the mixture of water and blood flowed into his eyes, blinding his path to the bridge. Calling upon the Almighty for help, Nathaniel hooked his arm about a secured line, pulled a scarf from his pocket and tied it about the wound, stopping the flow of blood. He must get to the wheel! He would not allow the storm to smash his ship to oblivion and his men along with it!

Once the ladder was reached, he pulled himself up the first rung. The force of the gale had now reached hurricane strength. He felt as though he was a mere straw, being blown back and forth at the will of something or someone else. It was a feeling he did not like.

"Damme,"[1] he thought. "I am in command of this ship and by thunder, command it I will."

Nathaniel conquered the fourth rung, then the fifth, until, at last, he reached the bridge. There he found Daniel alone and when the man saw his captain, the look of sheer relief flooded his features.

"A little rough, Daniel?" Nathaniel shouted, making his way toward the wheel.

"Aye, Cap'n, 'tis at that," replied Daniel as he continued to fight for control of the massive wheel.

"Can you use another hand?"

Daniel grinned. "Aye, Cap'n, and grateful for it."

Daniel had tied himself to the steering post, Nathaniel did likewise and together they were able to turn the wheel, heading the ship directly into the storm. All lamps on the ship had been smashed at the onslaught and except for flashes of lightning, the ship was bathed in darkness. In those flashes of light, however, Nathaniel had the opportunity to see the activity on deck. A surge of pride swept through him. No captain on the seven seas could boast of a better crew. Nevertheless, their efforts would be in vain if the ship were allowed to capsize.

The battle for survival raged on for hours. Without warning the

---

[1]"Damme" is a slang word created by Nathaniel that he uses instead of swearing.

wind, rain, and the sea ceased their battle. Walls of water surrounded the ship, and clouds sealed the heavens from view. They had entered the center of the storm. Nathaniel untied himself from the post and went in search of Haws. He found him below with the injured men.

"We're in the center of the storm," Nathaniel informed them. His exhaustion was evident by the tone of his voice, but his words were clear and concise. "Men, I'm proud of you all. By virtue of your actions, the STAR has made it through the first wall. Mistah Haws, see to it that the men have an extra ration of rum, and when we reach home, a bonus will be added to their share of the cargo."

He turned and asked. "How is the arm, Matthew?"

"Fit enough, Cap'n," was the answer.

"It was a mighty brave thing you did," replied Nathaniel, gripping the man's good arm. He fought to keep his emotion in control. "You saved my life, and I'll not be forgetting it."

"Twas Mistah Haws and the others that saved us both," Matthew informed him.

"If Matthew hadn't reached ye first," replied Haws. "Ye would be lost to our help."

"I did no more than what the Cap'n would do," insisted Matthew. "Nay, I did no more than that."

Tears of gratitude formed behind Nathaniel's eyes, and he quickly turned away lest the man should see them. "Remember the extra portion of rum, Mistah Haws," Nathaniel said, gaining control of his emotions.

"And whar do ye think yer going, Cap'n," came a voice from the rear.

Nathaniel looked into the face of the old man whose gray whiskers had never managed to form a beard. "To do my duty, Mistah Simmons," he responded.

"Ye can't be doing yer duty, Cap'n, by bleeding to death," replied the old man. "And why are ye calling me Mistah Simmons? Cookie is my name. Now, sit yerself down. I'll be tending that thar wound."

Nathaniel smiled and sat down. He loved this old man. It was Cookie who had befriended him, guiding him in the ways of the sea and whaling ships when Nathaniel first came aboard Captain Black's ship at the tender age of ten. Nathaniel had never forgotten him and when he heard Cookie had been forced to leave the sea due to his age, Nathaniel had brought him aboard the STAR as cook, doctor, and peacemaker. It was a decision Nathaniel had never regretted.

"Cap'n, Cap'n", ye best be coming," came a shout from the upper deck. "The outer wall is just ahead!"

The men who were well enough to join in the fighting followed Nathaniel to the upper deck. They fought through two nights and three days before the battle was won by the MORNING STAR! An exhausted Nathaniel left the deck to go below to his cabin. Once there, he took down the ship's log and began to write.

> *April 15, 1815*
>
> *We have survived the worse storm so far encountered on his hunt. I now take quill in hand to describe the heroics of my men. I make special mention of my second mate, Donald Matthew, who risked his life in saving mine. If he had not, I would have been swept out to sea.*
>
> *Henry Johnson jumped overboard to save the life of a fellow seaman and, though it looked like certain death for them both, Johnson refused to release his charge until they could both be plucked from the water. Never in all my years at sea, have I seen such bravery as was displayed this voyage. All the men deserve and will receive an extra bonus on our return home.*

He continued writing for almost an hour describing in full the heroics of the men of the MORNING STAR. He ended his entry by the following words,

> I thank the Almighty that not a soul was lost.
>> Signed, Nathaniel Lathrope,
>> captain of the MORNING STAR.

After Nathaniel finished writing in the logbook he put it back in its proper slot and took down his private journal.

> August 15, 1815
>> We are somewhere off the coast of Maui. Where exactly, I do not know. The storm has done a great deal of damage. Our cargo is intact; we can thank the Almighty for that and the dream of a lifetime within my grasp. With my share of the cargo, and with what I have managed to save, lo these many years, I shall have enough to buy the STAR. Then I will not only be her captain, but her master as well.

He laid aside the quill and lit his pipe. He took a deep puff; then, once again, began to write:

> "Jeremy Haws has a child awaiting him on the 'Little Gray Lady of the Sea'; my beloved Nantucket. I pray he will not, once again, be led to a tiny grave on the hillside.
> Young Samuel Tracy's bride awaits him, and Riley Timmons will not be returning to sea. He wants to buy a farm where he'll not be separated from his wife and sons. As for me—I shall stay at sea. This is the life that I have chosen for myself, yet there is an aching deep within me, the cause—I know not.
>> Signed, Nathaniel Lathrope,
>> captain of the MORNING STAR.

He put away his journal, pulled off his boots and fell into a dreamless sleep.

Chapter Twelve

◈

A faint glow fringed the far horizon. In a few minutes, the cry 'LAND HO' would rouse the men from their sleep. With the STAR firmly anchored in Alenuihaha Channel the water would be filled with canoes bearing men in search of rum and brown-skin girls eager to fill a man's hungry arms.

A movement off the starboard caught Nathaniel's attention. There was something moving in the sky! He was not sure exactly what it was. He whipped the spyglass from his waist and peered through it. "Damme!" he uttered looking through the glass. "If they're not falling stars!" A bad omen, indeed, he thought.

Nathaniel watched for several seconds more. Then a smile crossed his lips. "I feel like a blasted idiot making a mistake like that," he said, " 'tis not stars at all but white soaring birds."

Seconds later the alarm rang out! "LAND HO! LAND TO THE STARBOARD!"

The forecastle came alive! Men clamored from their bunks, pulling on their trousers as they made for their assigned posts. The officers ran from their cabins below to join their captain on deck.

"Mistah Haws!" commanded Nathaniel. "Prepare the men to disembark. I'm going to my quarters."

Once inside his cabin, Nathaniel opened his massive trunk and lifted out what he called his finery: a black silk shirt and satin trousers. The shirt emphasized his broad shoulders and muscular chest, molding perfectly to his lean waist. The trousers hugged his long legs, showing the power of his thighs. He tied a scarf around his throat.

"Now for the final touch," he mused, tucking his firearm into the waistband.

Once dressed, he went back to his men. Expecting to hear shouts of excitement, he was surprised at the silence. Nathaniel walked among them. Haws saw him and hurried to his side.

"Cap'n, thar be no canoes coming to see us. And look! Thar's not a person on shore to greet us. Cap'n, I think thar be trouble."

The rest of the men began to grumble.

"And the lasses! Whar be the lasses?"

Another voice was heard "'Tis too blooming quiet for me."

And yet another, "It fair raises me hair."

"Looks like a blooming graveyard to me," cried a man, standing next to the railing.

"'Tis haunted! Just like all them thar tales we be hearing."

One whaler came to Nathaniel, hat in hand. "Cap'n, 'tis better we go on to Hawaii. I've never been here before, but I've been 'earing 'bout this place since a wee lad. If we land 'ere, I'm thinking on staying 'board the STAR."

Nathaniel dashed to the bulkhead and climbed into his whaleboat. He looked down at his men, his fists on his hips. "Mistah Haws," he called out, "It appears the whalers of the MORNING STAR are afraid to go ashore! Tell me! Are these the same men who fought the worst storm in our history? Are they the same who has fought the mighty sperm whale and won? Is a little silence going to keep them from a well-deserved rest?

"Men, look ahead! Do you not see the same sandy beaches of other islands? Are not the palms swaying in the breeze from the trade winds? Do you not smell the aroma of fresh fruit? Does your body not ache with desire for a swim and a woman to hold? Are you really staying on board the STAR like whimpering children?"

The men did not move.

"Mistah Haws, you and the other officers come with me. Ahoy there!," he called to the men at the cranks, "Lower away the boats!"

Haws went to the bulkhead. "'Ow 'bout the whalers Cap'n? What will they do without an officer to tell them which way to jump?"

"Mistah Haws," Nathaniel said, "they're men, not boys."

"That was once me thought, Cap'n. Now, I not be knowing what's the truth."

The whalers shifted about looking at each other, not knowing what to do. Cookie was the first to speak. "I'll go with ye, Mistah Haws. I aim to 'ave me some fresh meat."

"Come ahead," cried Haws. "And any 'board that be a man, let him come!"

The officers jumped into their assigned boats. As the crane began to lower Nathaniel's boat, the men who had previously drawn lots to see who was to go and who was to stay, jumped in behind the officers. One by one the huge crane lowered each boat into the water. The men raised the oars and waited for the order to row toward shore. Once given, the men lowered their oars and the race was on to the deserted beach.

On a day like this it was not hard for Nathaniel to understand the men's feelings. In all his years at sea, this was one island he had never stepped foot on. He reflected back to the tales he had heard. Tales of blood curdling cries coming from off the mountain Haleakala where the sun never seemed to shine. There were other stories that now rushed to memory. Yarns about rocks that moved themselves from one place to another and of wanton women who, after making love, could turn themselves into trees, and come morning some poor man might wake up to find himself entwined in its branches.

He also recalled hearing about a magical pool somewhere on Maui where the witches who lived in its cool water could foretell a man's future. Ravishing witches who could lure a man into the depths of the water, never to return. But if the witches liked you, they could grant your wishes.

As he grew to manhood, such tales had been dismissed, however, on a day like this, well, one could never know for sure if it were fact or myth. The sun baked the earth. Nathaniel removed his scarf and mopped his brow with it. Never had he encountered such heat. They were now approaching land and the combination of flowers and ripening fruit gave off such a pungent odor it nearly suffocated him.

Water lapped gently against the boats as the men rowed silently toward the silvery shore. Flowers of every color laced the thick foliage. The presence of the men's fear was as striking as the fragrance of the flowers and fruit.

Once ashore the men collected into small groups, waiting for their captain to speak to them. Leaping to a large rock, Nathaniel spoke with a grin. "It looks as though our hosts are shy. Well, it matters not. I shall go and find them while the camp is being set up and the empty kegs are brought ashore." He looked at the officers. "Mistah Matthew, Mistah Timmons, take care of that duty while Mistah Haws and I walk a mite along the shore."

After a short distance, Nathaniel spoke again, only this time his voice held no mocking tone as it had in front of the crew. "I don't like this. Be sure and keep guards posted while I'm gone. At the first sign of trouble, don't wait for me, get the men back to the ship."

"Ye expect trouble?" questioned the first mate.

"It's best to always expect trouble," answered Nathaniel.

They continued to walk and discuss the duties of the day. The sound of crashing brush brought their conversation to a halt. Both men drew their pistols. Haws wiped the sweat from his face. "Do we shoot on sight?" he asked.

Nathaniel smiled. "And deprive someone of the pleasure of the first attack? No, we wait and see what happens." He smiled again. "The sight of the pistols may be enough to sober them." Nathaniel's pulse raced with excitement. His senses were alert for any trouble. This was all he needed to revive his spirit from the long sea voyage.

Hands parted the nearby foliage and a group of young boys dashed out of the woods. They had been chattering but stopped when they saw the two white men. Nathaniel walked the short distance ahead and spoke with the youngsters. When he returned, he told Haws they had told him the whole village had gone to the other side of the island to hear some missionaries. Now they were back, and the boys had volunteered to take him to see the white trader living in their village.

"Stay here," Nathaniel whispered. "It might be a trap, although I hardly think so. All the stories concerning this island have not included real violence."

"Aye, I'll be doing as ye say." Haws paused. "But I'll be coming to look for ye if yer not back in two hours."

Nathaniel's smile vanished. "If I'm not back, take the men out of danger. That is an order!"

The boys led Nathaniel through the thicket and into a dense forest. He followed them along a well-defined path. He kept them in sight until entering into a tunnel made of tangled branches, which appeared to be veering slightly to the right. The branch overhead grew thicker, shutting out more and more sunlight until, at last, he was encased in darkness. The air grew dank; his shirt clung to his chest in a cold sweat. He came to a fork in the trail. He looked in both direction and saw nothing. He called out to the youngsters. There was no answer. How could he have gotten so far behind them? Had they taken a path unseen by him? Or had they deliberately lost him? He did not know how it happened, but happened it did; he was totally alone, and lost. He could not hear the cooing of birds or breaking of twigs, except the ones he had stepped on. He had lost his sense of direction, and on account of all the bends in the trail, he didn't know whether he was going in circles, heading back toward the beach, or going toward the village. When he saw those lads again, he would tan their hides. He had given some thought about the possibility of being led into a trap, and he was well aware that he would be in no position to win unless he used his wits. But what could be the purpose of a trap? True, he had been surprised to see the STAR was the only ship anchored in the bay, and he wondered afresh, if there had been troubles with other ships. The men of the STAR had been busy on the hunt, and he had not taken the usual opportunity to rendezvous with passing ships where he would normally have gathered such information.

He continued his journey. The branches tore at his clothes, soon the material on his sleeves and trousers was ripped, his temper rose; they were, after all, his favorite apparel.

Nathaniel walked with more vigilance. There was a possibility that hostile natives were waiting for him, and he must make ready for a fight. He reached up and broke off a part of a sturdy branch. He held it tightly in one hand and his pistol in the other. Thus armed, he walked slowly ahead. He came to a fork in the tunnel. The path to the left ended in darkness, however, the path to the right contained a faint glow of light and this path he chose.

The nearer he came toward the light, the louder the sound of water.

He started to run. Finally, he burst into a clearing. To his uppermost gratitude, he found no one waiting for him. The sun shone brightly in a clear blue sky, where he saw multitudes of colorful birds soaring overhead while others paused in their flight to dip their beaks into the abundance of flowers. In the center of it all was a large pool of clear water, encased by moss covered rocks. A feeling of complete peace replaced the one of anxiety. He removed his torn and damp shirt and leaning over the edge, splashed some cool water over his chest, arms, face, and neck. He thought seriously about diving in for a swim, then discarded the idea. Not knowing the terrain or what might lurk just beyond the heavy foliage, he forced himself to be satisfied with the dousing. He had just finished putting on his soiled shirt when he heard the breaking of twigs. He picked up the branch and pistol and carefully headed in the direction where he heard the noise. Following the sound to a large boulder, he looked behind it and found nothing. *Must have been a bird.* The next thought that came to mind was, *I can't believe how jumpy, I am.*

He took a reading from the sun's position and started down a path opposite to whence he had come. He had not traveled far when the path widened to expose a ledge overlooking the bay. He walked to the edge of the clearing and was amazed as he watched the water change color. At first glance it seemed blue; then it changed to green before turning crystal clear, and as clear as the pool had been. "Remarkable place this Maui," he uttered, making his way down an undefined path that led him to a larger clearing. And there stood the boys he had met on the beach.

A look of relief flashed across the young leader's face. "You lost us," he stammered in his native tongue.

All anger toward the boys vanished. Nathaniel went to the one who had spoken and placing his own hand on the youngster's shoulder, said in the same tongue, "I did indeed. Now, shall we go see your white trader?"

The village appeared to be like so many others that Nathaniel had seen. Perhaps a little larger than most. He was near a large center hut with smaller huts forming a semi-circle about it. In the center of the compound were several large cooking pits with women sitting beside them. These women, he noticed, were dressed differently than ones of similar island villages, for they were covered above the waist and below the knees. He had never seen island women so covered. Perhaps the dressing habits in the islands were being changed by those missionaries about which the youths had spoken. In all honesty this new development was a disappointment to his eyes and he knew his men would feel the loss, just as he did.

Off to the side, some one hundred feet away, was a large wooden building with a wrap around verandah. As Nathaniel neared the larger hut, a man came out to meet him. He was tall, white-headed, and dressed completely in white. The man also studied Nathaniel.

"I am Nelson Leigh," he said, "late of the British Navy and the chief trader here. Is this your first visit to Maui?"

"Yes, it is," Nathaniel said, shaking the offered hand. "I am Nathaniel Lathrope from Nantucket Island and captain of whaling ship MORNING STAR. We usually weigh anchor in Hawaii, but a storm altered our plans; then showed us the way to your island."

The man smiled. "I'm sorry about your ordeal, yet thankful you did come here. How may I be of service?"

"We are running low on certain supplies," Nathaniel replied. "I hope to be able to satisfy all our needs on your enchanting island."

"Please," said Leigh. "Let's not stand in the hot sun. Come and join me on the verandah for a cool drink."

"Aye," Nathaniel replied, "I would like that very much." He

followed the trader to the shaded porch.

"What would you like to drink? Juice or perhaps a bit of rum?"

"Pineapple juice would taste mighty fine," Nathaniel told him.

"Pineapple juice, it is," replied Leigh, and quickly ordered it from a servant standing nearby.

"I thought the place deserted," Nathaniel said, taking the tall glass from the man. I might add that it was quite disarming to say the least, as was my journey here."

"I say," replied Leigh, "I was quite alarmed to hear of your getting lost. The lads were quite upset."

Nathaniel's eyes twinkled. "Were they now?"

"Yes, they were quite concerned. Didn't you see the natives that I sent to look for you?"

"I saw no one after the boys got ahead of me. I did, however, find a very inviting pool hidden among the thicket, and I took the opportunity to cool off, although, I could do nothing about the condition of my clothes."

"Was the pool near a stone archway?" ask the other man.

"As a matter of fact, I went through it."

"Then that explains why the natives never found you. The area is taboo to them."

"And why is that?" asked Nathaniel, moping his brow with his kerchief.

Seeing the gesture, Leigh asked, "Care for more juice?"

"Yes, thank you," replied Nathaniel. "When we dropped anchor in the bay we were quite surprised by the lack of greeting. Apparently the customs here are different than other islands we have visited."

"I do apologize," replied Leigh. "I was on the other side of the island as were most of the natives. The local minister insists we have a meeting in the middle of each month. The man is from England, but his ways are surely not mine. He and his household are a righteous lot. At first he attempted to have all the women and girls dress like English women."

"The people on the island are friendly and tried to accommodate them, but it was a disaster. The shoes hurt their feet, and the women smothered in the abundance of clothes. Finally, the minister had them drape themselves as you now see. I must say, a great deal of beauty has been lost to the eyes of man."

Nathaniel laughed. "Well, let me tell you it was quite an experience for my crew. When we found the shore deserted, my men didn't want to leave the ship."

Leigh joined in the laughter. "I suppose they have heard all the stories about Maui. I'm afraid most of those stories are lacking in substance. Shall we get back to your needed supplies?"

Nathaniel removed a slip of paper from his waistband. "I need a half a ton of yams, fifty-five hogs, forty-five fowls, some pineapples, and about four hundred coconuts. Then, of course, I'll need our water supply replenished. The STAR faced quite a storm. We'll be needing timber to repair her."

The men conversed a few minutes longer, then they shook hands and Nathaniel left. As he neared the beach, Haws came out to greet him. "I was about to send a searchin' party, Cap'n."

"Are the water kegs ashore, and has the camp been made ready?" asked Nathaniel.

"Aye, Cap'n."

"Good!"

It was almost dark when the food arrived carried by the beautiful native girls. They brought hot pork, poi, and vegetables in abundance along with the baskets of fruit. Everyone had a wonderful time enjoying the exotic dishes and the island music. The drums seemed to entwine with each lap of the sea. After the meal was finished, Nathaniel left the group and went to his tent. He lit the lamp. In the soft glow he could see that his pallet was on the canvas floor and his trunk placed in one of the corners. He sat on a barrel and removed his boots, undressed and crawled onto his pallet. Slowly his mind began to wander back to the placid, clear pool he had found in the Maui jungle. As the memory of its serenity filled his senses, he fell into a dreamless sleep.

Chapter Thirteen

❧

Early the next morning Mr. Jennings went looking for his wife. He found her in the sitting room. " I will not allow any more women to go to those men," he hotly declared. "No, I shall go myself and speak with Leigh. I will not have it, I tell you!"

"My dear Mr. Jennings," cried his wife in alarm. "What has happened? You look so very distraught." She put aside her needlepoint and hurried to his side. "What men? What women? Oh, please, explain yourself."

"Another ship of men have come ashore. Just when I get religion into them, a new group of men come to ruin all my teachings. I must put a stop to it."

"But how can you? The men won't listen to you. You have tried many times before, all to no avail." She took his hand. "Come, and sit in your chair. I'll fix you a nice cup of tea."

He allowed himself to be led to his chair. In a few minutes, she brought him a cup of steaming tea. "You know, Mr. Jennings," his wife continued, "the lot of a saint is not easy." He smiled. His wife continued, "Dear husband, I know all of this is a great trial to you. Nevertheless, it will add much strength to your faith."

Jennings patted his wife's hand. "You are my strength, my dear." He drained his cup. "I must see the trader. He cannot go on ignoring my wishes. No, I simply cannot have it."

"Can't this wait until you have seen the children? They so look forward to these early morning visits with you."

"Very well. But right afterwards I must visit with him."

Hearing a light knock upon the door, Jennings called out, "Enter."

Robert and Elizabeth, followed by Meghan came into the parlor. Meghan sat on a straight chair at the end of the room; the children stood in front of their father.

Meghan tried to give the Jennings all of her attention, but her mind kept going back to the events of yesterday. She had gone to the pool and was about to slip into the water when she heard the sound of running feet. She quickly darted behind a large boulder. From that position she was hidden from view, however, she could easily see who was coming. It was a man she had never seen before. He had a pistol in his hand, and seemed braced for a fight, yet he was alone. He was tall and well tanned. His shirt was torn and dirty. She watched while he removed it and splashed himself with the cool water from the pool. She took a step forward; her foot snapped a twig. He turned toward her; she fled in terror.

"Meghan!" Mrs. Jennings interrupted the young woman's thoughts.

Meghan jumped to her feet.

"Tell me! How many times must my husband speak to you before you reply?" The words were sharply spoken.

"'Tis that sorry, I am. I didn't hear him. I guess my mind was wandering, a bit," she replied still shaken by her memories.

"Very well," said the woman. "As for now, please leave us."

Just as Meghan stepped out on the verandah, Leah came running past her. It was not long afterwards that Mr. Jennings sought her out, a piece of paper in his hand.

"Meghan, child, I would like to see you in the library." Once inside, Mr. Jennings asked her to sit down. "Leah has brought a message from the main church in Hawaii, and it concerns you."

"Me?"

"Yes," came the reply.

"But what have I done?" she asked.

"Nothing, my child." He sat down at his desk. "If you will allow me to continue, I am sure it will become quite clear how it does concern you." He clasped his hands together; his eyes focused directly on her. "My dear child. Do you remember meeting The Most Reverend Mr. Bainbridge and his mother at the last conference in Hawaii?"

Meghan nodded. "I remember."

"He is coming here at the end of the week." Mr. Jennings said, "And his dear mother will be arriving this very evening."

"You need my room?" Meghan asked.

"No, of course not," his tone one of aggravation. He left his chair and stood before her. "Meghan," he said, "I want you to listen very carefully to what is said this evening. After all Mrs. Bainbridge's main purpose in for this visit is to speak with you."

"And what does she have to do with the likes of me?" questioned Meghan, a puzzled look on her face.

"That is what I'm trying very patiently to explain to you. You know Mrs. Jennings and I have tried to make you feel like one of the family. And I know you want to do everything in your power to make yourself worthy of our kindness toward you."

Meghan started to speak then decided to remain quiet and let him finish.

He returned to his chair. "That is all I have to say upon this matter. When the time comes, I'm sure you will do what is expected of you."

"Mr. Jennings, I'm at a loss to understand you. What can ye be expectin' me to do?"

Even though Meghan had been with the family for almost three years, she found it hard at times not to fall back to the old way of speaking.

"I will explain in due time, my dear," he replied. He picked up a book and was soon engrossed in its contents. Meghan knew by experience that it would do no good to try to get him to tell her more.

Several hours later, Elizabeth approached Meghan. "Mama would like you to come to her in the sitting room. She said to please hurry as Mrs. Bainbridge is here and wants to see you."

"Thank you, Elizabeth," Meghan said, pulling her hand from the girl's firm grip.

"Come in, Meghan," Mrs. Jennings said when she saw her standing in the doorway. "I am sure," indicating the woman seated next to her, "you remember Mrs. Bainbridge?"

Meghan said hello; then sat where Mrs. Jennings indicated.

"As I told you, Mildred," Mrs. Bainbridge said to Mrs. Jennings, "the girl will do nicely. She is a lovely thing. My son will be here this weekend to talk over the details. But for now, just let me assure you that she is exactly what my son needs." She absolutely radiated. " Yes, indeed, she will do very nicely," she repeated.

Mrs. Jennings beamed. "You may leave us, Meghan. There are many details that you need not bother about."

Meghan left the two women, more confused than ever. First it was Mr. Jennings saying things that did not make sense; now it was his wife and her friend. She shook her head in wonderment as she went to her own room.

The next morning there were the usual duties. Meghan helped the children get ready for breakfast in the kitchen. It was hard for her to understand why the family did not eat their meals together. At home they always did. Even after her father become angry with her, he insisted everyone be at the table for the evening meal.

The three had finished eating when Mrs. Jennings burst into the room.

"Meghan, my dear," she gushed. "How very proud we are of your acceptance by the Bainbridges'. I mean it is such an honor for them to even consider you. You are a dear sweet child but not of our faith. However, I am sure it won't be long until they teach you to see the light."

"Mrs. Jennings," Meghan said, "I'm a woman grown, but to be telling the truth, I don't know what you are talking about."

"The meaning is quite clear. Meghan, you are to marry The Most Reverend Mr. Bainbridge. He has found you worthy to become his bride. And, of course, his mother has also. Oh, the prospect of our little Meghan marrying and to one so well thought of by all who know him."

"I don't know him. I saw him only once, and then we didn't speak. I can't even remember what he looks like," Meghan told her.

"That doesn't matter. He has scheduled his time to be here at least a fortnight. That will give you ample time to get acquainted before you marry next month."

"Mrs. Jennings, I ran away from all I hold dear so I would not be marrying a man I didn't love. I didn't come half way around the world to be doing it here. And there is none to make me."

Mrs. Jennings bristled. "Why . . .why you ungrateful child! After all we have done for you, how dare you defy our wishes?"

"I'm not meaning to be ungrateful," Meghan replied, her temper barely under control as she faced the irate woman. "But have you been doing more for me than I be doing for you?

I watch your children; I see to it that they are always neat and clean, I see they are fed and have their lessons. And who but me keeps them from bothering their own parents? And for all of this, 'it's a prisoner I be in this beautiful land."

"I have never been so insulted," declared the furious woman. "I don't know what has come over you. I think it best if you go to your room immediately. I am sure Mr. Jennings will have something to say about your attitude."

Meghan went to her room, seething. "I can't believe I was sent around the world to be marrying against my will, and I won't be letting it happen. And I can't be wasting my time in bemoaning the fact. They'll not be seeing a tear from me. No, 'tis hard thinking I must be doing." Meghan finally went to sleep and when she dreamed, it was of the stranger at the pool.

Early the next morning, Meghan found Leah and told her of coming with the Jennings from Ireland to stop one wedding, and " I'll not be having one here either."

"What can you do? No one will go against the minister to help you," Leah informed her friend.

"I'm going to the pool," Meghan proclaimed. "and if there's a witch there, she'll not be hiding from me this day."

Just as Meghan was leaving the verandah, Mr. Jennings came out from the dining room. He had a letter in his hand. "Meghan, this came for you this morning. It's from Ireland. Leah can watch the children while you take it to your room and read it."

Meghan took the paper with trembling hands. Once in her room, she carefully removed the sealing stamp and began to read:

April 1814

"Meghan, dear child, your mother has asked me to answer your letter. Your father was with her, and I have never seen a man cry as he did. He has changed. He is sorry for the entire harm that has been done to you. He wants you to come home. I'm enclosing the passage money.

"Pack your things and be on the next ship to Ireland. Your mother wanted me to tell you that by the time you receive this letter your brother and Julianne will be married.

May the Saints be protecting you and bring you safely back home. Oh, yes. Another thing of importance was said. You will not be marrying Squire O'Shea.

Signed: Father James Ryan,
Parish Priest

Meghan had not tried stopping the flood of tears, for they were tears of happiness. She was going home; she was going back to her beloved Ireland! So with letter in hand, Meghan went to see Mr. Jennings; her words tumbled from her lips. "I'm to go home! My father wants me home, and he'll not be making me marry the squire. I'm to make passage on the next ship. Oh, Mr. Jennings, my da wants me home."

"Calm down, Meghan." Mr. Jennings said, trying to soothe her. " I am very happy that your father has had a transformation of heart, however, you must realize this letter cannot be allowed to change the plans that are in motion here."

"They'll be changed, right enough," she thundered. "I'm leaving Maui with or without your help. I'm going back to Ireland, and there's none to stop me." Without another word, Meghan left to go in search of Leah. She found the girl in the kitchen.

"Leah, I can be going home. My da wants me there. Mr. Jennings says that he can stop me. I guess he can, but I won't let that happen.

Leah, you say there's witches at the pool. You say they can grant wishes, and who am I to say they can't. Leah, come with me and speak to them. I know the Good Lady didn't bring me here to be marrying without love. Not when she helped me leave Ireland for the same reason."

"All right," agreed the other girl, "but you be changing your clothes and color your hair or I won't be going with you."

"There's no time," cried Meghan.

"You'll be going away, but I must stay. You change or I won't be going with you."

Chapter Fourteen

꙳

For a time Nathaniel lay quiet, watching shadows dance over the canvas shelter to the rhythmic sounds of lapping waves. He knew it would soon be light; the shadows would be gone, and so must he. Rising from the pallet, he took fresh clothes from his trunk and left the shelter. All was quiet in the camp. Some of the men were asleep on the sand while others were inside their shelters. The only ones that appeared to be awake were the guards on duty. Nathaniel left his clean clothes on a rock, waded into the water and swam out to the STAR, where the men on watch met him. After conversing with them for a few moments, he dove back into the water.

A faint glow spread across the horizon. It would not be long until the sun would once again spread its heat over the island, and the men would be awake. But for now, he was alone. The day before he had noticed a path going up the side of Haleakala Crater.

A good time to do a little exploring, he thought as he quickly dressed. It was not long until his boots were covered with a strange dust. Looking back on his trail he saw the dust had settled in tiny mounds of orange, black, and gray powder; erasing all sign of his passing. The path he had chosen was steep and gave his legs a good workout. He looked down into the channel. Another ship came over the horizon and he was grateful Leigh already had the list of supplies needed by the STAR.

A seagull swooped over his head, a thing of beauty, he thought. A cloud came out of nowhere, engulfing him in its mist. His visibility was no more than two feet in any given direction.

A surge of weakness swept through him. For an instant he thought he might lose consciousness. Chilled to the bone, his legs and arms lost their strength and he slumped to the ground. He was covered with sweat and his hands felt clammy his throat parched for the want of water.

"Damme!" he whispered, "I can't be getting the fever now, not after all this time."

A few weeks before the storm struck, a dozen men had come down with a hallucinating fever. They claimed to have seen a woman walking on the water and beckoning them into the sea. Several of the fevered men had jumped into the sea and had to be rescued from drowning. Nathaniel struggled to his feet. He reached out to where he had last seen the side of the mountain and was grateful to feel it still there. In a few minutes his strength returned. The mist thinned and he continued his walk up the mountain. He had traveled some twenty to thirty feet when the mist enveloped him again.

Suddenly, a blood-curdling cry pierced the air.

"By all that's holy, what's that!"

The cry came again.

Someone was in trouble! He had to think! He pulled his knife from beneath his shirt and waited for whatever would come. His head pounded; his pulse raced. He braced himself against the firm rocks beside him.

The cry came again, this time much closer. Distorted forms

appeared in the mist. They had huge bodies and long crooked necks with small heads.

"When the men of the STAR had the fever, they saw beautiful women, not monsters," he muttered.

The shadows he had seen were closer now.

Nathaniel slightly bent his knees and braced himself for the fight. Without warning, the mist cleared and revealed a band of geese. He tried laughing only no sound passed his lips. The geese marched passed him in single file. Then, as if to show their contempt for him, the last one turned and repeated the cry that had sent shivers down his spine. The hot finger of fever followed the chill. He continued in his descent. He prayed he would make it back to camp before all strength left him. As he neared camp, he heard voices and smelled food. His stomach revolted at the thought of eating. What he needed was not food but rest.

If I could only find the pool again, he thought, remembering the cool water. He had to think clearly. Was it only yesterday that he had stumbled upon the clearing? Where was it? Before the cloud had come, he had seen the village to his far right. There had been a place where two paths crossed. If he could get back there, it might lead him to the pool. With the help of the Almighty, he vowed he would make it. But first he must find Haws and let him know. He stumbled closer to the clearing and hid himself near the path. When one of the men came near, he called, "Hawkins, tell Mistah Haws I want to see him, now!"

It did not take long until his first mate arrived and Nathaniel informed him of his plans. At first Haws argued against him going off by himself, but in the end he had to accept his captain's orders.

"Mistah Haws," Nathaniel said. "I'll not have the men told. Do you understand?"

"They'll not be 'earing it from me, Cap'n." Haws promised.

The area was as beautiful and serene as Nathaniel had remembered it.

Birds flew about him, collecting nectar from the various flowers and plants.

He removed his boots and sat on the edge of the pool, enjoying the cooling mist rising from the water.

Chapter Fifteen

◈

Meghan and Leah knelt in a small clearing behind the waterfall. At Meghan's insistence, Leah began speaking, "Oh, spirit of the pool, my friend has come here for many, many, months, yet you have kept hidden from her. Please, won't you show her what her future holds?"

When Leah finished her chant, Meghan asked, "Do you see anything?"

"Be quiet, or they won't come."

They waited, they saw or heard nothing.

"Do you think they can see us here?" asked Meghan.

"Nay," came the reply. "Now hush," cautioned Leah, "'tis patience, you must be having."

Meghan settled back against a moss-covered rock, where Leah joined her. "Leah, I saw a man here, do you remember me telling you?"

"Aye, I do." replied the other girl.

"Think I'll ever see him again?" asked Meghan.

"Do you want to?"

"Aye," Meghan replied, "I do."

"Why?"

"Because he be more fair than any other."

"What kind of a reason is that? I hear the Reverend Bainbridge is fair in all his dealings, and you don't want to see him again."

"No. I mean he was a very handsome man."

"Oh."

"Oh? Is that all you can say?"

"Shhh, I think I hear something," Leah uttered.

"Can you see anything?" inquired Meghan as the mist started to lift.

"No," came the reply. "But I do hear something."

"How can that be? The waterfall is making so much noise I can barely hear you."

Leah smiled. "My hearing is better than yours." Through the mist from the waterfall, a form began to take shape. Neither girl could make out who or what it was. "Maybe it's the spirit come to answer our prayer," Leah said. "Watch and be quiet."

From their hiding place behind the waterfall, Leah and Meghan watched as a man appeared by the pool. They watched in silence as he sat on the pool's edge. When they saw him topple into the water, Meghan cried out. "He's about to drown. Come, we must help him."

"He must be a whaling man," insisted Leah. "Mr. Jennings said that whaling men are evil."

"Letting him drown would be evil, too." Meghan declared before leaving her hiding place, pulling her friend after her. "Leah, we can't let him drown."

They crept toward the man struggling to get out of the water. They saw him slip below the surface. For an instant Meghan could not believe her own eyes. She grabbed hold of Leah's arm. "It's the man I told you about."

"Are you sure?"

"I'll not be forgetting the looks of him if I live to be an old, old woman."

Both girls jumped into the water. In a matter of seconds, they pushed him up until his head and shoulders were clear, then Meghan pulled herself out and grabbed hold of his shoulders. Leah joined her and then both girls pulled on him until he was out of the water onto the ground.

Meghan knelt beside him, and asked, "Are you sick?"

The stranger opened his eyes; his lips barely moving, and mumbled something neither girl could understand. His body was hot, yet he was shivering.

"He has fever," explained Leah.

"How can he have a fever when his body is shaking?" Meghan had never seen a man so elegant looking. Even Gavin could not compare with this man, nor could she imagine her father more fair than this when he was young. She felt her own pulse racing, and the sensation frightened her.

A smile crossed over Leah's face. "Think the Spirit of the Pond sent him to you?"

"It won't make any difference if he dies," countered Meghan. Looking down at him, her eyes filled with tears. "Leah, what's do we do to keep him alive?"

"We must remove his wet clothes."

Meghan backed off. "We can't be doing any such thing."

"Then he'll die. Now," demanded Leah, "gather some of those ferns over there and bring them here. We'll cover him up and then pull off his wet things."

While Meghan gathered armloads of the foliage, Leah removed his wet shirt. "Now lay the leaves over him, then we'll pull off his boots and trousers."

Still, he shivered. "What else can we do?" cried Meghan.

"My uncle had the fever once. My aunt laid on top of him and he got plenty warm."

"We can't be doing such a thing."

"I can," Leah said. "You go for help and I'll stay here."

The thoughts of Leah being so near to the man of her dreams were too much for Meghan. She couldn't let that happen. "I'll do it." Meghan declared. "You best be off to find help. He could be a whaling man. Maybe someone from his ship is already looking for him."

A resentful Leah backed away. "'Tis you who should be going for help, not me."

"It has to be me that stays with him, Leah. It just has to be," Meghan insisted.

"All right. But if he dies, it will be your fault."

"He can't die," Meghan moaned. "He just can't."

Once Leah was out of sight, Meghan did what she had to do. She pushed off some of the leaves and eased her body over his and rubbed his shoulders and arms, trying to restore life into them. She tried to think of other things to calm her racing heart. There were the teaching lessons for the children. And later in the day she had promised to take them swimming, and after they returned to the compound the cook was going to show her how to cook bananas. Oh! It was no use! No matter how hard she tried; Meghan could not concentrate on anything except the man beneath her. She raised her eyes to look up at his strong jawbone, the molding of his nose, the dark fringes of his eyelashes, and noble forehead. She touched the blond strands of his thick hair. The temptation to kiss him became too great. She raised up and touched his lips with hers.

He opened his eyes. "Who . . . who are you?" his voice faltered.

She smiled. What harm would it do? "I'm the good witch of the pool."

"Good witch?"

"Aye. I've been sent to make you well."

"I won't be turned into a tree?"

"A tree?" Meghan asked, confused at his question.

"Just . . . leave . . . me . . . alone," he said, trying to push her off.

"I must kept you warm." Meghan insisted.

"No," he uttered, "You're . . . only . . . a dream."

"I'm real enough," Meghan told him. "Here, touch my hand."

He touched her. "You . . . are . . . real? No dream?" The words he spoke were mere whispers, then once again he entered the land of darkness.

Upon hearing the sound of running feet, Meghan slipped away into the dense forest. She saw two men kneel at the man's side. Meghan did not wait to hear what was being said. She ran through the forest, back to the compound.

Meghan found Leah waiting for her. With smoldering eyes, Leah inquired, "Did you get him warm enough?"

Meghan turned scarlet but did not reply.

Chapter Sixteen

&

"Mistah 'Aws, 'e be coming out of et," Matthew called to the man in the next room.

Nathaniel tried sitting up.

"Lie still, Cap'n. Ye've been taken with the fever."

"Where am I?" Nathaniel asked, his head spinning.

"At the trading post," answered Matthew. "Oh, 'ere's Mistah 'Aws; 'E can answer yer questions." Matthew left his captain's side to allow the first mate to occupy the chair.

"Mistah Haws, how long have I been here?"

"A few hours, Cap'n, no more."

Nathaniel listened quietly while the man explained how a young native girl had sought him out and begged him to help the white man at the pool.

"What about the other one?" Nathaniel asked.

"That was only one lass," Haws answered.

"There was a white girl," insisted Nathaniel. "She saved my life."

"Didn't see no white lass, Cap'n. 'Tis a bad dream, ye be having."

"It wasn't a dream," insisted Nathaniel. "She had a cloud of black hair, and emerald eyes. I felt her in my arms. She kissed me."

A look of alarm came into his first mate's eyes. "If ye saw anythin', 'twas a witch, for sure."

"She was no witch. And I didn't imagine her. I felt her in my arms." Nathaniel had half- risen from the bed, now he collapsed back into a deep sleep.

"Watch him," commanded Haws. "I'll be back."

◦❧◦

ACROSS THE ISLAND, two young women were arguing. "You can't go there," Leah said, trying to hold Meghan back.

"Let me go! I must see if he's all right," Meghan insisted, pulling free of Leah's grip.

"Someone will see you."

"I don't care. Leah, don't you see that I must go."

"I won't be going with you," Leah replied.

Meghan looked intently at her friend. "If that is how you feel, I can't make you go anymore than you can make me stay."

"What if Mrs. Jennings finds out you went there?"

"If anyone does see me, they won't know who I am. After all, I'm just one native girl among hundreds."

Meghan left Leah and hurried into the maze of trees and foliage. She saw no one until she arrived at the trading post. She had just about stepped into the clearing when one of the men she had seen at the pool, came out of the building and headed in her direction. She quickly darted behind a boulder and was well hidden by the time he walked by. She crept up to the window of the building and looked inside. There was a man laying on a cot and at that instant, he turned toward the window and her heart leaped as she recognized him. She eased herself over the windowsill.

"Who's there?"

"The good witch from the pond," she answered.

"Stay with me, please." With the word 'please', his head fell back on the pillow.

Meghan looked down at him, his eyes were closed, his breathing labored.

She leaned down and kissed him.

Six days later Leigh walked into the infirmary. Nathaniel was sitting up in bed. "I hear you are making a fine recovery," Leigh said, pulling up a chair and setting next to the bed.

"How long have I been here?" questioned Nathaniel.

"Almost a week," was the reply. "You did a lot of talking when the fever was high. Seems you saw some mysterious woman with green eyes, no less. I say, you were having some kind of a dream."

"It was no dream," Nathaniel told him.

"Wasn't it?"

"I know what I saw," Nathaniel insisted.

"Besides my wife," Leigh answered, "the only white women on the island are the missionary's wife, his young daughter and their Irish nanny." Leigh folded his arms, leaning back in his chair he continued, "I had an Irish nanny once, an elderly thing who was terrible afraid of snakes. It seems Ireland doesn't have any such creatures, and she would not allow me the privilege of owning one. I was terrible glad when she was sent packing to some other household."

Ignoring his remarks, Nathaniel asked another question. "Couldn't there be a white family on the island that you are not aware of?"

"There are white men who have settled down after marrying native women. I'm sorry to say there isn't a green-eyed girl among the lot."

"There was a girl there and she had green eyes," Nathaniel persisted. "She came here."

"She, what?" explored Leigh.

"She was here, in this very room."

"When did she come?" asked Leigh, leaning forward.

"I'm not sure. I seem to be drifting in and out of a fog."

Leigh filled his pipe; soon a sweet smelling tobacco filled the room. "My friend, I can assure you that whatever you saw was not of this world."

"Nor was it from your world of magic," Nathaniel interjected.

Leigh took another puff on his pipe. "Allow me," he said, "to fill you in on our magical pool. The witches of the pool have the power to cloud one's mind or to foretell one's future."

"And what has the pool told you?" mocked Nathaniel.

"Take it lightly, if you will," replied Leigh. "However, it did foretell my own meeting with my wife."

Nathaniel disbelief was apparent. "Surely, you can't be serious."

"Let me tell you something about my own history," Leigh said as he settled back in his chair. "I was once in the British Navy. I had been stationed in Hong Kong and on the way back to England I came down with a deadly fever. I begged the captain to allow me to die on land. He signaled a passing whaling ship, the PELIQUIN. Have you heard of it?"

"Aye," replied Nathaniel. "I sailed on her for a short duration, some years ago. Her captain was a friend of the man who raised me."

Leigh took another puff on his pipe. "I was transferred aboard the ship which brought me to Maui. The chief elder, a kind and wise man allowed me to stay with him. One night and I'll never know how, I found myself at the pool. Now, keep in mind there was no way I could have known of the pool. You see, it is actually forbidden to even speak of it. The natives were using it for an excuse to steal from their neighbor. They would say the witches living in the pool foretold it.

"I suppose one might say that I had a dream, but it was real enough for me. A mist rose from the water and out stepped the most beautiful creature I had ever seen. Her hair was as blond as the silk on golden corn, her eyes as the blue as the darkest sky. She embraced me, holding me tight in her arms until the fever broke."

"Did your wife live on the island?"

"No. I didn't actually meet her until a year later at an Admiralty tea in London. We fell in love and married. I was discharged from the Navy and was assigned trader on the island. Our sons were born here."

Nathaniel had his own theory on how they met. "It's obvious that she was someone you had met in the past and simply forgot the incident until you were ravished with fever."

"In one respect," Leigh agreed, "it might be a possibility. She was Navy; her father was in the Admiralty; our paths might have crossed. However, if that were the case, how would you explain the fact that I knew she had a birthmark on her thigh? No, my friend, she was revealed to me that day at the pool and was as real to me as your vision was to you. Mark my words, someday you will find the girl, but you'll not be finding her on Maui, of that I am certain."

"I do appreciate what you have told me," Nathaniel assured him, "Nevertheless, I don't believe the pool has anymore magical power than other pools on other islands. I didn't imagine her. There is no doubt in my mind that she is on the island. And," he hastened to add, "I'll find her."

"Since you are determined to look for her, how may I help you?" Leigh wanted to know.

"Ask your people about her. Surely, they must have seen her. Perhaps she is from one of the other islands and was here to visit someone."

Leigh smiled. "Yes, that might be a possibility."

Leigh left the room and was about to enter his own quarters when Haws came inside the building. He saw the trader and hurried over to him.

"'Ow's the Cap'n?" he asked.

"I'm worried about him, Mr. Haws. He really believes the girl he saw is real."

"Aye, 'e does at that," agreed Haws.

"When had you planned on leaving the island?" asked Leigh.

"We would 'ave been gone by now, if the Cap'n 'adn't taken sick," Haws told him.

"If that is the case, I would suggest you take your captain and leave now."

Haws shook his head. "Nay, 'e won't be leaving til 'e finds 'is lass."

"He's far from being a well man, Mr. Haws. I've seen many cases where a man seemed recovered only to slip back to the fever. He should be back on ship before that happens. There's nothing here for him. If there's anything I can do to help get him back on ship, let me know."

"I'll be doin' just that," replied Haws, his face grim.

Haws opened the door and looked inside. Nathaniel was struggling to get out of bed. He saw Haws and asked him for help. Haws assisted in helping him from the bed to a nearby chair. "Wall, Cap'n, 'pears to me, yer just 'bout ready to leave 'ere, and get 'board the STAR."

"Not yet, Mistah Haws. I'm not leaving here without her."

"Without who?" questioned the first mate.

"The girl at the pool."

Haws poured cool water from the table by the bed into a bowl. He wet a towel and handed it to Nathaniel. "'Ere, Cap'n. 'Twill cool ye."

Nathaniel took the towel and wiped sweat off his face and the back of his neck. He handed it back to his first mate. "Thank you, Mistah Haws."

"Let me 'elp ye back to the bed, Cap'n. Ye still be weak from the fever."

"Perhaps you are right. I'll be searching for her tomorrow. I'll not be leaving without her by my side."

"The men be anxious to 'ead for 'ome."

"I know. After I find her, we'll be on our way." He lay back on the cot, his eyes closed.

❧

ON THE OTHER side of the island, Meghan stood on the verandah, looking up at the star-filled night. She had not been able to see 'the man' again. It was a risk she dared not take. If she went to him as Meghan McGonigal, what reason could she give? If she went as a native girl, she would be sent away.

Meghan was so deep in thought she had not seen the approach of Elizabeth until the girl spoke to her. "Meghan, mama says you are to go to the study. Papa wants to see you."

"Thank you, Elizabeth."

"Meghan?"

"What is it, dear?"

"I'm worried about you. You seem so different, lately."

"Now, don't you worry yourself about me, Elizabeth, I'll be just fine. I best be off. I don't want to anger your Papa." Meghan hurried along the verandah until she reached the door of the study.

When she stepped into the room, Mr. Jennings removed his glasses.

"Meghan," he said, "my dear wife tells me that you have not been your bright and cheerful self these past few days. Is there something wrong? You're not ill, are you?"

"No, Mr. Jennings," Meghan assured him.

Pushing back his chair and rising, he went to the closed window and opened it. The room burst with the aroma of the sea, the sweet odor of ripening fruit, and the fragrance of the varied flowers. He took a deep breath. "Ah, the air is refreshing. Sometimes I get so very busy that I find myself forgetting the beauty of the island." He returned to his desk. "I have received a letter from the Most Reverend Mr. Bainbridge. He will not be able to come here as planned. He has asked Mrs. Jennings and I to join him on the big Island. I know you must be disappointed at not being able to see him again. However, he assures me that it won't be long until he can come and the two of you can become better acquainted." He cleared his throat, wiped his brow and then continued, "It seems there is a slight disagreement by the church board on this coming marriage since you are not of our faith, neverthe-less, he feels that in time, you will be converted to our way of thinking. Yes," he repeated, "it is only a matter of time until you will see the proper thing to do."

Proper, indeed! thought Meghan, *and just who is he to tell me that his way is better than mine?"* Aloud she asked, "And when will the family be leaving?"

"We'll be taking the boat tomorrow evening. Leah can spend the time here with you, and, of course, there is cook and the other servants, so you will not be alone. Now, if you have no other questions, you may return to your duties."

He stopped her at the door. "Who would have thought the day you came aboard the ship that you would find favor with such a man. Almost three years, is it not? You are a very fortunate young woman,

Meghan. Yes, indeed, a very fortunate young woman." With those words, he waved her out of his sight.

She did not, however, leave. "Mr. Jennings," she asked. "how long will you be gone?"

With annoyance in his voice, he replied. "Let me see. Today is Tuesday and I must be back for Sunday services. Now, if there is nothing else, Meghan, I must get back to my work."

Meghan left him without another word; her mind filled with rambling thoughts. Throwing caution to the wind, Meghan headed for the trading post. She would seek out the man of the pool as herself and see how he really felt about her. She would not stay here and marry against her will. Anything would be better than that. Arriving at the traders, she ducked behind some ferns as two men came out on the porch.

"Is he better, Mistah Haws?"

Ignoring the questions, the first mate replied. "I want ye to return to camp and tell Mistah Matthew to make the ship ready to sail."

"We're goin' 'ome, Mistah 'Aws?"

"Aye, lad, that we are." Haws left the compound and Meghan followed him. He went to the pool and Meghan crept close enough to hear him speak.

"If ye be listening, lass, I'll not be 'aving the man fooled. 'Tis not a witch, I'm thinkin', ye be, but some native lass who's wanting a way off the island. Wall, ye'll not be 'aving it 'appen on 'is 'eartache. And if ye be a witch and think ye 'ave 'im under yer spell, think again. 'E be a good man, and I'll not be letting ye 'ave 'im. There, I've said me mind." Haws looked about the clearing. "No," he repeated, "Ye'll not be 'aving 'im."

With tears rolling down her cheeks, Meghan watched him walk away.

Chapter Seventeen

❧

Very early the next morning, Meghan quietly left the parsonage. She tried to see Nathaniel, but his men blocked the way. She walked up to the bluff overlooking the channel. There were five ships anchored in the bay, she couldn't even guess which one he was on. With a heavy heart, she returned to the compound to find it a bed of activity.

"Where have you been?" demanded Mrs. Jennings. "You knew we had to leave on the morning boat and you haven't finished packing Robert's and Elizabeth's things."

"Mr. Jennings said you were leaving this evening."

"Our plans were changed this morning, and if you were here, where you were supposed to be, we could have told you."

"I'm sorry, Mrs. Jennings. I went for a walk. I'll hurry and finish putting their things into the trunks."

"See that you do."

Meghan left her and went to find her charges. They were in the kitchen eating their breakfast. Leah hurried to her side. "Where have you been? Mrs. Jennings has been looking for you."

"I just went for a walk," replied Meghan.

"To the trading post?" asked Leah.

"I was there, but I didn't see 'the man'."

"Why not?" Leah wanted to know.

"His friends were with him."

"Did you learn who he was?"

"No, only that he was from one of the whaling ships." Tears rolled down Meghan's face as she continued, "He's leaving the island and I'll never see him again." She could say no more and hurried away.

Leah went back to the children, a smile curling about her lips. Meghan would be staying on the island, after all.

Meghan finished with Elizabeth's things first and then started in on Robert's. She picked up a pair of his trousers. As she looked at them, a bold plan came to mind. "Why not?" she said aloud. After all, if Mrs. Jennings had not caught her, no one on the ship coming here would have discovered she was a girl. If it worked once, it would certainly work again. But what could she do? She didn't know enough to be a seaman, and it would be far too dangerous to be a cabin boy. She could cook, her mother had seen to that, and she had watched Caleb enough to know the type of food that was served on a ship and the amounts served. She smiled, then began to laugh. It was the perfect answer and it would be a dream come true! She could get away from the island and no one would ever guess how she did it. She would, of course, leave them a letter explaining why she had to go, and also leave some of the passage money her father had sent for the clothes she would be taking of Robert's. Her voice would not be a problem. Robert's voice was changing. Sometimes it became very low; then high, sometimes it actually squeaked. The more she thought about it, the more she knew it would work.

Meghan hurried to find Leah. She quickly explained her idea of escape, then waited for Leah's answer. At first the other girl refused to even consider Meghan's plan. "If they find out that I help you, they'll send me away," Leah said.

"They won't find out that you helped," Meghan assured her.

"Meghan, you can't be leaving. What will I be doing without you?"

"Leah, listen to me. If I'm forced to marry, I won't be here, anyway. There is no one else who could aid me."

"I'm afraid," confessed Leah.

"Please, Leah. Say that you'll help me," Meghan pleaded.

After some time, Leah finally consented to do what she could. The girls decided not to discuss the matter until after the family had left. It was with relief that Meghan waved a last goodbye.

The first thing that had to be done was to have her hair cut. She found a pair of scissors; then went looking for Leah. "My hair has to be cut," she explained handing the scissors to Leah.

When the chore was finished, Leah told her, "No one will recognize you." Then under her breath, added "Not even your handsome whaling man."

Meghan buried the lengths of hair deep in the ground outside the compound then covered the earth with leaves. Once the task was over, Meghan went back into the parsonage and dressed in Robert's clothes. This time she did not have to struggle to get them on. In three years he had grown taller than Meghan and weighed more. She met Leah in the hall.

"Do I look like a boy?" asked Meghan, laughing.

"Except for the swelling of your shirt, you could pass for a boy," Leah replied.

Meghan looked down at her chest and flamed. She hurried back into the room and bound her breasts as tight as she could. When she returned to Leah, asked, "Now what do you think?"

"You might pass for a lad, at that."

"Then I guess I'm ready for the test," Meghan replied, putting on Robert's cap.

On the way to the beach, Meghan met several of the local men. She held her breath until they passed. By the time she arrived at the beach, she beamed with confidence; no one had recognized her.

The first group of seaman told her their crew was filled. The second group waved her away before she could even open her mouth. The sun was high and sweat dotted Meghan's forehead and the back of her neck. The binding about her chest held the moisture in and made her skin itch. Meghan had just about covered the beach when she saw a boat pulling ashore containing five men. The one man with gray hair got out first.

"Ye best come back for me in two hours," she heard him say.

"Aye, that we will," answered one of the men.

Meghan waited for the man to reach her before she spoke. She lowered her voice and asked, "Would you know if your ship needs a cook's helper?"

The man stopped in his tracks. He looked her over. "Ye sayin' ye can cook?"

"Aye, that I can," she replied.

"Wait, lads," he called out to the men as they were pushing their boat back into the water.

"Ye come with me, he said to Meghan. We'll be seeing if 'tis a cook, ye be."

❧

ONCE ON BOARD the ship, the man took her to the galley. "Ere we be," he said. "Now, let's see ye start the mid-day meal."

"Where is the cook?" she asked.

"Ye be looking at 'im," the man told her, "and I be waiting to see what ye can do."

"How many men will I be feeding?" she asked.

"Twenty," he told her.

"You have a crew of twenty?"

"Nay, some of the men are still on shore."

Meghan found the size pot she needed and immediately added wood to the cook store. A good size piece of meat was selected along with potatoes, onions, and carrots. The vegetables were washed and then sliced before putting them all together in the large pot. She found fresh berries, which was soon made into pies. It was not long until the delicious aroma flowed through the open doorway to the men on deck.

One of the men poked his head in the gallery. "Mighty glad ye found us a cook," he said, jokingly. "Now we might be getting some good things to eat."

The cook smiled. "Looks like ye found yerself a berth, lad. That is, if the food be tasting as good as it smells."

After the men wolfed down the food, the cook motioned for Meghan to follow him back to the cook shack. "Why did ye leave yer last berth?" he questioned.

"'Tis homesick I was. And it would be a long time before the ship would return to Ireland. The captain said I might find a whaling ship to take me in that direction."

"What be yer name?"

Without hesitancy, she replied. "My name is Marty Ryan, and it has been a long time since I left Ireland. Ours was a British ship."

"Wall, Marty. Ye have a berth on the MORNING STAR. My name be John Simmons, but everyone calls me, Cookie."

Meghan returned to the compound elated at her good fortune, yet saddened by the thought of saying goodbye to Leah and all those with whom she had grown close over the passing years. Leah, of course, would be the hardest to leave. They had become like sisters, and Meghan would miss her dreadfully.

"Did they hire you on?" Leah asked when the two met.

"Yes. The cook is like Caleb; a good, kindly man."

"Did he really believe you were a boy?"

Meghan smiled. "No one could be telling the difference."

"Meghan, you'll be on ship for what . . . a year, maybe more. How can you keep such a secret?"

"I can't look that far ahead. All I know is that I can't stay here any longer."

"I suppose you do have to leave," Leah admitted, "but I'll be missing you just the same." "Leah, would you come with me for a walk?"

"What for?"

"To say goodbye to the island," Meghan told her.

"Now?" questioned Leah

"It'll be my last chance." Meghan reminded her.

"All right, but you best change into your own clothes," Leah said.

The girls reached the crater of Haleakala late in the afternoon. It was not until then that Meghan noticed the small bundle tied to Leah's waist, and was a surprise when the girl removed it and, after undoing the knot, handed Meghan a banana.

"Leah, thank you," she said accepting the piece of fruit. "I didn't even think of bringing something to eat."

When the banana was finished, Leah brought out thick slices of ham, bread, and pineapple. Soon the girls had eaten their fill, and it was time to continue their walk. "We go down the trail over there," Leah said, pointing to a wide path leading down into the center of the crater. After reaching the rim of the crater, the girls walked slowly down a trail of scorched stones where no plants or rich green foliage grew. Meghan did not like the place. She wanted to run back to the top, but Leah stopped her.

"It won't be long until we leave the crater and all will be green again,"

Leah assured her.

They walked in and out of dark shadows as they crossed the crater. Every so often they saw huge mounds of volcanic ash. Some of the mounds rose as high as a hundred feet. What was really surprising to Meghan was the plants growing out of the sides of the orange, black and gray mounds. The flowers on the plants were an exotic purple.

Meghan expressed her amazement and Leah replied, "There is beauty everywhere, if only we would look for it."

Meghan nodded, but did not reply. They continued walking until they came to a large black hole. Leah called out to her. "Meghan, get away from the edge, you might fall in and never could you find your way out."

"Has anybody ever tried to find the bottom of it?" Meghan asked, spellbound by its depth.

"I don't think anybody has ever tried," was the response. "Now, come away from the edge."

"All right," agreed Meghan.

As the girls left the rim, several women came into view. They stopped where the girls had been and threw something into the black hole. "I suppose," Meghan said, "if there is no bottom, it could be used to get rid of trash. Is that why the island is so clean of refuse? It is all brought here and thrown in?"

Leah pulled her away. "Before a baby is born they are in a special blanket of skin and afterward the skin must be thrown away where it can not be eaten by animals. So it is brought here where nothing can reach it, and then the babies grow strong and healthy."

"And what would happen if it is eaten by an animal?"

"The babies grow up weak and bad," Leah assured her.

"That's silly," Meghan said.

Leah looked alarmed. "Do you think you are wiser than all the people on the island?"

"Well, no," stammered Meghan.

"Then say no more about something you know nothing about," Leah told her.

Soon they had reached the eastern end of the crater. Here the trail began to descend toward Kaupo Gap. They walked over more lava rocks and bruised their feet on its jagged edges. Suddenly, a wild forlorn cry split the silence. It scared Meghan, but Leah only laughed.

"Surely you won't let a bunch of geese make a coward of you," Leah teased.

"I'm not a coward, but the noise did startle me."

"Haven't you ever heard them before?"

"I've never been to this part of the island," Meghan replied.

"In all your years at the parsonage you never heard the geese?" questioned Leah.

"No," said Meghan and the subject was not mentioned again.

Once across the crater, they found a path much easier to walk upon. It sloped gently upward, and Leah told Meghan that soon they would sight the sea. They walked through a forest of trees and the aroma was like nothing Meghan had ever encountered before.

"Leah, I've never seen trees like this before. Do they have a name?"

"I haven't heard them called anything special," Leah informed her. "But they are highly prized. Our chief makes our people work very hard cutting them down so he can trade the wood for things only the white man can give him. Our people have no time to plant the fields. Someday there will be no food, and we will all starve." Leah's voice trembled as she spoke.

"Please," begged Meghan, "don't think of sad things today."

Tears continued to form in the other girl's dark eyes. "After you've gone, I'll be sad all the time."

Meghan took Leah's hand in hers. "Leah, I promise I'll never forget you. And if it be possible, I'll be coming back for a visit. But you do see, don't you that I can't stay here any longer. Please say that you understand why I have to leave."

Leah whispered, "I understand."

There had been so many things the Jennings had not allowed Meghan to do, and there were so many wondrous things she had heard about that she had never seen nor would she be able to see now that she was leaving. After a long walk, they reached the bluff overlooking the Alenuihaha Channel.

Meghan cried out, "Look over there," pointing beyond the group of ships in the bay to a pod of whales. "It won't be long until I'm on a ship hunting them."

"And I'll be all alone," Leah bitterly replied.

The tone was not lost to Meghan. "I'm sorry if I'm hurting you by leaving. Even so, it is something that I must do. I will not be forced to marry without love."

Chapter Eighteen

✒

It was near dusk when Nathaniel awakened, his head throbbing, and his mouth dry. "Mistah Haws, are you about?"

"Aye, Cap'n, I be 'ere," Haws replied.

"Has Leigh found the girl?"

The trader had followed Haws into the room. "No, Captain. I sent runners out, as I said I would, and they have assured me there is not a another white woman on the island, other than the ones we have all ready discussed."

"What 'bout the nanny?" Haws asked, then quickly added, "Is she young?"

Leigh laughed. "I've never met the woman, but neither have I ever seen a young nanny. Besides, I hear she is too prim and proper to ever be seen with her skirt above her ankle, let alone in native garb. No, you can surely forget about that one."

Nathaniel repeated his vow. "I won't leave the island without her." He closed his eyes, remembering vividly the scene at the pool. He had fallen into the water and had no strength to pull himself out. Two women had pulled him out and down to the velvety moss. He had tried speaking, but no words passed his lips. His mind swirled. Could it have been witches who had rescued him? If so, one was the most exquisite creature he had ever seen with her emerald eyes and smoldering hair. "I must find her," he repeated.

And look he did. He searched every village on the island, asking if anyone had seen such a being. The answer was always the same. No one had ever seen her. Nathaniel returned to the pool. He had known beautiful women, but none had touched him as this one had. Could he have been wrong? Was there only the native girl who had helped him? No, he was not a man who would imagine such things. Yet, if she were real, where was she? "Damme! I know she was there and she was in my room. I know I didn't imagine it."

In one of the villages, he met several men and asked about a white woman with green eyes. They suggested he go to the parsonage. Upon his arrival, he found the doors locked and the windows barred. He saw the note on the door saying the family had gone to Hawaii and would not return for a week. In that instant Nathaniel felt completely drained of all emotion. He hated to admit that Leigh had been right. Was it all a figment of his feverish mind? Had he not seen her; did she not exist? He went back to camp and told Haws to get the men ready. They were to sail at high tide.

Returning to the mission, Meghan packed her personal things and took Robert's clothes, leaving the money for the clothing and some money for Elizabeth to buy something for herself. Next Meghan placed the money and a farewell letter on Mr. Jennings' desk.

Tears rolled down the faces of Leah and Meghan as they gave their final good-byes near the beach. Leah turned and ran toward the deep foliage.

A whaling man from the STAR stopped Leah as she headed up from the beach, and asked in the native tongue, if she knew the English family living in the village. When she nodded, he asked if there had been a white girl visiting in the past two weeks. She shook her head. He asked if there was a native girl on the island with green eyes.

At this she laughed, "Have you ever seen one?" she said, reverting to English.

With a grateful smile the man continued, "Good ye speak my tongue, so I'll be asking again. Be thar a native girl 'ere 'bout with green eyes?"

"Who wants to know?" the girl asked.

"Cap'n Lathrope, of the STAR," he answered.

"Are you the captain?"

"Nay, I be asking for 'im."

"Why doesn't he ask for her?"

After the fever left him, 'e did try."

"A fever?" questioned the girl.

"Aye."

"Where did he first see her?"

"At some pool. But enough questions. Do ye know such a lass, or not?"

Leah's mind whirled. Could this man's captain be the one that Meghan loved?

Meghan never told her the name of the ship she was sailing on, so what good would it do this man to learn of Meghan's existence. Besides, why should Meghan be happy if she, herself, could never be?

"Tell your captain, she's nothing more than a fever dream."

The whaling man thanked her and left.

The cook saw Meghan come on aboard and called out to her. "Glad ye came early, Marty. 'Tis almost time to be feedin' the lads, and thar be work to do before then."

Meghan washed potatoes, putting them into large pots to boil before she cut thick slices of beef to be fried.

"Can ye be fixing an apple pie?" he asked.

"Aye, that I can," Meghan told him. "And be mighty glad to do it."

Meghan stayed in the cook shack to eat her meal. The more she kept away from the crew so much the better. When it was time to retire, Meghan was not sure what to do. She approached Simmons. "Could I be sleeping in the storeroom?" she asked him.

The man did not speak for a time, and then he said he would partition off part of the cook shack where the vegetables were stored and she could have that place to sleep. Simmons had taken an instant liking to this shy young lad, and decided to become his protector. "I'll bring ye a cot with some covers," he said and left her, closing the door behind him.

Simmons knew it was hard for some lads to dress and undress amongst a lot of strangers, at times the whalers could be very rough on a newcomer, and he wanted to protect this shy youth, if he could. When the lad got used to the ways of whaling men, he reasoned, then that protection could be lifted.

Meghan removed her cap and shirt and released the binding holding her breasts flat.

Oh, that feels good, she thought. *If I keep the binding a bit loose, maybe no one will notice.* She heard a gasp behind her, and turned to see the cook staring at her . . .

"Yer . . . a . . . lass," he stammered.

Meghan paled, grabbed her shirt and quickly put it on. "Please, don't be telling. I've got to leave the island."

"Ye tricked old Cookie," he said, slumping down on a water keg. "Why ye be doing such a wicked thing?"

"Would you have taken me on board, if you knew I was a girl?"

He ignored the question. "Why did ye want to come 'board?"

"I was going to have to marry against my will," Meghan informed him. She quickly explained what brought her to the island from Ireland and what had forced her to make this dangerous decision. "This ship was my only hope," she told him.

"How did ye learn 'bout cooking and such?"

"My mum taught me to cook and when on the schooner the cook showed me his galley and I saw the kind and amount of food the men ate. He also taught me about hunting for whales and how to render the blubber, the name of different parts of the ship and the duties of the men. I have pretended to be a lad before, and the men on the schooner did not discover the truth."

"How long did the masquerade last?" Simmons asked.

"Not very long, but it was Mrs. Jennings and not the men who found out."

"Tarnation, lass, how long do ye think such a thing can be kept a secret on the STAR? Oh, Lordy, if Cap'n finds out, 'eaven 'elp us all."

"Then you'll not tell him what I have just told you?"

"Nay," he replied. "Thar's nothing to be done 'bout it now. The Cap'n just come on board and the sails 'ave been unfurled. 'Twill be a long time till we reach land, Marty. I dunno what might happen if the crew finds out."

"They wouldn't hurt me, would they?"

"I dunno know." He looked keenly at her. "What be yer real name?"

She started to say, but he stopped her. "Nay! I not be wantin' to know. I might be blurting it out by mistake. If that be happening, we'll both be tossed into the sea."

"The captain won't really do such a thing, will he?" For the first time Meghan was coming to terms with what she had done. Not only had she put herself in danger, she had brought trouble to this kind, caring man. "I'm sorry, Cookie, I never should have done it."

"I once saw him pick up a man and throw him overboard for breaking a ship's rule. Oh, 'tis a hard man our cap'n, when 'e be crossed."

Meghan sank back on the cot.

"Wall, 'tis best if ye be getting some sleep, Marty, " continued the man. "Ye'll 'ave to be on guard, for sure. Ye can't be careless, or 'tis death for us all."

"You can't mean your captain would have us killed?"

He looked stricken. "Who be sayin' a thing 'bout killing?"

"You said it would be our death."

"Aye, that I did," he admitted. "But I not be saying a thing about killing." He turned and shuffled to the door, muttering to himself, "'Tis my death if 'e be finding out."

Meghan waited until she heard him go on deck before getting ready for bed; sleep was long in coming. The next morning she awakened to the sound of banging pans. She hurried to dress. Stepping through the curtains, she saw the cook slicing thick pieces of pork.

"Be hurrying," Simmons said as Meghan came into the galley, "and take that basket and be gathering eggs for breakfast. Go aft and ye'll be seeing a passageway leading down into the hold. Once there, yer nose will be yer guide. Now, hurry along with ye. And Marty, don't be speaking to the men until ye forget yer English ways."

"My English ways? Why, Cookie, don't ye know I'm just a mere colleen from Ireland. English, indeed! My sainted granny would leap in her grave, if such a thing be thought true." She laughed as she left the shack.

Meghan had nearly finished gathering the eggs when she heard voices. She stepped out of view as two men walked pass and up the ladder to the deck.

"Something be wrong with Cap'n," one stated while the other replied, "'E's not the same as 'e once was, and that's the truth." The voices turned to whispers and she heard no more. As soon as they left the area Meghan finished gathering the eggs and took them back to the cook.

"While I was in the hold, I heard some of the men speaking about the captain. Has he been ill?"

"Thar be nothing wrong with Cap'n," the old man replied. He quickly cooked the eggs and dished them up. "Now, be taking these platters of food to the tables. I'll be seeing to the officers. When that chore be done, come back and we can eat. And don't be forgetting what I told ye about talking to the men. The lest ye say will be the better until ye learn to speak more like us."

Meghan could not help laughing. "Ye mean I should say ye and yer?"

"Aye, do ye think ye can be doin' et?"

"I'll be trying me very best," she assured him.

Meghan placed platters of eggs, fried potatoes, slices of pork and fresh fruit on the table and gave each man a glass of cool milk.

"So ye be called, Marty?' one of the men asked as she started to leave.

Meghan lowered her voice. "Aye, that I be."

"Now, whar do ye think the lad's from?" asked a tall, heavyset man. "'E don't rightly speak like one of us."

"I'm from Ireland." Meghan told him.

"From Ireland, is it?" said one, grabbing hold of her arm. "And just 'ow did ye get from thar to 'ere?"

"The wee folks brought me 'ere," she said.

"The wee folks, is it?" the same man said. "And why would they be doin' such a thing?"

"To get away from bullies like you," she hotly declared.

Cookie, coming up from the officer's quarters, heard the questioning of Meghan and put a stop to it. "Marty! Come along with me. Thar's no time to be idle."

She did not move. When Cookie came closer and saw the grip on her arm ordered, "Let the lad go, thar's work to be done in the galley." He turned to the rest the men. "I'm thinking ye all 'ave more work to do than tease a 'omesick lad."

The arm was dropped, and Meghan hurried back to the galley.

Once they were alone, the cook said, "'Tis an old man ye be making of me, Marty."

"I am sorry, Cookie," she said finding a keg to sit upon.

"Thar be no time for sitting," Cookie said, "'tis time to be eating."

Cookie and Meghan took their portion to a small table by the stern, a place where Meghan could watch the rolling sea and the rest of the ship. It was there that she saw a man come on deck. She leaned over to the cook and asked, "Who is that man, over there?"

"That thar be the first mate, Mistah Haws."

The color drained from Meghan's face. He was a friend of the man from the pool. She picked up her plate and hurried inside the shack. She was pouring hot water in the dish pan when Cookie came in.

"What's ailing ye?" he asked. "Ye look like ye've seen a ghost."

"Cookie," she asked, lathering the water with soap. "Has any man aboard the ship been sick of late?"

"Why the question?"

Marty ignored his question. "Is he all right now?"

"Aye."

"I haven't seen him, have I?"

Meghan was afraid to ask any more questions.

The next evening Meghan ran out of the galley to throw the slop over the railing and bumped into a man standing in the darkness. The impact almost knocked the buckets from her hands.

"Watch where ye stand," she grumbled. "Ye about tore the bucket from me hands. Next time I might be throwing it over ye."

The man stood his ground. "You must be the one signed on in Maui. What's your name?"

"Marty Ryan."

Ah, yes, one Marty Ryan. Well, Ryan, I suggest you put a bridle on your tongue in the future."

"And who might ye be to tell me what to do?"

"I am Nathaniel Lathrope, captain of the STAR."

The moon came from behind the sails, bathing the deck and the captain in its rays. Meghan gasped. It was he! Her face flamed from the remembrance of warming his body.

"Sorry . . . ." her words trailed off.

"Good," he replied. "Remember this, young Ryan, it is I who gives the command whether you live or die. I suggest you remember that in the upcoming months and guard your tongue." He turned on his heels and continued in his rounds.

Cookie had warned her to keep out of the captain's way and here she had insulted him with her wicked tongue. What would happen if he sought her out and realized she was not who she pretended to be. Would he have her killed, or would he set her adrift in the endless sea? What ever was she going to do? How could she keep him from finding out that it was she who was at the pool? The next question that leaped into her mind was why keep it from him? Wouldn't he want to know it was she who had saved his life? However, she had to admit, wouldn't it be wiser to wait? He might not want to be reminded of his weakness when he only wanted to show strength to his men. It might just be better to keep quiet about the whole thing. And she wondered afresh if he would really set her adrift when he found out that she had lied about herself. It was not a thought to give her comfort.

ᨠ᤻ᨠ

As the ship settled into its normal routine, things went pretty much the same from day to day; that is, until one of the whalers refused to obey a direct order given by Haws. Nathaniel had come on deck and heard the man's refusal.

Nathaniel turned to the second mate. "Mistah Matthew, summon all hands on deck."

Simmons was returning to the cook shack when he heard the order given, and he hurried to get Meghan. When she came on deck, Higgins saw her and his expression filled with loathing. Higgins had watched day after day as the new lad was passed over for a turn in the crow's nest.

"Mistah Haws, repeat your command," ordered Nathaniel.

"'Iggins, yer next to the crow's-nest," Haws repeated.

"I'll not be doing me watch till the new lad 'as 'is turn."

"Higgins, you'll do as Mistah Haws has ordered." Demanded a furious Nathaniel. "When I am not on duty, his voice and mine are the same."

"Cap'n," asked Higgins. "Every man 'ere be the same?"

"That is the rules as you well know," replied Nathaniel.

A sly grin came over the whaler's features, "Then it be Marty's turn. 'Taint fair Mistah 'Aws giv'n favors to the lad. Why, ye would think 'e's some dainty lass the way 'e's been coddled."

"That is not the issue here," snapped Nathaniel. "Mistah Haws gave an order. Obey it or be punished; the decision is yours!"

"I'll be doin' me duty, Cap'n, but ye being a fair man, if ye say the lad's not to be one of us, then that's the end of et." Higgins climbed the rigging and stood in the crow's nest.

Nathaniel turned to Haws. "Come with me," he said, leading the way down to his quarters.

"Mistah Haws, is there truth to what the man said? Has young Ryan been allowed favors?" Remembering the night of their encounter, continued, "He seems well able to take care of himself."

"Cap'n, 'e's not been told the watch is part of 'is duties. I've kept my eye on the lad. 'es not as strong as the rest of the men. Cookie feels the lad should be assigned only to 'elpin' 'im and to keepin' the tunnels filled with water when the fires are blazin'. The lad's a landlubber, for sure."

Nathaniel thought the matter through. "Mistah Haws, if the men feel favoritism is being shown, they'll take it out on the lad. I want you to wait two days, and then assign Marty the night watch. Is that clearly understood?"

"That be the time of yer rounds, Cap'n."

Nathaniel smiled. "I remember back to my first watch and well remember Captain Black doing the same for me. I can do no less for this lad."

Two days later Meghan stood at the bottom of the rigging, looking up at the crow's nest. She said a silent prayer, then put her right foot on the first rung, soon the other foot followed the first. She had climbed many a tree, but they stayed put, not swaying in the wind like this one made of rope. She continued her ascent, then made the mistake of looking down and grew dizzy. Between the wind and dizziness, she felt sure she would fall. She started to descend when a shout came from below. "Stay steady, and don't look down."

The palms of her hands were sweating, her legs turning to mush as she continued to sway back and forth. "Take one step at a time," continued the voice. "Keep your eyes on the crows-nest."

"Up 'ere, lad. Keep yer eyes up 'ere. Ye can make it, for sure, if ye listen to Cap'n."

Marty's heart sank. The captain was the one who shouted to her. What a failure she must be to him. It took most of her strength to make it to the next rung.

"Ye 'ave it now, lad," Higgins shouted down to her. "We'll yet be makin' a whaler of ye."

When Meghan finally made it to the top, Higgings handed her the spyglass. "Ye can't be fallin' from 'ere, 'tis far easier goin' down then comin' up."

Meghan took the spyglass and climbed into the nest. She looked down to see if the captain was still there. He was not. She looked out to the sky. The sun, barely poking its face over the horizon, cast shades of red across the still water. The taste of salt caressed her lips and tiny particles of its residue collected on her face. For the first time in weeks, she felt alive and vibrant.

Then the captain moved out of the shadows, and she watched him as he cupped his hand around his mouth and shouted up at her. "Ho, to the lookout, what see you?"

"The horizon be clear, Cap'n," Meghan hollered back.

Nathaniel moved on. He was amused at the way the lad's voice lowered and rose. He thought back to his own youth and wondered if he, too, sounded like a girl at times. No, he did not think that was the case. There was something wrong with a lad who never looked you in the eye. Was he running away from a cruel master as he himself had? Subconsciously, Nathaniel rubbed the scar on his hand; forcing the memory it evoked back into the deepest recesses of his mind, forcing his thoughts back to the newest member of his crew. He knew there was something vaguely familiar about Marty. Perhaps the lad reminded him of someone else, but for the life of him, he could not think who that might be. He leaned over the railing. The waves gently lapped against the side of the ship, otherwise, the sea was as smooth as glass. The moon was high; the stars glimmered in the heavens; they seemed to know they were guiding the STAR home. Home to Nantucket! And yet that fact made him feel lonelier than he had ever felt before. A part of him was missing—the part of him that he had left on Maui.

Chapter Nineteen

❧

Meghan's apprehension developed into admiration for the STAR's captain. She honored him for his ability to run his ship, to govern his men with fairness, to know when to be stern and when to show mercy. Over the following weeks that admiration grew into a deep respect and finally into a love that consumed her very existence; a love that she believed could never be shared.

One free afternoon Meghan became so frustrated in her failure to understand the art of knot tying, she did not see nor hear Nathaniel approaching her. "What seems to be the matter?" he asked her.

Meghan looked up at him, her cheeks burning, and said, "I can't be gettin' the knots right, no matter how hard I try."

"Let me show you," he said taking the rope from her. He quickly fashioned several different types of knots. He handed it back to her. "Now, let me see you do it,"

It was not long until they had an audience, each man giving her encouragement. For the first time Meghan actually felt a member of the crew. Even Higgins gave her some helpful instructions, then he made a suggestion, "When thar be time," he said, "I'll be showin' ye 'ow to be doin' some scrimshaw." He produced from his waistband a knife and a delicate figure of a small boy made out of whalebone.

The piece of art was breathtakingly intricate in form. She ran her finger deftly over the carved and polished bone. "Do ye really think I could be doin' such a thing?" she questioned.

"Aye," replied the man. "And after evening chores, I'll bring ye a knife and a piece of bone. Yer a smart lad, Marty. I'm thinkin' 'twon't be long till ye master the craft."

The STAR had been to sea one month when Meghan woke one morning to hear the yell from the crow's nest, **'Thar she bloooows! She blows! She bloows!"** She leaped from her cot, grabbed her clothes and quickly dressed. She arrived on deck in time to see the men getting ready to board the whaling boats.

"Whar away?" shouted Haws.

"Thar! Thar she bloows!" cried the lookout, pointing across the lee bow; the spray rose high from the whale and the man repeated the cry, "Thar she bloows!"

Nathaniel reached several rungs below the lookout. Reaching for his spyglass, he found the target he sought. "Humpbacks, to be sure," he said, then added, "but there's a whole pod. Mistah Haws," he shouted down to the first mate, "prepare the men for their stations."

Nathaniel climbed down the rigging. He paused in front of the cook shack long enough to order Meghan to come with him. "You might as well learn to handle an oar."

Meghan hung back. "I can't be going, Cookie. He'll know for sure that I'm a girl."

"There's no win to it," Simmons told her. "Ye 'ave to go."

Meghan pulled her cap lower over her eyes. She ran to the boat farthest from that of Nathaniel's. She had just about reached it when he called her back. "Marty! Come here. I need an extra hand." Begrudgingly, she did as commanded.

Harpoons and javelin were in perfect order. The attached lines neatly coiled in wooden buckets ready to whistle through the air when needed. The boats, filled with men, were lowered into the sea. Now, whaleboats are made for speed, and these were no exception, the men rowed with ease over the waves. Overhead, clouds drifted lazily across the sky impervious to the scene of activity below.

Nathaniel ordered the men to row toward the east where a black whale spouted water hundreds of feet into the air. Meghan closed her eyes and clung to the gunwale. This was not the same as watching a hunt from the schooner with Caleb by her side. The wind changed. It now came from the north, chilling her to the bone. "She sounds!" cried a whaler as the whale disappeared into the depths of the sea. The men stopped rowing. They waited for the whale to rise again. "She breaches," someone shouted.

With javelin in hand, Nathaniel stood in the bow, braced against the gunwale. Nearer and nearer the men rowed forward. Then the order was given and harpoons whistled through the air, pulling the ropes with them. Several struck the whale's thick hide. Four harpoons were anchored deep into the fifty-foot whale's side and anchored to the boat. The huge monster flipped its tail, covering the boat and occupants with salty water. The whale disappeared again from view. For a time all was quiet. Suddenly, and with a ferocious jerk, the boat was pulled through the waves at neck-breaking speed into the chilled wind from the north.

Meghan fought to turn her head to watch the STAR grow smaller and smaller as they were yanked by the whale further and further away from safety. For what seemed like hours, the whale sought to free itself from the lines. The sky grew black; the clouds, once floating peacefully overhead, now swirled violently. Thousands of droplets of salt pummeled her exposed skin as the sea, wind, and clouds became as one. Panic such as she had never known, ate at her until she thought her body might burst from the fill of it. Time meant nothing as the whale raced through the waves, pulling the boat miles and miles from their ship. The marathon was one of sheer terror for the girl from Ireland. Her eyes sought and found Nathaniel still standing braced against the bow of the boat, the javelin clutched in his hand. She searched his face for some sign of terror, all she saw was a look of sheer exhilaration and she forced herself to turn away.

Meghan's clothes were drenched and molded to her skin. A terrible thought flashed through her mind. If the binding was soaked, they could readily tell she was not a lad. The fear of dying was replaced by the fear of exposure. She fought the desire to cry. He could hate her for the lie she had been living, but she would not have him ashamed for her cowardice. From loss of concentration she lessened her grip on the gunwale, and the wind whipped her body across the wood plank to hit one of the men. He pushed her away and the wind sent her crashing back into the opposite side of the boat; she thought her ribs might be broken from the impact.

As suddenly as the race began, it ended. The whale stopped some 100 yards away. The men rowed steadily toward it. Nathaniel wiped the water from his hands. The whale was tiring; the men rowed until they were almost on top of the whale. Nathaniel thrust the tip of the javelin just below its eye. The kill was made; nevertheless, there were no shouts of joy. This was not the part of the job that the men enjoyed. They knelt in prayer and thanked God for saving their lives, once more.

Nathaniel looked toward Meghan, her head down, her eyes closed, her arms folded across her chest. "Lad," he said, "the kill has been made, all is well." She did not speak. "Let's go back to the ship," he said to his men.

Upon reaching the STAR, Meghan ran to her makeshift room. She found the slop jar and heaved.

Cookie found her there. "Marty, 'tis time to attend the fires."

A white-faced Meghan raised her head. "I need but a moment," she told him.

"A moment, but no more," he told her, leaving the room.

For the next three days, Meghan kept the tunnels filled with water. Her back and arms ached from carrying the heavy buckets full of water. More than once, she caught Nathaniel looking at her. The expression on his face puzzled her. Before the hunt he had been kind to her, even showing her how to accomplish the tying of knots. Once he had taken out his own knife for her to use in carving a piece of whalebone. His friendliness had vanished after the hunt. Now he avoided being anywhere near her, and if it looked as though they might be alone, he would turn and walk the other way.

She asked Cookie about it. "'Tis only yer imaginin'," he said. "Cap'n bein' a busy man, has no time for trainin' the crew. He leaves that up to the likes of me or one of the other men."

That was not why he was avoiding her, of that she was sure. It was the look of fear on her face. He was ashamed to have a coward on his precious ship. Well, she would show him she was no coward. She would go on all the hunts. And if he wanted to be left alone, she would not bother him again. If anyone were to turn away, it would be her.

On the third day of rendering, a hard wind came out of the south. The ship rocked back and forth with such force boiling oil sloshed over the tubs onto the deck. The stench of blubber absorbed the air, and it was impossible for Meghan to keep her stomach under control. She made her way to the railing and let nature have its way. Bringing her head up, she looked straight into the barbarous face of a charging whale. Its massive jaws opened wide, its jagged teeth ready for the kill. The waves tumbled about its gigantic hulk, sending whirlpools of water rushing toward the ship. Meghan, rooted to the spot, could not find voice to scream. Closer and closer, the monster of the deep came, its speed now at ramming force. And its target? The very place where she stood transfixed.

"It comes! It comes!" The lookout shouted, his arms waving frantically. "The sea-devil's rammin' us."

His voice finally cut through Meghan's frozen mind. She stepped away from the railing, but it was too late. The colossal head struck the boat. The vicious impact knocked her over the railing. Her body hit the whale; then rolled off it into the tempestuous sea as it swam away. The lookout sounded the alarm, "Man overboard, on the lee side."

Haws looked in that direction, saw Meghan and threw her a line. She grabbed hold of it and impelled herself hand over hand up the knotted rope. He laughed as he seized her hand. His laughter stopped when she came aboard. He quickly removed his oilskin and wrapped her in it. She collapsed in his arms. Simmons had been sent for and he hurried to Haws.

"I'll be taking the lad," he told Haws.

"Lad, is it," Haws seethed. "I think we both know better than that. Now, get Marty to his quarters, I'll be seein' ye both, later."

Simmons put her on the cot. "Well, lass, ye can open your eyes, the worst has happened."

"Oh, Cookie, he knows." Meghan sobbed.

"Aye, Marty, he does. Now ye best be changin' yer clothes before ye catch the fever."

Meghan had just finished dressing and was attempting to dry her hair when she heard someone come into the cook shack. She threw the towel on the chair, her hair curled about her head in ringlets. She straightened her shoulders, and left her room. She took one look at Cookie's stricken face and knew something was awfully wrong.

"'Tis the Cap'n, Marty. The fever's got 'im."

Meghan's heart sank. "He's not going to die, is he?"

Simmons shook his head. "Can't be tellin' for sure, Marty. 'E's mighty sick." He took a pail of cool water and rags back to Nathaniel's quarters. Meghan followed. "Thar's nothin' ye can be doin' for him," he told her. "Ye best get back before ye get sick."

"I'm going with you," she insisted, "and there's none to stop me."

Simmons gave her a long, searching look and then nodded for her to follow him. A single candle burned on the nightstand. The old man quickly dipped a rag into the cool water and bathed Nathaniel's face; his fever raged; his body shivered.

"Over in that trunk, ye'll find a blanket, bring it to me," Simmons instructed Meghan.

"Will he be living?" Meghan asked, giving the blanket to the old man.

Simmons saw the tears forming in Meghan's eyes. "Ye best be gettin' any fancy notions out of yer 'ead," he told her. "I 'ear tell the Cap'n lost his heart to some little native lass on Maui."

"A native lass, are you sure?"

"Thar's no time for gossip," he told her. "Cap'n need to be warmed. 'Tis some warmin' bricks 'e be needin'. Ye stay here. I best be gettin' the warmin' bricks and brew some herbs to make 'im a broth. Listen to me, Marty, thar be no time for weepin', I won't be tellin' ye again." He hurried out of the room.

Meghan removed her cap and laid it on the bed. In the candlelight her hair became a dark cloud about her head. As she looked down at the feverish man, her tears freely flowed.

You can't be loving another, she thought, *Not when I love you so."*

"Who's here? He asked, then added, "Cookie?" There was no sound. "Someone's there, speak up. Who are you?"

Nathaniel opened his eyes. A faint smile crossed over his lips. He lifted his hand, caught hold of her shoulder length hair and forced her head down to his; their faces mere inches apart; his voice no more than a whisper.

"I knew . . . you'd . . . come . . . back. or are you a dream?" he asked, struggling to sit up.

"I'm real enough," Meghan said.

"Then, kiss . . . me," he pleaded.

Their lips met a gentle caress; but that did not satisfy him. He kissed her until her senses reeled. She loved him, while his heart was somewhere on Maui. She did not try to check the flow of tears.

"Why are you crying?" he asked. "Such beautiful green eyes should never be touched by tears."

He touched her hair. "I can't see the color. But I remember it was as black as raven's wings, and your body soft against mine. My love, tell me your name."

"It's Meghan," she whispered.

He closed his eyes.

Hearing running footsteps, Meghan stepped away from the bed, and quickly pulled her hair under the cap.

Simmons burst into the room carrying two bricks wrapped in a cloth. "Pull back the covers," he ordered. "The Cap'n needs his feet warmed." Meghan hurried to do so, and Simmons put the bricks in place.

"Don't leave me," Nathaniel said, reaching out.

"I won't, Cap'n," Simmons told him, then turning to Meghan ordered her to leave the room.

"Oh, Cookie, please let me stay. I want to help."

"Ye'll be helpin' by leavin'," the man informed her. "No use the Cap'n seein' ye like this."

Meghan left and returned to her sanctuary, her heart singing with the knowledge that he wasn't dreaming about any native girl. He dreamed of her and the short time they had together. Yet, how could she tell him that she was the young whaling man Marty Ryan? Would he feel she had made a fool of him? Oh, why had she listened to Cookie? Why hadn't she gone immediately to Nathaniel and told him the truth?

Two hours later Haws relieved Simmons from his watch. Nathaniel motioned for Haws to come closer and the first mate put his ear next to the captain's mouth.

Chapter Twenty

❧

Simmons helped himself to a cup of coffee.

"'E opened 'is eyes just after ye left. 'E looked about, then asked where SHE was. I told 'im thar was just the two of us, and 'e said that SHE had been there. I asked him who that was, and 'e said it was the one from the pool. Oh, Marty. 'E's plumb lost 'is 'ead, and I don't know what to do."

"Cookie, please let me go to him," begged Meghan.

"And what can ye do? I tell ye, 'e wants the witch from that blasted pool."

"There was no witch at the pool, 'twas me." Meghan left him and went to her own room. When she returned, she was wearing the native dress.

"I can't believe me own eyes," Cookie stammered.

"You can see, can't you, that I must tell him who I am," pleaded Meghan.

"Nay, ye can't be doin' that," Haws said as he came into the room with a mug of steaming coffee. Haws eyes swept over her.

"Ye are a beauty, just like our Cap'n said," he admitted, taking another sip of coffee. "I'm no fool," he continued. "I can see the truth of it. Ye are in love with Cap'n, and maybe 'e loves ye, but the men must be thought of. And 'avin' a lass on board the ship is a bad thing for them. We 'ave a long ways to go before we see 'ome. The men be lonely, and thar's no tellin' what they might do to ye, if they knew the truth. So I'm askin' ye to put aside yer feelin's for the Cap'n and be a lad once more."

"My feelings don't matter," Meghan assured him. "I'm only thinking of the captain. I promised him I would never again leave him. I'll not be going back on that promise. Besides, what will you tell him when he wakes and asks for me?"

"'Tain't likely 'e'll be rememberin'," Haws told her.

"More likely than not, 'e'll be thinkin' 'twas only a dream."

"He knows my name's Meghan. I told him so."

"Thar ain't no Meghan on board the STAR, only a new lad called Marty," Haws replied.

"I can't be giving him up, Mistah Haws. I just can't."

A look of compassion came over the first mate's features. "Aye, I know 'tis a hard task I'm givin' ye, but 'tis best for the STAR."

"Is it also best for the Captain," she asked.

"The STAR 'as always come first with Cap'n. I reckon it still does," Haws replied.

"I won't make any decision, now," Meghan told him. "I have to think hard on what's the right of it, Mistah Haws."

Haws bid the two of them goodnight and left. Simmons did likewise, leaving her alone with her own thoughts.

Meghan slowly changed into Marty's clothes and sat on the edge of the bed, thinking. She knew, of course, that Haws was right. It was not fair to the men, but was it fair to her and her captain? She had kissed him. Oh, he would think himself gone crazed if he could not find her. She put her cap on, tucking the curls underneath. She looked into the reflection of her mirror. There was no sparkle in her eyes, only sadness. She tenderly traced the outline of her lips remembering the feel of his when she had kissed him. Those memories would have to last a lifetime. After the hunt how could she go to him and say who she was? She did not believe he would ever forgive her for the deception.

The hardest thing for the girl to do in the next days was to be near him while attending to the fever. On one occasion, as Simmons was standing beside her, Meghan asked, "Cookie, he would want to know the truth, wouldn't he?"

"He be a strange one," Simmons said. "Not given to talk like most. But I know 'bout 'im when 'e first went to sea. Couldn't 'ave been more than ten years old. A darky brought him to Captain Black from Virginny. The captain knew the lad's papa, 'im bein' dead at sea. Wall, I sort of took 'im under me wing, so to speak.

"One night 'e woke up from a bad dream, 'oldin' one little 'and in the other. The right one there, turn it palm up. See the scar?" Meghan nodded her head, and Simmons continued, "I asked Captain Black 'bout it and 'e told me the story. Be ye wantin' to 'ear it?" Again she nodded her head.

Simmons settled back in a chair, his eyes focused on his captain's face.

"Cap'n Lathrope as a babe, was raised by 'is mama's brother. Not that the Cap'n be knowin' that fact, 'im bein' raised as a slave on the plantation. Ran away the first time when 'e be a mite of eight. With the 'elp of his darky friend, they made it to Nantucket. I 'ear 'e be thar 'bout six months when 'is uncle came for 'im. The man took him back to Virginny. He didn't like the Quaker way of speakin', and he beat 'im every time 'e opened 'is mouth."

"But," interrupted Meghan, "he doesn't speak with an accent now."

"I'm comin' to that, if ye be lettin' me." Simmons told her, mopping Nathaniel's brow with a cool rag.

"I'm sorry," Meghan replied, taking the rag from Simmons and dipping it into the cool water.

"As I remember it, 'is uncle took a fit of temper and held the lad's 'and, palm down, over a flame. 'Held it thar till the lad fainted, dead away, and he nary spoke the Quaker brogue 'gain."

"How he must be hating his uncle," Meghan said.

"I can't be sayin' as to that," Simmons told her. "The one thing I do know is that 'e can't 'bide lyin' or deceit. I dread the day 'e be findin' out ye be a lass and not a lad."

A short time later they were relieved of duty by one of the other whalers. Meghan and Simmons left and she did not see the captain until the next night. Meghan stood in the shadows until she saw Haws come on deck. She slipped down the ladder and eased open Nathaniel's door. The only light in the room came from one small candle, flickering on the side table. Tracy was sitting on a chair alongside the bed.

"I come to sit with the Cap'n," she said. "Ye best be getting some rest."

"'Aye," replied the youth. "'Tis been a long day."

"Has the cap'n been sleeping?" she asked him.

"'E's a bit fretful," stated Tracy. "Keeps mumblin' somethin' that I can't be hearin' true."

""Like what?" she wanted to know.

"Don't rightly know. It sounds crazy to me," Tracy admitted. He left the cabin and closed the door.

A sudden roll of the ship knocked Meghan off balance and she fell across the bed, waking Nathaniel.

"You . . . came . . . back," he stammered. "I.. waited.. all day. Now that you . . . have . . . come, please, hold me close."

She held his head close against her.

"Kiss..me. . . ," He pleaded. She obeyed his request. "You're . . . real," he stammered. "It's not . . . a dream?"

"It's not a dream," she confessed. "I'm here."

"And ye'll never leave me?"

"Never," she promised, for she knew that she truly loved him. She felt her heart soar from its resting place to nestle deep within him and she knew the two hearts would intermingle forever.

"Come, lie beside me. I want to feel you close."

She slipped onto bed and held him close. She stayed nestled in his arms until morning. At the sound of the door opening, she slid off the bed, to return the next night and the next. Sometimes in his delirium, he would call out her name and others in the room supposed she was someone from his past. To her, it was a stab in her heart. She wished with all her heart that the trip was over and she was once more in Ireland. She told Simmons as much.

On the seventh day the fever broke. "Are you sure he'll be all right?" she asked Simmons.

"Aye, Marty, 'e'll be up and 'bout in no time," came the reply.

Nathaniel came out of his world of dreams to ponder on the things that had happened. In his fever, the spirit of the pool had visited him, and she said her name was Meghan. She had kissed him and lay beside him. He remembered traces of freckles over the bridge of her nose and speckles of gold all around the edges of her green eyes. Her mouth was soft and supple. He could still feel her warm and soft body by his side. It was all so very real. But how could it be? If they were on land, he would swear she had actually been there, but in the middle of the hunt? No, it was impossible to have happened.

Nathaniel splashed his face with water, his mind in a twirl of activity.

It doesn't make sense, does it? he asked himself. *How could there be a woman on board ship? I must shake myself of the dream before it turns into a nightmare. My lovely Meghan with midnight hair and emerald eyes does not exist. But if it wasn't her, who was it?*

Later that very day Haws went to Nathaniel's quarters. "'Tis mighty good to see ye sittin' up, Cap'n. Ye 'ad us all worried." He paused. "Bad dreams gone?"

'Was I having bad dreams?" asked Nathaniel.

"Aye, Cap'n. Ye be callin' out the name Meghan. I dunno ye know anyone by that name. Somebody ye left behind on Nantucket? Somebody ye did not tell me 'bout?"

"There was no one here by that name?" he asked, knowing very well what Haws' reaction would be, and him feeling like a fool because he had asked the question.

"'Ow, could that be, Cap'n? Ye know all on board the STAR."

"The dream has come back to haunt me, Jeremy. I know now that no matter how much I wished it were true my lovely Meghan with her raven hair and emerald eyes, does not exist."

Compassion filled his first mate's features.

"I've been thinkin' Cap'n," he said, "young Marty Ryan 'as been helpin' care for ye, and 'e 'as green eyes, but as far as 'is 'air, 'tis the color of the setting sun. 'E must 'ave been mixed up in yer dreams. 'Tis that blasted island, Cap'n. I 'ope never to see it again." Nathaniel did not reply, and Haws hastened to add, "I best be goin'. The men will be pleased ye be well, once again."

"Marty? Could it be?" wondered Nathaniel. "I felt drawn to him on that first hunt. There was something about the lad that I felt I must protect. But could I have reached out for him in my fever?" The very thought of it sent cold shiver down his back. He shook his head to dash the notion from the depths of his mind. Yet the thought did not leave.

Nathaniel straightened his shoulders. "Mistah Haws, have Cookie fix me some food. I must have strength to face my men. And Mr. Haws, have him bring it, himself."

"Aye, Cap'n, that be my plan," replied the first officer, and he quickly left. He hated to deceive his captain about the girl, but it had to be done. And the lie between them made it impossible for Haws to stay there any longer.

Nathaniel had been embarrassed by the thought he might have reached out for the young seaman in his delusions and decided to avoid him as best he could. On the ship the size of STAR, this was not an easy task. Although they did not speak, Nathaniel could not help but notice how Marty was improving in his duties. He was well on his way of becoming a real whaler; there was not a man who could scamper up the riggings nor sight a whale any faster than the lad. One afternoon Nathaniel and Meghan came face to face. "I understand you took care of me a night or two when I had the fever, Marty," he said.

"'Twas nothing, Cap'n," came the reply.

He looked deep within Marty's eyes, and saw they were the same as in his feverish dream. It shook him to the core. "Be that as it may. I must ask you to forget anything that I might have said or done. I understand that for a time I was delirious with the fever and not in my right mind."

"You don't remember anything?" she asked.

Nathaniel, barely recovered from the first truth, reeled from the possibility his worst fears had happened. "If there is anything I should remember, tell me."

"Nay, Cap'n. There be nothin' to remember."

Relief coursed through his veins. He smiled. "I do thank you for your assistance. Perhaps the time will come when I might be of service to you." He turned and went about his duties.

Meghan fought to control her emotions. He had not remembered her as she thought he had. It was only his fever. Once again teary-eyed, she hurried to the cook shack and found Simmons waiting for her.

"Cookie, I must get off the ship."

"And whar be ye goin' in the middle of the ocean?"

She could not answer.

"I see ye talkin' to Cap'n. Be he the reason for yer flight?"

"Aye," she said, breaking into sobs. "I can say no more," she fled to her room, away from his probing eyes.

Chapter Twenty-One

~~~
ᕉᖬ
~~~

Many long months had passed since the STAR left Maui. Nathaniel was completely recovered from the fever, and it had not returned. His dreams of the pool spirit had grown less and less until there were no more. However, a day never passed that he did not sense her presence. In fact one morning he thought he caught a whiff of her fragrance. For an instance he was stunned. Then he realized it was only his imagination.

Meghan brought the scissors to Simmons. "Time for the cutting," she said, handing them to him.

"Aye," he said, touching her tresses, "and 'tis a pity to see a thing of beauty destroyed."

"In just a few weeks it will be time to do the cutting, again," she told him.

There was a smile on her lips, yet her heart was heavy. Nathaniel seemed to be avoiding her since his illness. Meghan felt as if her heart would break from the lack of his warmth. She tried in every way she could think of to make him proud of her. She worked harder than the other whalers doing their assigned tasks, or so it seemed to her. What she lacked in strength, she made up for it by accomplishing a new goal each day. Even Higgins had commented on her improvement. She had, under his direction, carved a beautiful tree out of whalebone. It reminded her of the trees of Ireland and Maui, although they were different in form. Perhaps it was just a longing she had for seeing the lush green land she had left behind.

Time moved on as the STAR sailed through the great sea toward the narrow strip of water between Alaska and Russia. Once through, the STAR would be in the Arctic Ocean. But for now the men were engaged in the business of whaling. Time and time again the whale-boats were lowered into the sea. The frypots were kept busy, and Meghan hurried to keep the tunnels full of water.

As they neared the Bering Strait, Meghan thought she would freeze. Never in her life had she been so cold. She wore all of Robert's clothes and even tucked her petticoats into the trousers, yet to no anvil. Higgins saw her plight and decided to take her some warm clothes of his own and on his way back, he slipped on the icy deck and broke his arm. Meghan hurried to find Simmons. Together, they managed to get the man to his bunk.

"Ye're a good lad, Marty," Higgins told her. "Now, ye be taking those clothes and 'tis that sorry I'm for the times I treated ye badly."

"'Tis hardly more than a fleeting memory," Meghan responded as she helped set his arm.

Meghan woke one morning to see they were no longer alone in the icy water. There were at least thirty-five ships heading in the same direction as the STAR. That is they were moving, the STAR was not. She dressed and dashed onto the deck. She skidded across a thin layer of ice to the bulkhead and her assigned position. The men were already in their boats, bobbing in the freezing water. That day three whales were sighted and killed. It took six days of rendering before the bones were sent back to the sea.

The following day Meghan had the watch. "There's something in the water ahead," she shouted. "'Tis all white and it be floating."

"Thar be ice floes, Marty," said Higgins, relieving her of the watch. "'Tis thin layers of ice. When we get to the Arctic, thar be large enough to stove us in." Later, Meghan watched while walrus skimmed across the ice and plunged into patches of open water.

"A new experience for you?" spoke a voice from behind her.

Meghan did not have to turn around to know who it was; her heart gave the answer. It was a miracle she kept her voice from shaking. "Aye, I've not seen such things."

Simmons joined them.

"Marty, I be needin' ye in the cook shack." He looked at Nathaniel. "Sorry, Cap'n, I didn't see ye."

"Good morning, Cookie," replied Nathaniel and continued on his rounds. After he left Simmons looked hard at Meghan.

"Ye best keep away from Cap'n, Marty. Ye be playin' with fire."

"I didn't seek him out," protested Meghan. "But I know what ye say be the truth of it."

Later that morning it began to snow; the flakes soon turning to more ice. The decks became near impossible to walk on. The men skidded from one end of the ship to the other. The fear of hitting the floes, or getting so ice-bound they could not move, was slowly becoming a reality. Just ahead the ice-laden DENVER LEE split in half, and disappeared from view; her men perishing in the frigid water.

Meghan's courage began to fail. She wished she could be as brave as the whaling men. She confessed as much to Simmons.

"Wall, Marty," he began. "'Tis true ye be new to whalin', but I dare say, ye be feelin' no worse than any man 'er 'bouts."

"And the cap'n?" Meghan said.

"E be a man set apart," was the instant reply.

In the afternoon, the STAR anchored itself to a medium size floe. A whaleboat was lowered, and Nathaniel and Haws left immediately for a rendezvous with the captains in the area. They had been gone several hours when Meghan heard the laughter of children. At first she thought she had been mistaken. However, she saw several at play on the ship anchored next to them.

Simmons joined her on deck. "Where did the children come from?" she asked him.

"That be Cap'n Hedrick's ship, and he brought his family with him."

Meghan thought it would be a terrible worry to have children aboard a whaling ship. What would happen if one of the children fell into a vat of boiling blubber? While absorbed in such thoughts, a ball was thrown from the ship. It rolled over the deck and dropped into the icy water. Meghan screamed as she saw a boy run after it. He had not gone very far when his feet went out from under him; he slid across the deck hitting the rail with such force he lost his balance and fell over it onto the floe; then rolled down into the water.

"Man overboard," she cried, and without hesitation, jumped in after him. She caught him by his coat and brought him up to the surface where strong hands plucked her and the boy from the sea. She had lost her cap, and her hair floated about her face in abundance. She saw Nathaniel looking down at her and then she moved into a tunnel of darkness and saw no more.

Nathaniel turned ashen. This was no boy, but an exquisite young woman. In fact, it was his spirit of the pool. Why her hair was now red instead of black, he had no idea. He pulled her limp body from the water and covered her in a blanket.

"Row, lads!" shouted Haws. "Row back to the ship!"

Once aboard the STAR Nathaniel, with the cook at his heels, carried Meghan into her room. Simmons tried to take Meghan from him, but Nathaniel brushed the cook aside and carried Meghan to her bed. Haws and Simmons had followed him into the small room. "Get out," he commanded, "and let no man enter." They closed the door behind them.

He threw her wet things to the floor and wrapped her into thick quilts and held her close to add warmth.. He rubbed her arms and legs trying to bring life back into her small, cold frame. She had helped to save his life, of this he had no doubt, now it was up to him to keep that same radiance safe within her.

"Oh, Lord," he prayed, "don't take her from me. Not now, when I know the truth."

Haws and Simmons barred the door to the cook shack, allowing no one to enter. The lad was near death, they told the men, and the captain was doing his best to save his life. They kept an all night vigil. It was near dawn when Nathaniel opened the door.

"Will Marty live?" the men asked.

"He will live," Nathaniel assured them. "But for now, he must rest. Cookie will be taking care of him." He turned to his first mate. "Mistah Haws, come with me."

Once the door was closed, Nathaniel faced his first mate. He was doing his level best to keep his emotions under control. "There is very little about the STAR and her crew that you do not know. I'm asking you now, did you know of this deception?"

"I did," replied the first mate.

Nathaniel sat at his desk. "How long have you known that Marty was actually the girl on the island?"

Haws remained standing. "Think back to the time the whale rammed the ship. Marty fell into the sea and I pulled her out. That's when I learned the truth of it."

"And you let me think I was crazy?" Nathaniel looked up at Haws, his eyes red-rimmed, his face bloodless, and asked, "Why, Jeremy, why?"

"Ye were sick just after it was made known to me. To tell ye the truth, the lass wanted to tell ye, and I stopped her. I told her 'twasn't fair to the men to know she be a lass, nor would it be safe for the men to know. She said she loved ye more than life itself, and I knew the truth was spoken. But it couldn't be changin' the fact that the truth be kept from the crew."

"The men needn't have known," replied Nathaniel. "You could have come to me and told me the truth. You of all people, knew the torment of my soul for the want of her."

"Cap'n," Haws replied. "It whar the best for the STAR. I knew it was what ye would 'ave done be the roles reversed."

Nathaniel could say nothing. He knew reason when he heard it. He buried his head in his hands. For several minutes neither man spoke; then it was Haws who broke the silence. "What say ye, Cap'n. Shall the truth be known or kept?"

Nathaniel raised his head, and Haws saw the tears of anguish in his captain's eyes. His heart went out to him. He knew how he would feel if his own dear wife were aboard ship, and he could not hold her in his arms. He wondered if he could be as strong as he wanted his captain to be.

Nathaniel rose from the desk to the water pitcher and splashed water over his face. He reached for the towel and dried off. "You are right, Mistah Haws. There is nothing I can do but agree with you."

Haws started for the door, and it was the captain who stopped him. "Let the girl be told that it was Cookie who pulled her from the sea and took care of her. She won't remember what really happened. And, Mistah Haws, let the word go forth that it would not be right for the lad to know the captain took care of him. The men will understand the order."

The men did understand the order. There was not a one who, at some time or another, did not owe their lives to the captain. At the time of the incident the captain had asked them not to make it known to the others, they had obeyed his wishes.

Simmons was summoned to Nathaniel's quarters. "Sit yerself down," Haws informed him. "Cap'n wants to ask ye some questions."

"Aye, Cap'n," Simmons responded.

"I'll get right to the point." Nathaniel told him. "It can't be unknown to you that Marty Ryan is not what he claimed to be. That he, in fact, is a girl. Is her name known to you?"

"I dunno know, and that's the truth. She was goin' to tell me, but I feared I'd let it slip."

"How did she happen to come aboard?" Haws interjected.

"She came to me on the beach and asked to come aboard as a cook's helper. Said she'd been on another ship, and wanted to go back to Ireland. I signed 'er on thinkin' she be a lad, and that's the truth of it."

"Did she say why she left Ireland?" questioned Nathaniel.

"Was she in trouble with the law?" demanded Haws.

"Nay, Mistah Haws. 'Twasn't nothin' of the sort. 'Er papa wanted her to marry some man she didn't love, so she ran away to become a nanny for the preacher's children."

"Then why did she want to go back to Ireland?" asked Nathaniel, leaning forward to hear the answer.

"By virtue of the fact the preacher wanted her to marry someone on the island."

"And she had no love for this man?"

"Nay, Cap'n. 'Tis ye that she loves, she told me so."

Nathaniel's expression did not reveal the joy that leaped within him. And his voice was quite calm when he continued speaking. "Cookie, I don't want the men to know of our discovery. Nor do I want Marty to know the truth is known to me. Do you understand?"

"Why can't she be knowin'? Cap'n, if ye could see how she suffers, you'd be changin' yer mind about tellin' 'er."

"Do you question my orders?"

"Nay, Cap'n," he said, turning away. "But 'tis a mistake. Aye, 'tis a blunder to be sure," he continued to mumble as he left his captain's quarters to return to his own room.

A week later Meghan was able to return to her duties and all seemed normal once more. Except for the fact that Nathaniel could hardly keep his eyes off her. What a fool he had been, he told himself. How could he have ever thought she was a lad? The way she walked, the way she had a habit of brushing the hair away from her eyes, and her laugh; it was a musical thing to hear. Also, he began to notice little things he had overlooked in the past. Like the fact that Higgins, who had once hated her, was always by her side. And Tracy, who was married, seemed far too attentive toward her. As for Matthews, had he deliberately brushed against her? And Mistah Haws . . . . No, he must stop these thoughts. He must not allow his suspicions to bring disaster to his ship.

At long last the wind came up, and the STAR's sails bellowed, but it did not move. One side of the ship was sealed in ice against a floe. No matter how hard they tried, the ice would not release the ship. The only thing they could do was to melt the ice.

Furniture was brought on deck and set on fire. Pieces of the burning wood were thrown on the ice. Sometime during the night, the ice released the whaling ship, and the wind moved the STAR into the open sea.

Chapter Twenty-Two

❧

EXCEPTS FROM THE CAPTAIN'S SHIP LOG

July 5,
>   We are nearing the entrance of the Bering Strait. We are not alone. There are at least twenty other whaling ships here.

July 10,
>   The hunting has been good. We have added many barrels of oil to our store.

July 20,
>   We sighted ice this morning. We are not far from the entrance.

July 30, —
>   We have commenced our journey into the unknown. Every time is like the first time.

August 5,

We entered the Arctic early this morning. The men of the PELIQUIN are hunting walrus on the ice. I pray they have luck.

August 10,

Tomorrow, I hope to be able to put a whaling boat on a chase. STAR has taken on ice. If we make two knots a day, we deem ourselves fortunate.

August 12,

The MARY HOUSTON sank this morning. It was terrifying to behold. Her deck was heavy with ice. Her captain shouted to have the ice anchors removed, but it was too late. The ice had worked under her midsection and pushed her back against the floe. The whole side stoved in, all was lost in the frigid water.

August 20,

We have not moved in two days. The weather is near unbearable. I take time to report that the men have withstood all that life has dealt them. I'm proud to be their captain.

August 22,

Higgins, attempting to walk across the icy deck, slipped and broke his arm.

August 30,

Will this trial never end? The bitter cold and hardships are eating at our hope and courage.

September 3,

We continue to be frozen from movement. The DENVER LEE sank this day. Her crew was lost.

September 5,

　　Marty Ryan showed great courage this day. Marty jumped into the water in an attempt to rescue a small boy from drowning, however, the attempt failed. The lad was the son of the captain of the KYLA ROSE. Marty Ryan almost died of exposure. A new life has come to the ship.

September 8,

　　At long last, the main group of ships have begun to slowly move. We spied a whale, killed and rendered same.

September 10,

　　We are stopped, again. Our port side is encased in ice. Another captain's meeting will be held tomorrow. Something must be done, or we all perish.

September 11,

　　A few of the captains voted to abandon ship and try to get through on foot across the ice. This I am against; the risk to the men is far too great to even consider.

September 12,

　　Some crews have left their ships mired in ice. The ships must be burned to clear the Strait.

September 18,

　　We have taken our meager furniture and built fires on deck to melt the ice frozen to the sides of the ship. If all goes well, we may find ourselves free.

September 20,

THE GLORY caught fire and burned. Her men were rescued.

September 22,

A NE wind has come in a heavy gale. We are inching ourselves from the ice. If the Almighty grants us this privilege, we may live to begin anew.

September 27,

We are moving slowly, and we have had our first casualty. A piece of iceberg broke loose and fell on William Blake, crushing him to death.

October 15,

We have broken free!

November 28,

I thank the Almighty for his favors. We have left the Arctic, and are heading for home.

Chapter Twenty-Three

ৡ

The hunt was over. The MORNING STAR lay anchored in the shipping lanes off Ireland. Meghan knew it was just a matter of time until she must leave the ship and the men of which she had grown so fond. The thoughts of leaving Simmons were bad enough, but the thought of never seeing her captain again was more than she could bear.

Meghan and Simmons were standing at the bow of the ship when he said, "Won't be long, lass, till ye must leave us. Now's the time to be tellin' Cap'n of yer love."

"Nay," she replied. "I couldn't bear to face him. My thanks be to you and all you have done for me. I can't ever thank you enough for taking care of me that terrible night when I almost froze."

"Marty, I can't be keepin' the truth from ye any longer. 'Twas not me, but Cap'n who took care of ye."

"The captain?" Meghan reeled from the shock.

Simmons nodded his head.

"Then he has known the truth all this time?"

Again Simmons nodded his head.

"And he hasn't cared enough to mention it to me?"

"'Tis that sorry I be, lass," Simmons said, vowing to himself that the first thing in the morning, he would see the captain.

ᕱᕒ

TRUE TO HIS vow, the next morning Simmons found himself in front of the captain's quarters. He straightened his shoulders and knocked upon the door. "Cap'n, might I speak with ye?" he asked he entered.

Nathaniel looked into the pale face of the man standing so ill at ease in front of him. Alarmed, he asked, "Cookie, are you ill?"

"Nay, Cap'n, 'tis not me I worry 'bout."

"Then, who?" came the response.

"'Tis Marty, Cap'n."

A shadow crossed the captain's features. "Is she ill?"

"Nay, Cap'n. Not in the way ye mean."

Nathaniel rose and stood looking out of the porthole; the sea ever rolling; the sunlight reflected from off the water, blinding.

"Go on, Cookie. Say what you came to say."

"She be knowin' 'twas ye that saved 'er. I told 'er so."

"I asked you not to," Nathaniel said.

"I know ye did, Cap'n, but she be hurtin' so. She loves ye. I only spoke me mind in 'opes she'd tell ye so. She's feelin' mighty bad thinkin' ye know who she be and 'aven't gone to 'er. She want's to leave the STAR and go 'ome."

Nathaniel turned to face the other man.

"Is there anything else you wish to say?" Nathaniel asked.

"Cap'n, ye'll not be lettin' 'er go without tellin' 'er of yer love? Nay, Cap'n, ye can't be doin' such a thing."

Nathaniel looked intently at his friend and cook.

"You may leave now, and do not tell her of this visit."

"I won't be doin' that, Cap'n. 'Twould only 'urt 'er more."

Two days later the schooner SEA WITCH was spotted. Haws sent a boat out to stop her and to obtain passage for Meghan. With a heavy heart she dressed for the last time as Marty Ryan. Once aboard the SEA WITCH, she would revert back to being Meghan McGonigal of Ireland.

Meghan came on deck and quickly said her good-byes to the crew. She could not afford for it to be lengthy, she must get away before the dam of tears were released. She could not bear to see the crew's reaction to such a show of emotion. Meghan had hoped to get a glimpse of the captain before leaving. She had asked his whereabouts and was told he was charting the course to Nantucket. Heartsick, she climbed down the rope ladder into the waiting boat. The men did not lower the oars, they sat as if waiting for another passenger. Then it happened. Another trunk was taken aboard and then she saw the long legs of the captain step into the boat and sit beside her.

"Well, Marty," he said, starting a conversation with her. "I see you are homeward bound."

"Aye, Cap'n, I am," she said, trying to keep the tears in check. "And where are you going?"

He smiled down at her. "I have a package to deliver."

"Ready, Cap'n?" one of the men asked.

"Row, away," he replied. The men lowered their oars into the sea and rowed toward the waiting schooner.

Meghan cleared the lump in her throat.

"After you deliver the package, you'll be returning to Nantucket? With tears streaming down her face, she turned her head away from his view.

"Marty, are you crying because you'll miss the STAR and her crew?

If so, do not feel badly. I've seen grown men weep when a hunt is over and the men say their final farewells. On a whaling ship, each man has to rely on another for his very existence. They grow very close in friendship."

Meghan could not speak, and they rode the rest of the way in silence. After climbing aboard the schooner, her things were brought up and she followed the steward to her cabin.

"Why didn't I tell him the truth?" Meghan sobbed, sprawling across the bed. "Now, I'll never see him again. Not that he cares! Oh, why did I ever have to fall in love with such a callused man?"

A tap came on the door. Meghan opened it, expecting to see the steward and gasped when she saw Nathaniel in the doorway.

"What are you doing here? I thought you would have returned to the STAR by now."

"May I come in?" he asked.

"Of course," she replied with a shaky voice.

"How do you like your quarters?" he asked, stepping inside the room.

"'Tis fine," she answered, her eyes downcast.

"Much better than the STAR could provide?"

Her eyes blazed. "I loved the STAR. And I'll be missing her something fierce."

"Will ye now?" A smile played about the corners of his mouth.

"You're making fun of me. Nay, Cap'n, 'tis not worthy of you."

He ignored her outburst. "It's a trifle warm, and you are still in a heavy coat.

Do you need assistance in taking it off?"

Remembering she had not bound herself, she flushed red. "I'm just fine," she told him.

"Sit down, Marty, you look faint." He brought a chair and sat down; his long legs straddled the seat. He removed his pipe from his coat, putting it between his strong teeth without lighting it.

"What will you be doing now that you are no longer a whaling-man?" he asked.

"I . . . . I . . . hadn't thought that far ahead," Meghan replied going to the door. "Best be getting off," she said, opening the door.

He lit his pipe. "I'm in no hurry," he told her.

Nathaniel rose from the chair to stand in front of her.

"Is there nothing you wish to tell me?"

Meghan stood mute.

"If that is the case, I'll be saying good day to you."

Meghan leaned against the closed door with her eyes closed and tears rolling down her cheeks. Why hadn't she been able to find the words to tell him who she was? Now, he was gone and the opportunity for such a confession was forever lost to her. She left the door and tossed her cap and coat on top of the bed. She opened her trunk and took the brush to her tangled hair.

A knock summoned her to the door. "Who is it?" she asked in a clear voice.

"A tub and bathing water," was the reply.

Meghan hurried into the little alcove where the chamber pot reposed.

"Enter," she called out.

The door opened. She heard the pouring of water, and then heard the door closing. She came out of hiding and saw a full length-bathing receptacle. She trailed her fingers along the water's edge. It was perfect. She dipped into one of her canvas bags and brought out her hidden soft underwear. Next came a heavy wrapped package. She removed the paper and shook loose the satin folds of the emerald dress that had been made for her from the exquisite material young Elizabeth had given her aboard the schooner, oh, so many years ago. It now joined her other finery lying across the bed.

Meghan found a wooden screen and placed it between the tub and the rest of the room. Once her clothes were removed, she slipped into the tub, the warm water caressing her body. She fell asleep, for how long she could not even guess. The water was cool; she was shivering; and the ship was moving. THE SHIP WAS MOVING! Meghan leaped from the tub. Water splashed over onto the floor, but she took no heed. She dashed to the porthole and saw that they were moving away from the whaling ship. The STAR had unfurled its sails and was racing away; taking her love with it. Slowly Meghan dried off her shivering body. She was about to dress when a knock came at the door. A deep voice spoke through the closed door.

"Miss McGonigal, the Captain would like to have you join him for dinner."

The Captain? If only it was her captain and not the captain of the schooner, her answer would have been different.

"I'm tired," she told the door. "I don't feel up to eating."

Still undressed, Meghan laid on the bed for some time before the name she had been called registered with her.

"Miss McGonigal. Was that the name he called me? How did he know?"

Her mind cleared.

"It must have been on the request Haws sent over for my passage. Of course, that had to be it. He knew that I wasn't going to remain a boy on the trip to Ireland."

An exhausted sleep soon had her in its power.

When Meghan awakened, the tub was gone and in its place were a lace-covered table and a placing for two. Leaning against a glass was a card stating: *The Captain will be joining you in an hour.*

So some stranger had taken upon himself to be host for the evening meal, she thought. Well, stranger or not, she could not face him dressed only in a towel. Standing in front of a full-length mirror that she had not noticed before, Meghan arranged her hair with one long curl escaping the upsweep to caress her slender throat and golden shoulder. Dipping into the small bottle of perfume made from crushed flowers, she ran her wet fingers down the sides of her neck to the hollow of her throat, then down her arms to her wrists. With the sweet smell, she thought herself back on Maui.

A light knock, the door opened and a man stepped inside the room.

"Miss McGonigal, may I present the Captain."

A tall, lean form appeared in the doorway. Meghan gasped as Nathaniel came in. The other man quietly left the room.

" I . . . I . . . thought you had left." sobbed Meghan.

Nathaniel pulled her into his arms. He kissed her eyelids and tasted her tears.

"Don't cry, my darling."

"Did you say . . . my darling?"

"I did. Oh, Marty, girl, haven't you guessed how very much you mean to me?"

"How could I? You never said one word about caring for me. Cookie told me it was you that pulled me from the sea and spent the night warming me. You knew who I was and yet you said nothing."

"Be reasonable. How was I to know that the raven haired girl on Maui was one Marty Ryan, a red-headed lad from Ireland? The facts seemed to be that it was the lad Marty, and not my witch of the pool, that tended my fever. I had fallen in love with that girl on Maui. Later I found myself drawn to the lad, and when I found out that lad was you, I still didn't know you were the one of my dreams. Not until Cookie told me the truth."

"But that was over a year ago. You could have said something then."

"Could I be less strong than you? It was a decision you made with Haws, and I felt honor bound to accept it. But we are no longer under that vow. We have no one now to consider but ourselves."

Meghan could not believe what was happening to her. He was kissing her and awaking emotions she never knew existed.

"Cap'n," she moaned. "'Tis not right to be making me feel this way."

Nathaniel removed his lips from the hollow of her throat.

"Oh, Marty Girl. I love you more than life itself. I have loved you and only you since the day at the pool when you saved my life. It was only after talking with Cookie that I realized you and she were one and the same. Tell me, do you love me?"

"I love you, Captain, with all my heart," she assured him.

The words were simple, yet they struck his heart as a bolt of lightning and he looked deeply into her eyes. He entwined his fingers in the strands of her hair, knocking the pins to the floor.

Her pulse beat with the sounds of drums. Never had she been without control, and now, all she had was slipping away. She wrapped her arms about his neck, pulling him down to her. He responded with a passion to match her own.

Suddenly Meghan struggled to free herself.

"I can't be doing it, Captain. I can't be giving myself to you in such a reckless moment. Nay, Captain, 'tis married first we must be."

He raised his head, "I've all ready spoken with the Captain Miller. He has the power to marry us, and will do so tomorrow." He lowered his head once more, his lips softly caressing the hollow of her slender throat.

"Captain, please stop." Meghan moaned.

"Nathaniel," he whispered, not stopping his delicate quest, "my name is Nathaniel, Marty Girl."

With all her strength, she pushed him from her.

"No more till we're wed, Nathaniel. And my name is Meghan."

"Meghan! Aye, 'tis a name of beauty, but for me, you will always be my Marty Girl. Give me another kiss and I'll go fetch the captain to wed us, now."

"Nay! You have to ask my father first."

"WHAT!" he exploded.

"It would not be proper to marry without his consent."

"So we must wait?" He sat on the edge of the bed. "Do you realize it will take weeks and weeks before we reach your home? Beloved, we have waited so long to become as one, please don't be asking me to wait any longer."

"Tis as long for me, my darling," Meghan whispered. "But it has to be proper."

"If that is your wish, I'll not force myself on you."

He left the bed, retrieved his coat from the floor and had his hand on the handle of the door when she called out to him.

"Nathaniel, are you leaving, now?"

He turned to face her. "I'm afraid to stay."

Reaching out to him, she whispered, "Nathaniel, hold me."

"I want to, my darling, more than I've wanted any thing, but first I must find the Captain."

Chapter Twenty-Four

❧

When the SEA WITCH landed in Ireland, Nathaniel rented a coach in the village of Kilcrohane and soon they were on their way. Meghan could hardly sit still.

"We're almost home," she said excitingly. "Oh, I can hardly wait to have you meet me mum and da."

"How will you break the news that we have all ready wed?" asked Nathaniel with a twinkle in his eyes.

"It's that relieved they'll be knowing that we've not been living in sin."

His face sobered. "Can you call our love a thing of sin?"

"Nay, beloved, not our love." she assured him. "but if the marriage vows were not spoken, the bedding would be."

Stopping the carriage, Nathaniel took Meghan into his arms. "Since we were married that first night, the matter does not concern us." He kissed her soundly, then once again took the reins. "Marty Girl, I never realized how very beautiful your Ireland is."

Meghan laughed. "Now what will me mum and da be thinking

when they hear you call me Marty Girl? Nathaniel, you best be remembering to call me Meghan."

"To me you shall always be my Marty Girl. However, while we are here, I shall try to remember to call you Meghan." He paused. "There is something I wish to say before we see your parents. If you leave with me to live on Nantucket, the chances are very slim that you will ever return. I want you to be very sure of your decision."

Meghan touched his face ever so gently. "You are my husband, Nathaniel. My home is wherever you are.

Nathaniel raised her hand to his lips and tenderly kissed the gold band around her slim finger. "Mistress Lathrope, I love you with all the breath in my body."

Reaching the stone fence by the cottage, Meghan asked Nathaniel to stop the horses, and he complied. "There's 'Old Woolly'," she cried out. "Do you think he'll still remember me?"

"Marty Girl. Meghan, how could anyone or anything once they have met you, ever forget you."

"Oh, Nathaniel, I'm thinking there's a bit of blarney in you."

Before he could take her in his arms, Meghan jumped down and ran to the gate, flinging it open. The ram looked up from his munching and stared at her; then came running. With a cry of delight, Meghan threw her arms about his thick, shaggy neck. "Oh, you do remember your little Meghan after all these years."

Kathleen McGonigal was pulling a pail of water up from the well when she heard the carriage approaching. "John!" she called. "'Tis Meghan, home at last."

"Our colleen be home!" John took his wife into an embrace. A shadow crossed his features. "Do ye think she'll be forgivin' me?"

Kathleen smiled. "I have. Can she be doin' less?" The couple stood together as they waited for the carriage to stop. When the passengers stepped down, Kathleen cried, tears flowing from her eyes. "Oh, John. Our Meghan is no longer a child, but a woman grown."

Meghan ran to her mother, throwing herself into the woman's arms. "Mum! Oh, Mum! I'm home."

Tears were also streaming down her father's face as he took her into his arms. "Can ye ever be forgivin' the terrible wrong that forced ye to run away from all ye held dear?" he asked, trembling as he waited for the answer.

"'Tis but a fleeting memory," Meghan assured him, returning his embrace.

Then holding out her hand to Nathaniel, continued, "Mum, Da, I want you to meet m'man. Captain Nathaniel Lathrope of the whaling ship MORNING STAR. And he be worth all the heartaches of the past."

"Aye," exclaimed her father. "'Tis that glad I be in knowin' ye." The men shook hands, Nathaniel bowed to her mother. "And," continued Meghan's father, "our heartfelt thanks for sendin' word ahead of yer arrival. I don't believe my dear Katie, could have stood the shock of seein' Meghan without bein' warned of yer comin'."

Meghan looked up at Nathaniel. "You sent word? Oh, Nathaniel, how grand you are. And me not even thinking of it." She thought for a moment. "But when did you send the message?"

"While you were shopping, beloved. I also told them of our marriage."

Meghan quickly looked at her parents. "Are you angry because we didn't wait to be married here, all proper in the church?"

Kathleen smiled. "I'm thinkin' it be a wise decision, not to wait."

Meghan blushed. "I bought some dresses for you, Mum and a coat and pipe for you, Da."

"I can hardly wait to be seein' them," Kathleen assured her, "As for now, the sup be waitin'."

Meghan hurried off with her mother while the two men unloaded the carriage. Meghan stepped through the opened door. Somehow the room seemed smaller than she had remembered and there was a feeling in the air that she couldn't quite understand, yet she knew it was something she had experienced before. But the smell of baking bread was an aroma that she could never forget.

"Fresh bread," Meghan exclaimed, going into the kitchen. "Oh, how I have longed to smell and taste your bread." Meghan broke off a piece and popped it into her mouth. She savored the taste.

Kathleen hugged her. "Oh, 'tis that grand to have ye home, me darlin'. Tell me, true. Are ye as happy as ye look and sound?"

"Aye, that I am. Oh, Mum, there is so much to be telling."

"The tellin' can be waitin'," boomed her father, coming into the room with packages in his arms. He turned to Nathaniel. "Ye both must be starving."

Nathaniel laughed. "I wasn't until I smelled the bread."

"Let's be sittin' down," said John, leading the way to the table.

During a lull in the conversation, Meghan asked, "Where are Gavin and Julianne?

Am I not to see them?"

"'Tis more the pity," remarked her mother. "They left for Dublin before the message of yer comin' arrived, but they'll be home by week's end. Can ye be stayin' till then?

If the answer be aye, ye are more than welcome."

"Can we, Nathaniel?" inquired Meghan.

"We can," was the instant reply.

The rest of the evening was spent discussing the past years of being apart. Meghan told them all about her life as a whaling man. They asked a lot of questions until it was apparent to everyone that Meghan could no longer keep her eyes opened.

"My wife has had a long and exciting day," said Nathaniel.

"Aye," agreed her mother. "'Tis best we all be off to bed."

Meghan took Nathaniel's hand. "My room is beyond the hearth," she said, leading him to her room.

With Nathaniel standing in the center of the bedroom, the room seemed very small, indeed. The bed was clearly not large enough for the two of them, nor was it anywhere near the length Nathaniel would need.

"Come," he said, lifting Meghan up over the windowsill; then taking several blankets with him, he followed her out. "Lead the way to the barn," he told her. "We'll spend the night there."

John McGonigal stood by the open window in his bedroom. He motioned for Kathleen to join him, just as the young couple ran into the barn.

"'Tis late with the milkin', I'll be," he said.

John turned to see the moonlight bath his 'Katie' in its glow. "Ye look like a young bride, yerself," he said, kissing her tenderly.

"I feel like a bride," she replied, taking his hand in hers as they returned to their own bed.

Nathaniel and Meghan climbed the loft where he spread one of the thick quilts on fresh hay. He tucked the quilts under the hay; then pulled Meghan down to him.

"Oh, Marty Girl, my life did not begin until we wed."

It was late the next morning, when Nathaniel and Meghan entered the cottage. Her parents were sitting at the table. Kathleen rose to greet them.

"'Tis hungry ye both must be. Now, be sittin' down and I'll be dishin' it up."

Meghan started to help her mother. "Be ye sittin' down," her father said. "There's things to be said between ye and me."

"Please, Da," Meghan pleaded. "Don't be thinking more about it. 'Tis in the past, so be letting it die." Meghan looked at Nathaniel for support; it was not given.

"Meghan," he said "a man must rid himself of guilt, or he is no more a man, but a thing to be pitied. Do you want that for your father?"

"My thanks be to ye," McGonigal said. "And never were truer words spoken."

After breakfast Meghan and her father left the cottage to find a shady spot under a spreading tree. They talked for over an hour before Nathaniel joined them; then Meghan returned alone to the cottage.

In the early afternoon Meghan took Nathaniel horseback riding, over the glen.

"Where does this Squire O'Shea live:?" he asked.

"Just over the next rise," she told him. Then she looked intently at him. "Why do you want to know?" she asked.

"I thought I might have a word or two with the man."

"Oh, Nathaniel. There mustn't be trouble to weary me mum and da after we leave."

Nathaniel laughed.

"And what trouble could come with two sensible men just talking? You just point out the place to me, and I'll go by and see him before we leave."

"He is a big man, Nathaniel, and a mean one at that."

Nathaniel laughed again.

"'Tis not a laughing matter," Meghan told him.

"Beloved," he replied. "Don't you know by now that I can take care of myself?"

"Aye, but ye'll be fighting fair. Not so with the squire."

"Now," Nathaniel replied, "who said a thing about fighting?"

"Promise me, there won't be any trouble."

"Now, Marty Girl, show me where you stood on the cliff and wondered about the passing ships." The rest of the day was spent introducing Nathaniel to her friends and showing him all the places that meant so much to her as a young girl.

The next morning Meghan awoke to find herself alone in the loft. She quickly dressed and climbed down the ladder. Nathaniel was nowhere in sight. She hurried into the cottage and sought her mother.

"Mum," she asked. "Have ye seen m'man?"

"I saw him speakin' with yer da a bit ago."

"Maybe they went off together," reasoned Meghan.

"Aye, they probably did just that." Kathleen smiled.

"Come, and sit beside me," Kathleen said, indicating space on the settle. "We haven't had a chance to talk alone."

Once seated, Meghan inquired, "Mum, do ye like m'man?"

"Aye, I do. And yer da be likin' him, too."

"Mum," Meghan asked, "what made da change back to the man he was?"

"He didn't speak of it yesterday?" asked her mother.

"He asked me to forgive him for the past, and to speak of it to you."

Neither heard the door open until John spoke out, "I've been a foolish man. I believed the lies of my brother and his words haunted me for years; then the words in me ears stopped ringin', that is, until I took ye ridin' in the cart I labored for ye. Be ye rememberin' it?"

Meghan nodded, and he continued, "'Twas after ye wrote from

the island that the hurtin' came out in the open."

"I remember it as if it were yesterday," Kathleen said as she relived the incident afresh.

Kathleen was once again at the kitchen sink and McGonigal stood behind her with a letter in his hand.

"And who might this be from?" he demanded.

"'Tis a letter from Meghan," Kathleen replied.

McGonigal threw it down on the table, it slipped to the floor. Kathleen hurried to retrieve the precious letter. "Do you want to be hearin' for yerself what she had to say?"

"I not be carin', and that's the truth of it," he told her.

"John, she be yer own child, and she's so very far from home."

"Me own? Let there be no more lies betwixt us," McGonigal snorted. "I be knowin' the truth all these years. She be no more mine than Gavin; they both came from the loins of me brother David."

Kathleen gripped the corner of the counter. Her face draining of color. "What nonsense be ye speakin'?"

"Nonsense is it? I heard the truth from David's own lips."

"And what truth might that be?" Kathleen demanded.

"He came to me on our weddin' night, and he said he had taken your innocence and that I was welcome to the spoils."

Kathleen gasped, "And if ye believed it, why did you take me to wife?"

"I married ye because I be lovin' ye so, and all the time the both of ye were laughin' at me."

Kathleen stared at her husband. "Ye, yerself, saw the spots of me virtue."

"Aye, ye fooled me, right enough." McGonigal moved away from her. "I tried to drive the truth from me mind, but it came back when

Gavin arrived early. Ye convinced me that because of yer fall, he came ahead of his time."

"'Tis the truth yer speakin'," Kathleen told him. "Ye be knowin' it yerself, the doctor told ye so."

"Ye convinced him of yer lie, but ye did not fool me. And ye allowed David to take ye again and father Meghan."

"By all that's Holy, 'tis not true. Not one word of it," argued Kathleen.

"Don't be addin' blasphemy to yer sins," he cautioned.

"'I haven't sinned," replied his wife.

"Katie, why keep up the lie? I saw ye with me own eyes enter the barn minutes after David. For five years we had no other but Gavin, then just nine months after ye saw David, ye have Meghan. Do ye think me a fool?"

"A fool? Nay! But a foolish man ye be and prove it, I can." Kathleen went to their bedroom. When she returned, there was a yellowed piece of paper in her hand. "Read it and be prayin' for forgiveness."

McGonigal took the paper from his wife's hand, and slowly began to read its contents.

April 22nd

And I take paper in hand to write a few words to you, dear Kathleen. I would give anything if you were here beside me, instead of hundreds of miles away. Oh, me darling, it was more thnt I could bear to keep from taking you into me arms and kissing your sweet lips after you bandaged my wounds. But your words stopped me cold. A wee one in the basket, you said, and I knew you could never be mine.

"From what I've been told, John cares little for his son. If I had fought for you, Gavin would have been ours instead of my brother's. I did a terrible

wrong to me brother and told him some lies. But after all these years, I don't suppose it matters.

"I'm mending my wounds, but I can never come back, for my identity be known. All that keeps me going is the hope that what I do is just. Remember always, my beloved, that I love you, and if you ever need me, I'll be sending someone to bring you to me."

David

McGonigal put the paper aside. He put his hands on Kathleen's shoulders and looked deeply into her eyes. "Be this letter true?" All Kathleen could do was nod.

McGonigal released her and sank into a chair, his head in his hands. After a space of time, he looked up, staring into her pale face.

"Can ye ever be forgivin' me for the foul things I've done and said?" he begged.

Kathleen cupped his face with her hands.

"John, if only ye had come to me long ago, we could have been spared so many years of pain."

McGonigal stood. Kathleen went into his arms. It had taken time for the wounds to heal, and when they did, a letter was sent to bring Meghan home.

Meghan had listened to her parents' story with tears streaming down her face. So many things now made sense to her. That is, all except what happened the day he destroyed her cart. When she mentioned it, her father explained it to her.

"The blasted woman asked me if I had ever noticed that ye looked just like my younger brother David. It was too much for me. I went crazy and that's the truth of that."

"Da, how could you have believed those lies?"

"I knew my brother a lot longer than I had known yer mum. I believed his lies."

"'Tis all in the past," Kathleen interjected. "Let's not be spoilin' the day in a burst of rememberin' the past."

"Aye," agreed John, "and what a grand day 'tis." He looked about the room. "Where is Nathaniel? Not still sleepin', is he?"

"Nay, he left before I woke. I thought he might be with you." Meghan said.

"Wherever he might be," Kathleen said, "he's bound to be hungry when he comes."

"Hello, am I too late to break the fast with my new family?" Nathaniel asked, coming into the cottage.

Seeing him, McGonigal smiled and declared, "Just in time. Katie has been planning this meal ever since we got your message."

Thick slices of beef and an ample supply of coddled eggs with plenty of fresh bread, butter and homemade jam were placed on the table in front of the two men. The two women joined them and it wasn't long until the platters were clean.

"Mrs. McGonigal," said a contented Nathaniel, "that was, by far, the finest meal I have ever eaten."

"He be right, ye know," Meghan's father answered, "She be the best cook in all the glen." Thus saying he motioned for Nathaniel to follow him outside for a smoke and conversation while the dishes were cleared away.

The following week seemed a fleeting moment as old acquaintances were renewed and the McGonigal family was reunited. Gavin and Julieanne came to visit, and there was many a tale to repeat. Gavin told Meghan about their father's visit to him and he had asked for forgiveness for the things that had happened between them. McGonigal had given Gavin his birthright and the young couple had settled on the land west of the meadow. They had built themselves a home and were very happy, especially with the coming birth of their first child.

⟨♋⟩

NATHANIEL DISLIKED TAKING Meghan away from her family after so short a visit, but they had to return to Nantucket as soon as possible. The carriage was loaded, and Nathaniel asked McGonigal to join him for a short walk while Meghan said her final good-byes to her mother and brother. Once out of earshot, Nathaniel handed McGonigal a packet of papers.

"What's this?" asked McGonigal, taking the papers and looking through them.

"The ownership of the grounds once held by Squire O'Shea and promised to you. We had a chat and he was most anxious for you to obtain the land."

"No, I couldn't possibly own it now. It holds a bitter memory of how I treated me wee child."

"Then the bad memory must be wiped away, and replaced with the truth that if it weren't for the land, I would not have met your daughter. Mr. McGonigal, my life was incomplete until Meghan became a part of it. I obtained this land and now give it to you as a gesture of my eternal gratitude that she is now my wife."

"I heard a rumor that O'Shea had an accident a day or two past; he has a black eye and swollen lips. He claimed to have tripped and fallen in a rock field. Be ye knowin' a thing or two about that?" inquired McGonigal.

"I know nothing about a rock field," Nathaniel assured his father-in-law with a twinkle in his eyes.

The men returned to the conveyance. Nathaniel helped Meghan to sit down; then with the reins in his capable hands and a final wave good-bye, they were on their way. "Are you content to leave, my darling," Nathaniel asked, kissing her on the forehead. "Are there no regrets?"

"I'm content, Nathaniel. I can leave Ireland knowing all is well with my family," she assured him.

Chapter Twenty-Five

꩜

Nathaniel and his bride boarded on the WILLA MAE just minutes before it disembarked and before dark made the rendezvous with the MORNING STAR. Meghan, attired in a lovely peach silk gown, covered by a wine colored cloak and bonnet, sat in the wooden chair while it was being pulled aboard her husband's ship. Haws and Cookie had already informed the men of the true identity of one Marty Ryan who was now their captain's bride, and they nervously awaited the arrival.

Once aboard, the men offered their best wishes to the couple for a long and happy marriage. Their anxiousness was apparent to Meghan.

"Please," she begged. "don't be treating me any different than before. I'm the same as I once was."

Nathaniel stepped forward. "No, Mistress Lathrope, you are not the same as before. The men know it, and so must you." He turned to face them. "I know it will be hard on you to remember she is no longer Marty Ryan but your Captain's Lady." He smiled, but the smile could not be contained and he began to laugh. The men looked at each other, but none spoke. "It was even hard for me to learn, but learn it

I did," Nathaniel continued. The men nudged one another; Meghan blushed; and the tension was broken.

With a roar of approval from the men, Nathaniel swept Meghan into his powerful arms and carried her down the ladder into his quarters. Meghan had been there before, but under very different circumstances, also it was at night then and now the sunlight streamed in through the portholes. The bed was large enough for the both of them. Through the connecting doors Meghan could see Nathaniel's cabin where he studied his charts and kept his journals. Down the passageway was the salon where she would be eating her meals with her husband and officers. It was not a great amount of space, but she rationalized, there was the whole ship at her disposal.

Sensing her thoughts, Nathaniel put her down. "Meghan, love, the rest of the ship is now off limits to you."

"You can't be meaning I can only have these rooms? Oh, Nathaniel, that is far too cruel," she said with trembling lips, remembering her time on the schooner going to Maui. "I would die without the sun upon me and the wind in my hair."

"I'll have a small place fixed under the bridge where you may sit and watch the sea." He saw the look on her face and held her in his arms. "Marty Girl, it is a hard life for the captain's lady aboard ship. That is why so few wives travel with their husbands. They stay at home to raise their children."

"That's what I'll be doing?"

"That is something we don't have to decide now," he said, untying her cloak and hanging it and her bonnet on a clothes hook. "Can I help you change?"

"Nathaniel! The men?" she gasped as he lifted her into his arms and carried her to the bed.

He kissed her tenderly. "You were saying?"

She was silent.

❧

THE NEXT DAY as the sun's rays burst through the overhead glass window and lit upon Nathaniel's hand, Meghan could clearly see the scar; it commenced at the tips of his fingers and traveled up the palm to his wrist. He woke to find her staring down at it.

"Not a very pretty sight for a young bride," he said pulling her down to him. "Come, give me a kiss."

She wiggled closer to him, welcoming his lips searing onto her own. When the kiss ended, she reached out and took his hand. "Does it still pain you?" she asked him, quietly.

"Sometimes, when I tire," he admitted.

"Cookie told me some of the story," she admitted. "Will you tell me about it?"

"Are you sure you want to hear it? It was not a time of my life when there was much joy."Nathaniel stared up through the skylight. Overhead, white clouds swirled though a field of bright blue. The ship was quiet. All about was peace and tranquillity, however, his heart pounded with the hatred he still harbored deep within his restless soul.

Meghan felt the tension and did not break the silence. She waited for him to begin his story. In a few moments he began to speak.

"My father was a seafaring man like myself. He was captain of his own whaling ship. He went to New Bedford to order another ship for his fleet and in the town he met my mother, Rebecca Stewart. He had been invited to attend a concert and there she was in the box across from his. They fell in love and wanted to marry, but she was under age and was forbidden to do so by her brother, William Stewart.

"They ran away and were married at sea by Captain Black. On Nantucket Island my father built a fine home for her and for the child she was to bear him. He went to sea on a hunt and left his first mate on land to take care of her and me after I was born. The man's name was Toby Hastings. My father had been gone for some months when his ship was stoved in by a whale; five lives were lost, including his. By this time my mother's brother found her and wrote she should return home, to him. She wrote back that she had promised her husband to have their child on the island and thought that had ended the matter. She was wrong in that assumption. William Stewart came and forced her from the island.

"He took her back to Stewart Hall, there she died giving birth to her son. Then, the son, I, was taken to the slave quarters and until I was five years old, I thought the slave, Mattie, was my mother. On my fifth birthday I was taken before William Stewart, my uncle, the master of Stewart Hall. He told me that I was the bastard son of a man named Jeremiah Lathrope. That Lathrope had forced himself upon his sister, my real mother, Rebecca. That Lathrope had refused to marry her and when she became with child, Lathrope abandoned her. My uncle then said my real mother had died as a result of my birth and that he wanted me to remember the cruelty of my father for the rest of my life. Then he ordered me out of the house and back to the slave quarters."

Tears streamed down Meghan's cheeks. She wished she could say or do something to take away his pain. "What happened then?" she asked, trying to keep her voice steady.

"I ran to Toby. He picked me up and held me tight. I told him what had been said and he told me the truth. I can hear his words, even now.

"'Dat's true about yer papa dying at sea, but dat's not wot killed yer dear Mama. She had promised yer papa ye wud be born on Nantucket. She begged yer uncle to let her stay til after the birthing; he refused. She showed him the wedding papers and he threw them away. But I was there when they wed. Then he made her go with him back to Virginny. Nathaniel, yer dear mama died of a broken heart.

Yer mama made me promise to help ye get back to the sea, and I thinks it's time to be doin' et.'"

"With Toby's help I did make it to Nantucket. I signed aboard the FLAGG as cabin boy under Captain Black, a dear friend of my father, and the man who married them. In the six months that I lived with the Black family, I not only learned the meaning of a mother's love, but I mastered their way of speaking. Before the ship could sail away, Stewart's men found me and dragged me back to Stewart's Hall. It was several days before I was summoned before its master who finally took the time to speak with me, and when he did, the sound of my accent drove him to the brink of madness."

"'Is it not enough,' he screeched, 'that you killed my dear sister, must you mock me with the tongue of the man who stole her and sired you?'"

"I told him that my father was a far better man than he could ever be. With a barbaric look in his eye, he grabbed my hand and held it over a fire until I lost consciousness from agony. When I came to my senses, he was bending over me.

"'Your pa,' he said, 'may he rot in hell, forced my sister to be with him and I am cursed with raising his whelp. If I ever hear you speak with his voice, I'll have your tongue struck from your body. Promise me that you'll abide my words.'

"I shook my head, and he again lowered my hand to the fire. Again and again he said the same thing and I continued to shake my head. Finally, I could bear the pain no more, I agreed to obey his wishes. That, of course, was good enough to satisfy the evil within him, and he took a whip and lashed my back. He would have killed me if one of his friends had not come upon the scene and stopped him.

"When the time came, Toby helped me to escape. This time it was successful. I sailed with Captain Black, and I have never seen Stewart again."

"And what has happened to Toby?"

"When I returned from the sea," Nathaniel said, sitting up, "I found that Stewart had found Toby and hanged him. I vowed that one day, I would return and do the same to the master of Stewart Hall."

Almost afraid to hear the answer, Meghan asked, "Will you kill him?"

Nathaniel replied. "That would be too easy. When I have the opportunity, and it is close in coming, I shall ruin him and take from him all that he holds dear. I'll leave him nothing! Then I'll hang him."

"Nathaniel, dearest," soothed Meghan. "The hate he's holding in his heart will destroy him. Even his own family must hate him for what he did to you. Killing him will only ease his pain."

Nathaniel lay down. "Only you would have thought of that. But, come, let's not spoil our time together by talking." He pulled her to him and she was lost in a haze of love.

As the days continued, the room below deck became Meghan's prison. The porthole was a narrow slit, and all Meghan could see was the sea. When it rained, which it did a great deal of the time, the water seeped down from the glass skylight and ran down the walls. Nathaniel spent as much time with her as he could and each of those moments seemed like being in heaven, but those times were rare. The little shelter on deck was even worse. She grew to hate the sea and vowed that once on land, she would never set foot on a ship again.

As Marty Ryan she had the run of the ship, as the captain's lady she was a prisoner. She would give anything to be able to climb the riggings and stand her watch in the crow's-nest. Even to help Cookie was denied her. She was treated like some fragile piece of china, and she hated it.

During her brief stays on deck, it was obvious to every man on shipboard that she was miserable. Several of the seamen approached

Haws, who in turn went to their captain. When Nathaniel faced the men, Haws said, "Cap'n, the lads be worried about yer lady. They seen 'tis a 'ard thing for 'er to be confined below deck when once she 'ad the run of the ship. They be sendin' me 'ere to ask if she be allowed such freedom, now."

Nathaniel looked into the concern faces of the men and told them to speak their minds. It was Higgins who stepped forward. "Cap'n, she should have the run of the ship. And I promise ye that she'll be treated due respect."

"It's an unusual request," said Nathaniel, "but if that is your desire, then so be it."

Meghan was delighted to hear the news. But when she wanted to dress as Marty again, Nathaniel forbade her to do so. "I wore men's clothes for a long time on this very ship," she reminded him. "Why can't I do it again?"

"On account of I say you can't. Damme, Meghan, what would the men be thinking if such a thing was permitted?"

"So 'tis Meghan, is it?" she snapped. "What happened to your 'Marty Girl'?"

He ignored her outburst. "You are my wife, and I want the men to remember that." He held his hand out to her. "Will you come on deck with me?" She turned away. "Please, don't fight me on this. Believe me when I say it is best for the ship if you always dress as my lady." She did not answer. Nathaniel opened the door and left.

Some time later, Simmons knocked on the door, and Meghan let him in. Seeing the tray of food, she commented. "I'm not hungry."

"Ye best be eatin' somethin'," he said, putting the tray on the table.

"Oh, Cookie," she sobbed. "He won't let me dress as I did before."

"Yer not as before. Ye be the Cap'n's lady and ye must act the part."

"He is m'man, Cookie. He is not my master."

"'Board this ship, he be. Ah, can't ye be seein' if a wife's not willin' to obey the Cap'n's laws, 'ow can 'is men be expected to obey?" Thus saying, Simmons left the cabin.

For some time Meghan did not move; then a smile blossomed in her eyes and around her mouth. Nathaniel was her life. What did it really matter to her how she dressed, but if it was important to Nathaniel, it would be important to her. She put on a pink dress of muslin. The full skirt falling just above her ankles, the blouse was draping gently across her shoulders. She brushed her thick hair until it shone. After arranging it in a becoming style, she went on deck to find her husband. He was speaking to Haws and turned as she approached. Her heart leaped when she saw his expression was not of a gloating nature, but one of love and devotion.

He raised her fingers to his lips, sending quivering sensations spiraling up her arms. "I worship you, my lady," he whispered, heard by her alone.

"And I, you," she whispered back.

He took her arm, "Come," he said, "and walk around the deck with me."

Chapter Twenty-Six

Nathaniel's days were filled with his duties, while his nights were spent with his beloved Marty Girl. Up till this time, he had not been able to bring himself to describe his homeland to her. It would be a shock to her, he knew, after living in the green field of Ireland, and those years in the tropical garden of Maui, to see his barren island. However, the time had come when he could no longer put off the telling. He handed the watch over to Haws and went below. He found Meghan lying on the bed, looking up at the blue sky.

She smiled as he entered the cabin. "Come, lie with me," she said, holding her hand toward him.

He lay beside her. "Are you still happy being my bride?" he asked her, a somber look in his expression.

"Happier than I can be saying," she replied.

A knock came at the door, and a voice called out, "Cap'n ye asked to be told when land's sighted." The voice went away.

Meghan jumped from the bed. "Oh, Nathaniel. Is my new home so very near?"

"Wait! There's something I must tell you about Nantucket."

For an instant the alarm in his voice startled her. "You don't have another wife awaiting your arrival, do you?" she asked part in jest and part in apprehension.

The question stopped him. "No, of course not."

"That's good, " she remarked as she opened the door and listened to the watch.

"'LAND HO! LAND TO THE LEE SIDE."

"Nathaniel! 'Tis my new home to be seeing," and she ran out the door and went up the ladder, without waiting for her husband.

"Wait," he hollered, but she was already gone.

Meghan was staring at the island when Nathaniel came to stand beside her. "Oh, Nathaniel, where are the rolling hills and the beautiful green trees? I see nothing except sand and barren waste." She looked at him and was surprised by his expression of love and pride in his eyes. She wondered how he could love such a desolate place. Yet, he loved it. There was no doubt in her mind about that! And, she decided, if he saw beauty there, well then, so would she; although she had to admit it might take some doing. Meghan took his hand in hers. "I love you Captain Lathrope; your homeland is now mine, and I'll be growing to love it, too."

He squeezed her hand. "There is beauty here, Marty Girl. Look at the vivid blue sky with it's fleecy, white clouds. Now, look toward the bay. See the ships anchored there? And over to the right, see those ships sailing in while others are sailing out? There is life and excitement here.

"It's true we are just a speck in the vast ocean, yet what we do has changed the course of the world. If it wasn't for the men who go to sea and face the danger of life and death, there would be no candles or oil to fills the lamps to light the cottages of the people, nor medicine for the sick. Despite the necessity of oil there is always the feeling of sorrow for the killing of the whales. Those gallant beasts of the sea are honored by the men who must destroy them, and are respected by those same men for their valiant fight for life. Never is a whale killed for the joy of killing. As soon as our barrels are filled, the hunt is over and we return home.

"As for the men, they are living the life the Almighty has chosen for them. They live with courageous and noble hearts. Their women are as stalwart as the men. For they must watch their loved ones leave, not knowing when or if they shall see them once again. They give their men the peace of mind they need, knowing their wives are at home and watching over the spirits that God has given them to raise. It is truly hard on a woman. The strong will survive; the weak will leave. But who can blame them if they do? Not even their husbands say naught against them."

Their conversation was getting far too serious for Meghan. She did not want to think about the sea, death, nor the sadness it brought. It was a beautiful day, and her man was standing beside her. "Was the island always barren?" she asked, looking once again to the sandy rock before them.

"No," he replied. "There was a time when the land was full of tall grass and majestic trees. Animals were abundant and ran free. Men came from the mainland to hunt. The Indians that were living here were a friendly lot and welcomed them.

"Then it was discovered that meat could be stored without spoiling, if it was covered with salt, and the ocean was abundant with that product."

"But how did they get the salt from the water?" Meghan asked.

"That was soon figured out. The seawater was put into buckets and brought to a boil over a wood fire. And on the island wood was abundant. Over the following forty years trees were cut down to produce those fires. When the trees and bushes were gone, grass was pulled out by their roots and burned. At that time no one thought to replant, and now there is nothing left."

Nathaniel wrapped his arms about her slim waist. "I did not know how to tell you this before. I love you and was afraid if you knew the truth; you might not come with me. And I would have died of a shattered heart if you had let me go without you."

Her eyes shone bright through her tears. "Nothing really matters, except our love and being together." She smiled. "Even this is better than being married to the Reverend or the Squire." She thought he would see the jest, and was not prepared for the hard, cold look that came over his handsome countenance.

"Did you marry me only to get away from those men?" he demanded.

"Oh, Nathaniel. I spoke only in jest," she assured him. "Please, take me into your arms and say all is forgiven."

He locked her into an embrace. "Never tease about our love," he whispered against her hair.

"I promise I'll never be doing it again," Meghan sobbed.

Haws joined them at the railing. "Cap'n," he said, "'tis time to be leavin'. Yer trunks are in the longboat."

Nathaniel took Meghan's arm and led her to the boat. The crane cranked the boat over the side and into the calm water. Once on shore, the men took out the luggage and placed it in a waiting wagon, then the crew hurried off to greet their waiting families. Nathaniel and Meghan walked up the path leading from the beach to a bluff overlooking the sea. From this rise, Meghan caught sight of the hundreds of whaling ships anchored on the opposite side of the island. Behind them the STAR looked like a lone sentinel.

"I own this part of the island," he told her. "And over there on that rise, I shall build you a grand home. The home my father built for my mother was burned down by her brother, William Stewart."

"At least, we won't be having anything spoiling our view of the sea," Meghan said, smiling once again.

A turn in the lane and she could see the village. "Oh, how grand. Never have I seen the likes. Nathaniel, why do the houses have porches on the roof?"

"Those homes belong to the captains' families. The porches are called 'Widows' Walk.'" He did not look at her as he continued speaking. "That is where the wives stand to watch for their husbands' ships to return."

Knowing he would have to leave her soon, she blurted out, "When will you be leaving?"

"Not for a long time," he assured her. "And not until I build you your own 'Widows' Walk.'"

"How long will you be gone on the next hunt?" Meghan asked, not really wanting to hear the answer.

"I don't rightly know. We'll return when the cargo is full."

The thundering waves crashed onto the rocks below and began what was to be their chant over the coming years. "He's mine! He's mine!" Meghan covered her ears, trying to keep from hearing the words.

Nathaniel held her close, stroking her hair. "I won't be leaving for a long, long, time," he assured her.

Meghan snuggled closer to him. Here she was making them both miserable long before the time of his leaving. "I won't be thinking such thoughts again," she responded. She took a deep breath. "Now, let's be looking at where we'll be living."

Nathaniel took her to his cabin made of logs he had shipped there from New York. Upon entering, Meghan could see everything needed a good sweeping and washing. It was a well-built cabin, which consisted of three rooms. In the bedroom was a large four poster bed made out of oak. There was also an oak chest of drawers, which stood by a huge window with a marvelous view of the sea, and a standing wardrobe closet. The living room had several oak benches and some straight chairs, too. The kitchen area had a pump that actually brought water into the room. The hearth was huge with several iron arms fastened steadfast into the brick lining to hold the cooking pots.

"Why would you be wanting another cottage when you have one so grand?" Meghan asked her husband.

"Because," he said, kissing her tenderly, "it's not grand enough for you."

"Nathaniel, I've been doing a heap of thinking, and seems to me, if I had a wee one I wouldn't feel so alone while you are gone."

Immediately Nathaniel sensed what he thought Haws must have gone through knowing his wife was with child when he left on the hunt. Nathaniel was not sure he could leave Meghan in such a condition. "It is something we can talk about later," he told her. He kissed her again. "The ship must be taken to the harbor and unloaded, and arrangements must be made to sell the cargo and pay the crew. I probably won't be back until this evening. However, I promise you won't have to be alone. I'll send someone to help you with the unpacking and cleaning."

Nathaniel hurried to the home of Captain Henry and Aggie Black. Although the captain was not at home, his wife was.

"I heard thee were back," Aggie said. "I also heard thee did not come back alone."

Nathaniel picked up the frail-looking women, and gave her a bear hug. Frail-looking, she might be. Frail in strength or in courage and understanding, she was not. Aggie Starbuck Black was born to the Nantucket Starbucks' and in her younger days she had fought off an Indian war party alone for nearly seven hours before help could arrive.

Over the years she had lost none of her abilities nor her sense of humor. She loved Nathaniel with all the fierceness a "mother of the heart" can give.

"What kind of a lass, is she?" asked Aggie. When she saw the light burst into the man's eyes, she said, "Never mind! I'll do the judgin' for myself. Won't be hearin' any truth from a lovesick puppy. Now, whar she be?"

"That's one of the reasons I came to see you. I wondered if you might know of someone who could help her with the unpacking and the cleaning. Not that she isn't strong. She came aboard the STAR dressed as a lad and did a man's share of the work," the last was said with apparent pride.

"Dressed as a lad? Nathaniel, what's goin' on?"

"One of these days, I'll tell you all about it," Nathaniel assured her. "You'll be loving her as much as any mother could. I'm sorry, Aggie. I haven't asked about the Captain. Is he at home?"

"He's on the hunt. He should be back any month now."

A serious look came over Nathaniel. "How is Haws' wife. And does the child live?"

"She's fine, and the babe is a strappin' lad."

Nathaniel laughed with relief. "So my first mate has himself a son." He paused, then added, "And is all well on the rest of the island."

"As well as might be expected with so many of the men gone."

"The STAR is back as are other ships in the harbor."

"And for how long? Tell me! Does thy wife know 'bout the time when thee are gone?"

"She knows, Aggie."

"And how be she takin' it?"

"I imagine the same as you when you realized your destiny."

"Aye," Aggie replied. "With a smile on her face and tears in her shattered heart, I dare say."

Nathaniel gave her another hug. "You'll be finding someone to go to her?"

"I'll be helpin' her myself, but I dare say, thee knew that well enough."

"Just another one for thee to mother," he replied, smiling.

Arriving at the cabin, Aggie called through the open door. "Anybody here?"

Meghan came to the door. She had on a apron and kerchief tied about her shoulder length hair. There was also a streak of dirt on her forehead and down her cheek. "Did m'man send you?" she asked, smiling.

"Aye, that he did. The name's Aggie Black."

"Then you be Cap'n Black's wife. Nathaniel told me about how kind you and the Cap'n have been to him."

Aggie looked Meghan over. "I heard from one of the men ye be a thing of beauty. I couldn't ask Nathaniel, so I came to see myself. I brought a kettle of soup and some fresh baked bread. We can eat' now, and clean later."

"M'man told me I would feel at home, and he's right. Let's not stand here. Come into the kitchen, I started the cleaning and the table is ready."

Aggie had brought a tablecloth, dishes, cups and eating utilities. It was not long until the house had taken on the luscious smell of food. "Did Nathaniel tell ye about his childhood?' queried Aggie.

"He told me some of the things," Meghan replied, buttering another slice of the warm bread. "He told me he ran away from his uncle's plantation and came to live with you and Cap'n Black. He told me that he was helped by his friend, Toby."

"Did he also tell you that Toby was colored and his pa's first mate aboard his ship, and that his mama's brother had Toby hung when he helped Nathaniel come back to us?"

"Aye, that he did," assured Meghan. "My poor Nathaniel. How he must have suffered."

"To say nothin' about poor Toby," replied Aggie.

"Oh, I didn't mean . . ." Meghan started the sentence, but Aggie did not let her finish.

"Of course, thee didn't," Aggie replied with a smile. "Now, we best put away the vittles and get to cleanin'."

"Mrs. Black."

Again Aggie interrupted Meghan.

"Thee must call me Aggie. All the loved ones do."

Meghan smiled at being included in the loved ones. "My thanks be upon you."

The two women cleaned for the rest of the day. With a hug between them, Aggie left the cabin and met Nathaniel at the base of the cliff. "Thy wife is waitin' for thee, Nathaniel. She is a grand lass. See that thee deserve her."

"I will, Aggie. She is my life."

"Thee life is the hunt!" Aggie replied. "Thee will never change. Thee are like my Henry. The call of the sea is too powerful to ever leave her." Nathaniel started to speak, but Aggie stopped him. "Don't be denying the truth as we both know it," she said. Reaching up on her toes, she kissed his cheek; then hurried on her way.

Nathaniel hurried up the steps until he stood in front of the cabin. With hands on his hips and his legs wide apart, he called out, "Hello in the cabin! Marty Girl, come welcome the master home."

The door flew open and Meghan leaped into Nathaniel's waiting arms. He carried her to a wooden bench in front of the cabin, and sat down, keeping her on his lap.

"There is soup on the stove and bread on the table. You must be starved. Would you like to go in and eat supper?"

"Marty Girl, all I want to do is sit here with you and watch the sun disappear below the sea."

"That would be wonderful," Meghan said, snuggling deeper into his arms. And thus they sat while clouds mingled with the sun's departing embers and seagulls soared across the panorama of color.

"Are you happy, beloved?" Nathaniel asked.

"Happier than I ever dreamed of being," she responded.

"And you're not sorry to have left your emerald island?"

"Nay, m'man. I only want to be with you."

Nathaniel removed her kerchief and stroked her scarlet hair. "Marty Girl, I want you to love it here as much as I do. I want all our children born here. I want for them what I never had for myself." The sadness in his voice alarmed her.

"Please, don't be downhearted, I promise you all our babies will be Nantucketers."

"And you'll never leave me?"

"Now, why would I be doing such a thing? I love you, Nathaniel. You are my whole world."

"You might get lonely and want to return home to your parents."

"This is my home," Meghan assured him. "Besides, with you by my side, how could I ever be lonely?"

"Marty Girl, I . . . ," he could not finish the words.

"What were you about to say?" she asked looking up into his face.

"Nothing important," he told her. He carried her into his cabin and up the stairs.

The next morning the couple went visiting. Nathaniel introduced Meghan to the other captains' families where she was well received. After which, he took her to the various shops in the picturesque hamlet. He desired her to meet the shop owners and become acquainted with the merchandise they stocked.

At each place he left a large sum of money to be used as she saw fit, a custom utilized by the captains for the convenience of their wives. After having a light repast in a hostelry catering to families, Nathaniel took her exploring the various places he found interesting. One such place was in a cove he owned; a natural rock pool, where Nathaniel, as a young boy, had learned to swim.

"Marty Girl," he asked. "Would you care for a swim?" He sat on the sand and started to remove his boots.

"I haven't any bathing clothes," she said, blushing.

"Nor do I," he exclaimed, as he removed the last article of his clothing. " Please, Marty Girl, we can refresh ourselves."

"What if someone sees us?"

"No one will come," he told her. A twinkle came into his eyes. "It is forbidden." He held out his arms, and she hurried to join him in the cool water.

There was another place on Nathaniel's land that was soon to become Meghan's favorite hide-a-way. From there she could see the STAR anchored in the bay amongst hundreds of other ships. At first it had been hard for her to recognize his ship in a sea of other tall masts, but Nathaniel showed her how to identify his.

"Every captain has designed his banner and when he is on board, the emblem is flown above all others."

And knowing that Nathaniel was on aboard made her feel closer to him. Sometimes in the late afternoon, Meghan would walk down to the water's edge and meet his long boat. Once ashore he would take her hand and together they would walk up the path to sit on the bluff until the sky filled with stars.

This particular day Nathaniel had gone to New Bedford on business and she was alone on the bluff. She leaned against one of the large boulders, awaiting his return; it wasn't long until she was fast asleep. Nathaniel found her there and taking a piece of string from his pocket gently pulled it across her face. He watched as she brushed it away. He leaned closer and kissed her. Her eyes flew open, her arms encircled his neck, pulling him down to sit beside her.

"You were gone when I awoke this morning," she chided him.

He smiled and kissed her again. "I could not have left, if you had been awake." He stood and pulled her up to him. "Come, walk with me."

"Where are we going?" she asked as she stood beside him.

"Does it matter, little one, as long as we are together?"

"I'll go wherever you take me," she answered.

They walked down the steps, hand in hand. Once on shore he said, "Marty Girl, I want to introduce you to the new master and captain of the STAR."

Meghan stopped and looked up at him. The alarm in her voice was evident. "You're no longer cap'n of your ship? Oh, Nathaniel, what ever happened?" Not waiting for an answer, she ranted, "If only I could get my hands on him, he'd think twice about taking your ship away from you."

"Hold on, Marty Girl," Nathaniel interjected. "I wanted to wait until we were aboard the STAR to tell you, but I can't let you worry so. I'm now the master of the STAR."

Meghan laughed. "What a fright you be giving me. You were able to buy the ship, oh, how proud you must be, her master as well as her Cap'n. But in all the maze of ships, I don't see yours. Where is it?"

"It's there, somewhere," he answered lazily. "Now, with you as my wife, and the STAR as my own, all my dreams have come true." For a moment there was silence, and then he asked her, "Now, beloved, what dreams do you dream?"

A wistful look came into her eyes. "I would be having a tree growing in my favorite place on the bluff. A tree whose branches I could sit under and watch for the STAR to bring you safely home to me. Aye, that would be my wish."

"Close your eyes, and don't open them till I say the word,"

"What foolishment are you up to," Meghan asked, still closing her eyes as instructed. And for what seemed like an eternity, Meghan kept her eyes shut.

"Now, turn around and open them," Nathaniel told her, "tell me what you see."

Meghan gasped. "What magic have you been weaving?" she asked.

There, on top of the bluff, was a tree whose magnificent branches swayed in the light breeze. "Have I surprised thee, my lady?" Nathaniel whispered as his lips caressed her slim throat.

Tears clouded her vision. "Aye, that you have. Oh, Nathaniel, where ever did you find such a tree? And how did you bring it here?"

"Such questions can wait. Come, you must see it up close." He took her hand and together they walked up the path to stand on the bluff.

"Oh, Nathaniel, it's a wondrous thing you have done." she told him. "To give me my very own sentinel to watch over me and to guide you safely home. Tell me, dear husband, how came this about?"

"We lay anchor in the cove and while I was taking you down to the shoreline, the men carried the tree up. They prepared the land earlier and they tell me you gave them quite a start when you came up and sat down. However, while you slept, they were able to finish the digging. Everything was ready and upon my signal, they raised and secured the tree."

"And a grand tree, it be," Meghan said. "The grandest I have ever seen."

Nathaniel removed his hat and began to speak: "I name thee the SENTINEL, and I commission thee to stand guard over my lady while I'm away. Protect her from the elements, give her comfort when she is sad, give protection to the birds who seek shelter amongst your mighty branches so they may sing away my lady's melancholy." Nathaniel held out his arms and Meghan entered his embrace.

The repairs to the STAR were finished; the supplies for the hunt carried aboard. All was ready for the departure, and still Nathaniel had not informed his wife. The past year had been wonderful for the couple and Nathaniel knew it might be years before they were together again. Also the house was finished. Something else Nathaniel had not told her.

Meghan was taking bread out of the oven when Nathaniel came into the room. "I have a surprise for you, beloved. The house is finished." He took her hand in his. "I hope it will meet with your approval. Come with me now."

To Meghan's surprise the house was not made of logs, but brick and three stories high. The doors and wood shutters were brilliant white and Meghan hoped her friends would not be envious of her new home. Nathaniel opened the door and carried her across the threshold. The wooden floors gleamed with layers of wax, and the winding staircase was highly polished. He carried her up the staircase into their bedroom. He turned in a circle to show her the interior. A massive four poster bed dominated the large room. The front windows faced the harbor; the side windows revealed the massive tree. A fire burned in the hearth and white damask curtains fluttered at the opened windows.

In the middle of the highly polished wood floor lay her very own rag-rug; the one her granny made so many years ago.

She wiggled to be free; then knelt beside it.

"Does it meet with your pleasure?" he asked her. She lifted her face to him, and he saw tears rolling down her cheeks.

"Marty Girl, I didn't mean to make you sad for your home, in Ireland," he exclaimed as he knelt beside her.

"Nay, 'tis not the home of my youth that I shed these tears. It's for my new home and m'man who thinks of everything." Her gaze sifted to the top of her new set of drawers and spied her mother's raised rose lace.

"I don't understand how it happened. I never even dared hope to see my lovely things again, and here they are." At the foot of the bed stood her wedding chest. She opened the lid and marveled again what miracle brought it all about, for before her wet-stained eyes were all of the things she cherished.

"How did it happen? I mean, when did it come? I mean, how long have you had it? Oh, I'm not thinking straight. Nathaniel, why are you laughing?"

"You're like a little girl and it's Christmas. We'll speak of this later. Come along, Marty Girl, and I'll show you the rest of the house and then your very own 'Widows' Walk.'"

"Can we go there, first?" Meghan asked, hardly being able to take her eyes away for a treasure she thought to never see again.

"If you wish," he replied.

Meghan followed him out of the house and up the stairs by the kitchen door. Once on the roof she walked around her own balustrade, stopping at the front to gaze out to sea. "There's the STAR," she gasped with delight.

Nathaniel put his arms about her waist, her back to his chest.

"Marty Girl, there's something that I must tell you. And it's the hardest thing that I have ever had to do."

Meghan wiggled around in his arms until she faced him. "I'll say it for you, Nathaniel. You're leaving for the hunt tomorrow." Seeing his utter look of amazement, she added, "'Tis not a thing to be kept secret; I've know it for some weeks now. 'Tis our last night together, but as long as you are by my side, there is no tomorrow, only tonight." Silence prevailed as they watched the sun disappear.

The next morning found Meghan standing with other wives saying goodbye to their men. "Please be here when I return," Nathaniel pleaded as their lips met.

"And where would I be going?" she asked, smiling. "My love, I'll be waiting, even if it takes years," she promised. One last kiss and he was gone.

Meghan waved until she could no longer see the STAR; then she turned and ran up the bluff to the home where she and Nathaniel had only shared one night. Last night his presence filled each room. Today there was only emptiness, the house cold without him. When she could stand the silence no longer, she ran to her tree of refuge, but the sea would not allow her solace, and it began to thunder its chant, 'He's mine! He's mine!'

"I won't be listening to you," she cried, holding her hands over her ears. "He's not yours! He's mine, and he will be coming back to me," she threw herself down and began to sob. "He is mine. He loves me. Oh, Nathaniel, please come back to me."

"That will be doin' thee no good," said Aggie looking down at the weeping girl. "Thee must not let the sea know thee fears her. If thee do, she'll win him, for sure."

"She already has," admitted Meghan, drying her tears.

"Has she?" retorted Aggie. "Well, we shall see. For now, come with me. 'Tis a hot cup of tea, thee be needin'."

Meghan followed Aggie back to the house. Once inside, she slumped into a chair, making no attempt to help Aggie prepare the hot drink. In a few minutes the tea's sweet aroma filled the room. Meghan sipped the drink and the liquid did help to warm her shivering body.

"Thee feelin' better, child?" Aggie asked, putting down her own cup.

"Aye," admitted Meghan. "And 'tis that ashamed I am for not being more brave."

"Nonsense!" snapped Aggie. "It happens to us all. Why, when my Henry leaves, thar's buckets of tears, I be shedding."

"How long did you say he's been gone?" Meghan asked, taking another sip of tea.

"Let me see," pondered the woman. "Aye, 'tis almost seven years."

"Seven years? Aggie, how can you stand the loneliness?"

"'Tis three sons, I have. One is now sailing with his pa; one is in New Bedford; the third lives with me. He's a great comfort to me as the child within thee will be in years to come."

"A child! How . . . how did you know?"

"The point is, does Nathaniel know?"

"I couldn't tell him, Aggie. I just didn't want him to worry."

Aggie looked straight into Meghan's eyes. "Will thee go home to have this babe?"

"This is my home, Aggie. Besides, I promised Nathaniel all our children will be born on his beloved Nantucket." Meghan put aside her cup. For a moment she stood at the window looking towards the tree; then, finally, she turned back to face the older woman. "Forgive me, Aggie. I've never asked what you do to keep your heart light while Captain Henry is away."

"Thar's plenty for me to do. I'm mid-wife on the island, and I help look out for the younguns who have no parents. I try to be a granny to them all. Of course, I've grandchildren of my own and that keeps me busy. I never have time to be sorry for myself."

"Then I won't either," Meghan declared. Then to herself, she thought, *I'm thinking I won't be lonely after all.*

Chapter Twenty-Seven

❧

The dream had started pleasant enough; then it took Nathaniel into a shattering nightmare. He woke with sweat dotting his forehead and upper lip. He leaped from bed, dressing quickly. He left his quarters and dashed up the ladder to find his first mate. The man was on the bridge. "Mistah Haws, set sail for Nantucket," Nathaniel ordered. "We are going home!"

"Goin' 'ome!" Haws questioned. "Cap'n, we've been gone less than five months."

"Turn the ship about. 'Tis by my order!" Nathaniel left the bridge to return to his quarters. He sat on the edge of his bed. Once they were at sea, the hunt for the sperm whale had taken control of all his thoughts. Now, this blasted dream, three nights in a row. He had seen the anguish face of his beloved Marty Girl, and it fairly tore his heart apart. She needed him, he did not know why, but he was going home just as fast as the wind allowed.

The bay was quiet as the STAR dropped anchor. He heard the bell ringing their arrival. Nathaniel scanned the shoreline to see if she was there; she was not among the waiting families. She had plenty of time to be there. Had she left him? Could that be the source of his nightmare? Once on shore he ran up the pathway. Lights flickered in the Great House, as the village called their home. The door flung opened and there stood his friend, Captain Henry Black.

"Bless my soul if it isn't Nathaniel. But what is it, lad? What brings you back so soon?"

"Where's my wife?" demanded Nathaniel. "Why wasn't she on the shore to greet me?"

"Best we speak quietly in the parlor," replied Captain Black, leading the way.

Once inside, Nathaniel questioned, "Has she left me?"

"Left thee? What gave thee such a thought? Yer wife is upstairs. Aggie's with her. Nathaniel, my boy, thee are about to become a father."

A father? Never in his wildest dreams had that possibility emerged. Nathaniel bolted out of the room and up the stairs. He opened his bedroom door and was about to enter when Aggie's pale face stopped him. She pushed him back out of the room, closing the door.

"I heard the bell ringin' and knew 'twas thee. I've been prayin' to the Almighty to bring thee home in time to say goodbye to thy lady and perhaps thy child, also. Meghan's right bad. We have sent for the doctor in New Bedford. Only the Good Lord knows if he arrives in time."

Meghan cried out. Nathaniel brushed Aggie aside and went to his wife. Meghan looked at him in disbelief. "You're here? You left her to come back to me?"

Wonderment splashed across Nathaniel's face. "Left who?" he asked.

"Aggie said she wouldn't win." Meghan closed her eyes and sank back on the pillows.

"What does she mean, Aggie? Who does she believe I have been with? Doesn't she know she is the only woman I want in my life?"

"'Tis only the pain making her speak so," explained Aggie. Another scream and Aggie hurried back to the bed. One quick look told Aggie what had happened. "The wee one has turned. The babe's feet come first. Nathaniel, thee must leave me to my work."

"What does it mean? The feet comes first?"

"Thee must leave!"

"I'll not go. Tell me how I can help?"

"Get a damp cloth and sponge her face."

Aggie thrust her hand into the opening and turned the baby about. Meghan screamed; then fainted.

"Thee has a wee lass, and her hair be as fiery as her mama's."

"And my wife?"

"She lives! But, Nathaniel, she'll nary have another, I'm thinkin'."

"She lives! That's all that matters! She lives!" cried Nathaniel, with tear-rimmed eyes.

Captain Black appeared in the doorway. "Tell me. Is all well?"

Aggie nodded her head and ordered both men out. This time Nathaniel did not argue. He led the way down to the kitchen where both men collapsed in chairs.

Some hours later, Meghan opened her eyes to see Nathaniel sitting in the chair beside her bed. "I thought it be a dream," whispered Meghan. "But you're here, beside me."

He leaned on the bed. "I love you with all my being," he told her, kissing her lightly on the mouth. "And we have a daughter."

Aggie carried the baby to the bed and handed her to Meghan. When the child was secured in her mother's loving arms, Aggie left the room, quietly closing the door behind her. She went to the kitchen and began fixing the mid-day meal.

Upstairs Meghan was asking, "What shall we name her?"

"I leave the naming up to you," he said, holding the little hand.

"Could we name her after our mothers?"

"If that is your wish," replied Nathaniel, taking the baby into his own arms.

Meghan smiled. "Rebecca Kathleen Lathrope. Oh, Nathaniel. 'Tis a grand name for so little a colleen."

A grave look came over Nathaniel. "I never knew my mother," he said. "You have done her and me a great honor."

Dawn found Nathaniel walking along the shoreline. He had not been able to sleep. He had tossed and turned for several hours. Then, being afraid he might wake Meghan, dressed and left the house while it was still night. Sometime later Captain Black also took to walking on the beach. Upon seeing him, Nathaniel called out, "Henry, I'm over here. Come, join me."

The captain raised his hand. "I see thee, lad. I couldn't sleep myself. Thy little one woke me up, crying."

"Crying? What was the matter with her? Was she ill?" Nathaniel wanted to know.

"Not a bit of it," assured the other man. "Just hungry, I expect. The wife finally fixed her a sugar tit, and she quieted right down."

They walked in silence, each deep in their own thoughts. It was Henry Black who first spoke. "Nathaniel, I've something to talk over with thee. It came to Aggie's mind first. With us both leaving soon, Aggie thought it wise if she came to stay with Meghan until we come home. What say thee to such a suggestion?"

"I'll say it is an answer to my prayers. It will ease my mind knowing my wife is not alone. But, Henry, what about your own home?"

"Our son is getting married. He can bring his bride to the house.

Aye, it is an answer to all our prayers," continued Black. They proceeded in their walk.

Dawn had brought a new day; the air freshens their lungs and clears their vision. The harbor was alive with men and ships all getting ready for the next hunt.

"When will you be leaving?" Nathaniel asked his friend.

"The beginning of fall," was the reply. "Thar's still work to be done on old FLAGG." He paused. "There's something I need to speak with thee about. Sometime back I received a letter from your uncle to be opened when I received word that he had died. In the letter he wrote of his sorrow for his actions in the past and asked thy forgiveness. It also states that if he still lived when you returned, he would send word of his coming to visit you. Nathaniel, at the time of his death he was a broken man. You spoke of the nightmare you had for three nights, he has had them for years. Lad, he asks for your forgiveness."

Nathaniel stopped walking. "He robbed me of my birthright! How can I forgive that?"

"That be betwixt thee and thy maker, lad. I can only pass yer uncle's thoughts along to thee. Now, we best hurry or Aggie will be serving us a cold breakfast."

The two men lengthened their stride and were soon on the porch. "How is Meghan and little Becky?" was the first thing Nathaniel said as Aggie opened the kitchen door.

"Both are still asleep," she said. "And don't be making noise to wake them."

Nathaniel went upstairs. Seeing that Meghan's eyes were shut, he started to back out of the room, but Meghan stopped him. "Nathaniel, please don't go. I'm awake," she said softly, holding out her arms to him.

He leaned down and gently kissed her. "How is the new mama, this morning?" he asked.

"Wonderful," she replied. "And 'tis a grand day, isn't it?" A sudden thought came to her and she quickly voiced, "Oh, I must look a fright. I haven't even combed my hair."

He smiled. "Would you like me to brush it?"

"Aye," she replied. "Would be kindness, itself."

He took the brush from the small table. And after helping Meghan to sit, he sat himself down behind her and began to brush her crimson tresses. "Have you given any thought to you and Becky coming with me on the next hunt?"

Tears sprung to her gentle eyes. "You be knowing how much I love you, but I can't be thinking only of you and me. There is Becky to be considered, and the STAR is no place for her. Nathaniel, you know I would go anywhere with you, if was only me.

"You have your life, and I never want you to change. Your mind on the hunt must be clear, and it wouldn't be, if we were there to fog your judgments."

"Other wives have taken their children on their husband's ship. You saw that for yourself," explained Nathaniel.

"Would you be wanting our daughter to fall into the sea and freeze? Remember. I saw that for myself, too," Meghan reminded him.

"And since you saw it," Nathaniel said, still brushing her hair, "You wouldn't let that happen to our daughter."

"Nathaniel, how can you even think so cruel?" she said, pulling away from him.

"You know how much I love you. You say that you love me, too. And if that is the truth, how could you want us to be prisoners in your quarters or wedged into that tiny space on deck. Oh, I can't believe you would want that for us?"

"I want you by my side, at any cost," Nathaniel insisted. "How can you want us to be separated?" He left the bed to stand before the huge window. He was shaken for the want of her and the memory of being at sea without her.

"You said nothing about me joining you before the baby was born. Why are you so insistent now?" she asked.

His shoulders shook, his voice quivered, "I never knew how lonely I could be without you."

This was their first quarrel and it left them both shaken. "We'll speak of this later," Nathaniel informed her. "When you have your strength about you."

"I'll not be changing my mind, Nathaniel. Nay, I'll not be doing that."

His shoulder's straightened. "You're being stubborn, Mrs. Lathrope."

"As you are, Cap'n Lathrope."

Nathaniel turned from the window. Meghan looked lost in the large bed.

He started to go to her then turned from that path when he noticed the determined look about her eyes. She was robbing him not only of her presence on his ship, but also that of his daughter. "This is not the end of the discussion," he declared, taking his leave of her.

Aggie was preparing Meghan's tray when Nathaniel bolted into the spacious kitchen. She started to ask him what was the matter when the expression on his face stopped her. Instead, she called to her husband, telling him breakfast was prepared.

The man took one look at his friend and asked, "What's wrong, lad?"

"Nothing at all," stormed Nathaniel, his voice ringing with anger.

Aggie put a platter of ham, eggs and fried potatoes in front of the two men. Captain Henry helped himself to the food, and was about to take his first bite when Nathaniel pushed himself away from the table. "She refuses to go with me!" he told the pair.

"Who refuses to go with thee? Nathaniel, what are thee talkin' about?" asked Aggie.

"Meghan! That's who! I want her to come with me on the next hunt, and she has refused."

"She would never leave the child," responded Aggie, looking at her husband, with a raised eyebrow.

"I would never ask her to leave Becky at home. No! I asked her to bring our daughter with her."

"Are thee serious?" questioned Aggie.

"Other wives have done it. I've been talking to some of the husbands and they feel it is the wife's duty to make the trip."

"Duty, is it? Let me tell thee about duty." Aggie's eyes blazed. "No! Better still, allow Henry to tell thee."

A woeful expression came into the older man's eyes. "It brings back tormenting memories, Nathaniel. However, I think thee should know what thee ask of thy wife." Henry pushed his food away. He looked at his wife and she nodded her head. He took his pipe and packed the bowl. In a few moments, smoke puffed into the air. "When we first married, Aggie came on board with me. It was hard on her being confined to such a small area, yet she never complained. Her only thoughts were to make me comfortable, and the men liked having her on board. Aggie was always one to listen to the men's misfortunes and many the time she was able to smooth the trouble waters amongst them.

"One day she came to me and said we were going to have a baby. What a jolt that was. There we were in the middle of the hunt, with land not to be sighted for a year. I was, to say the least, in a troubled state of my own. I knew nothing about the birthing of a baby, although I had helped bring many a kid or piglet into existence. But a child, and mine to boot, no, I had never experience such a thing. When the time came, we were in a massive hunt and word was sent out if any of the ships had a doctor aboard. Well, glory be to God, our prayers were answered. One of the passing ships had a doctor aboard. You can imagine our thanksgiving when he came on deck and helped in the birthing of a beautiful little girl."

"I never knew you had a daughter," interrupted Nathaniel.

"It was long before thy time, Nathaniel. Anyway, to get back to my tale. We named her Charity. She was a joy to be around. As the years went by, we allowed her more and more freedom. She was about four years old when a terrible storm swept over the ship, interrupting the rendering. All of our attention centered on keeping the fires alive. Aggie had been in our room with Charity when one of the crew got badly burned.

"One thing led to another, and Aggie had to stay on deck longer than anticipated. The storm finally passed and she was able to go below. Charity was no where to be found. A search of the entire ship could not find her. Charity had simply disappeared. The only clue we had to what happened was her little doll wedged between two barrels of water near the railing. What we had to accept was that Charity had become frightened and came up on deck and the storm swept her away."

Nathaniel was stunned at this revelation. "Forgive me," he said. "I had no idea you both had lived through such a terrible time. How have you managed to keep your sanity?"

"There has been compensations," replied the old captain. "Now, I have my sons with me."

"Thee are a forgetful old man," laughed Aggie. "Thee only has one son who goes to sea."

Henry flamed red. "An old man's slip of the tongue, my dear." He said as he pierced a slice of ham. "Drat it all," he uttered. "My food is cold."

Aggie retrieved the plate and refilled it with hot food. After she handed it to him, she filled a plate for Meghan. "Thee must take the tray to thy wife. 'Tis time to put her mind to rest."

"To rest?"

"If thee left her with the same look on thy face as thee entered this room; then, she, too, must be upset, and she's in no condition to be troubled."

Meghan had not been able to rest. Time was too short to waste with quarrels. She wanted to go to Nathaniel and say something to ease his thoughts, but what could she possibly say? The years had not diminished the sight of that little boy falling into the sea, and to know he would never, in this lifetime, run into his mother's arms and say I love you. No, never again say those little words of magic. She held her daughter in her arms and looking down at her sleeping child, thoughts of those little eyes never opening again, was more than she could bear.

She glanced up when she heard her husband come into the room. Nathaniel looked into her red-rimmed eyes. "Marty Girl, I'm sorry for what transpired between us. Please forgive me."

"'Tis nothing to forgive, my darling. I do want to be with you as much as you want us with you. Nathaniel, I wouldn't ask you to give up the sea, any more than you can ask me to put our wee one's life in danger, for that is what I'd be doing, and I'd never forgive you or me if her life be taken in such a horrible way."

"I wasn't thinking about danger," admitted Nathaniel. "Could you really believe that I wanted either of you in jeopardy?"

"No, my darling, not for one moment," she said smiling.

The next six months were fulfilling ones for the three of them. Little Rebecca would laugh and hold up her arms whenever Nathaniel came into the room. He would scoop her up and twirl her about, and she would squeal with delight.

❧

THE STAR HAD just returned from a short hunt, and Nathaniel was anxious to get home. He stepped out of the long boat with Haws by his side. It was a beautiful, balmy day. Before parting, Haws took a deep breath and said, "The men 'ave been askin' 'bout our next long hunt. What should I be tellin' them?"

"We leave the first of September," Nathaniel answered. "It gives us two weeks to bid our good-byes."

Haws grinned. "'Tis a fair time," he said.

It was not a sudden decision for Nathaniel. He had been thinking about it for several weeks. He had not mentioned this fact to Meghan. He did not know how to explain it. He left Haws and headed for home.

❧

AS NATHANIEL APPROACHED their home, he stood spread-legged in front of the house and called out, "Hello in the house! Marty Girl, come, welcome the master home.

The door burst open. Meghan, carrying baby Rebecca, ran down the steps and fell into his arms. "Oh, Marty Girl, how I have missed you both."

He held them close to him, their hearts beating as one. He picked them up and carried them to their tree. The three sat together under the protection of the massive branches. Birds hidden among the leaves sang their songs of love.

"Marty Girl, we'll be leaving for the long hunt in two weeks. And my darling, I'll leave some maps and charts behind so you'll be able to know the route we plan to sail."

"Nathaniel, 'tis a hard thing for me to say, but say it I must. I know the lonely life of a whaling man, and if there be a time when my memory is dim, all I ask is that I'll never know if you take another to ease your pain."

"There can never be another for me," he said kissing her lips. "Oh, beloved, you are forever lodged in the deep recesses of my heart and mind. No, never fear, my Marty Girl, you will never be just a memory to me."

Meghan knew her journey was over. She need never run away again. She was home at last. Home in her very own safe harbor, building hope for the future and for their tiny Rebecca.

The babe, Nathaniel, born in 1788 under the most incredible of circumstances, had indeed become the man his father was, fulfilling his mother, Rebecca's hope.

❧

Book two, *Widow's Walk*, from the Endless Sea Series continues the story of the Lathrope family of Nantucket Island, Massachusetts. As the story begins, Nathaniel and Meghan's only daughter, Rebecca, is a spoiled, rich twelve-year-old who longs to join her father on the sea. The years involved in this book begin in 1828.

❧